Orille :

A DEADLY THAW

The York Factory Connection

With warm wishes

F R E D E R I C K   R O S S

[signature]
Sept, 2021

◆ FriesenPress

Suite 300 - 990 Fort St
Victoria, BC, V8V 3K2
Canada

www.friesenpress.com

ISBN
978-1-5255-1825-6 (Hardcover)
978-1-5255-1826-3 (Paperback)
978-1-5255-1827-0 (eBook)

1. FICTION

Distributed to the trade by The Ingram Book Company

"If you can think like a virus, then you can begin to understand why a virus does what it does. A smallpox particle gets into a person's body and, in a way, it's thinking, I'm this one particle sitting here surrounded by an angry immune system. I have to multiply fast. Then I have to get out of this host fast. It escapes into the air before the pustules develop."

-Dr.D.A. Henderson
Centre for Disease Control

"If a work of fiction can create, in the reader, the belief that the plot could happen, then it's well on its way to being an enjoyable read. Frederick Ross is offering a well researched novel that brims with possibilities which moves the improbable into the possible category with characters and situations with whom we can relate. Even ordinary mortals can follow the science - bonus!!

As a first fictional effort, Dr. Ross has done an excellent job weaving history and exotic locales (such as northern Manitoba) into a suspenseful story worth reading."

Rodney S. Brown M.A.

Preface

I wrote this book because of my concern regarding the resurgence of the smallpox virus as a clinical entity. After 9/11, the media generated considerable fear that smallpox could conceivably become an agent of bioterrorism. I started saving newspaper clippings which reviewed the various ways whereby smallpox could return and become 'weaponized.' Lab accidents, release from permafrost, and viral DNA biosynthesis are all present-day possibilities for the return of this deadly scourge. Smallpox can now be potentially created in a lab, making the world far more vulnerable to an epidemic than ever before. Virtually everyone on the planet is currently susceptible to this infection, with vaccinations lasting only ten years at best. Moreover, relatively few people have been vaccinated.

This book approaches these possibilities within an historical fiction dating back to the fur trade on the shores of Hudson Bay. Visiting the cemetery at York Factory last year, I was overwhelmed with the hundreds of tombs dating back to the eighteenth century. What would happen if an archaeological dig were to take place there and, by breaching the permafrost, the lethal pathogen was inadvertently released? If this happened, the world would be faced with a plague of such apocalyptic proportions as to dwarf all other infectious diseases combined. Frightening as it seems, scientists and politicians must be prepared to deal with this possibility. Current stocks of live smallpox virus still exist in two major labs in the world and perhaps others concealed in unknown labs. It is therefore no longer possible for society to rid itself entirely of the threat of variola virus or, for that matter, other lethal pathogens.

This book introduces a bright young archaeologist and her team, who find themselves immersed in the history of York Factory during an exhumation as part of an archaeological research project. An unlikely romance follows with an unusual discovery that jeopardizes the life of every human being on the planet. *A Deadly Thaw* is a cautionary tale about ignoring certain events that occurred centuries ago as if history could not possibly repeat itself.

'So the story of man runs in a dreary circle, because he is not yet master of the earth that holds him.'

– Will Durant

Prologue

They walked down a series of splintered wooden steps across a small creek known as Sloop Creek. Numerous trees and saplings had overgrown what was once a clearing. Grey weather-beaten picket fence enclosures surrounded many of the ancient graves. Several boards were broken and only a few headstones were still standing. As Boudreau had described, a thicket of willows and poplar had taken over the graveyard and partially hid this unique historic site from view. Enthralled by an overwhelming sense of history, Rachel bent over to read some of the epitaphs on the tombstones.

"There are so many unmarked graves in this cemetery that it's difficult not to walk on them," Boudreau cautioned. He was painfully aware that a few of his ancestors were likely buried somewhere in this cemetery. Numerous small fenced enclosures indicated the graves of children. Several tombstones nearby were adorned with brightly coloured ribbons.

"Why do they have ribbons on those tombstones?" Rachel asked.

"These ribbons were placed by First Nations people who recently visited the cemetery to honour their ancestors buried here. The ribbons are attached to the tombstones either to invoke good spirits or to keep away bad ones, I suppose. It's a way of honouring their ancestors and showing that they are not forgotten. This cemetery is unique as it includes Europeans and native people together, often side by side. The Hudson's Bay Company didn't believe in segregation," Boudreau explained.

They arrived at one headstone but could barely read the name as it was so weathered. At another plot, a headstone rested right beside a wooden cross, suggesting the interment of two bodies on the same site. Rachel immediately took notice of this unusual anomaly.

Chapter 1

Little Duck

Pro pelle cutem

The ice had just broken up on the northern rivers draining into Hudson Bay, creating easy avenues for the transportation of furs from trapping grounds in Canada's northern hinterland. The year was 1782 and the fur trade was thriving. One of the Indian paddlers on the trip that year was a twenty-two-year-old Chipewyan named Little Duck.

Little Duck grew up on the limitless space of the rough rolling grounds known as the Barrens. Like most Chipewyan, he was adept at living off the land; it was this ability that attracted the Bay men to enlist his services. Hard as nails and of few words, Little Duck proved to be a strong paddler and a capable hunter during the five-week annual trip to the fort at York Factory. This was his third year making the journey with the Company men to York Factory. He wore a caribou skin shirt like a poncho, cut with points at the back and front. It was from this style of dress that the Cree gave his people their name: 'pointed skins' or Chipewyan. This style of clothing kept the Indians warm without restricting them in paddling their canoes or the eight-man York boats of the Hudson's Bay Company.

Little Duck was only a teenager when he first met the white fur traders known as the 'Company men' in the great Barren Lands of Canada's northern tundra. The Barrens was a desolate and treeless biome, which occupied most of the endless tundra. Barely able to hold vegetation except for scant patches of lichen and grasses, the Barrens stretched westward from Hudson Bay to Great Slave Lake and Great Bear Lake and beyond, all the way to the shores of the Arctic Ocean. The Barrens was stark, vast, and limitless. So dry was this godforsaken land, it could take a hundred years for a spruce tree to grow only a few feet. Yet the Chipewyan had dwelt on it for eons, surviving the rigours of climate and distance.

The Company enlisted Little Duck as a paddler to help transport the thousands of pounds of furs to the Hudson's Bay fort at York Factory, a forty-day paddle to the northeast. He lived in a small village on the shores of one of the thousands of unnamed gunmetal lakes in the subarctic tundra of Canada's Northwest Territories. Standing nearly six feet tall, with a hawkish nose, Little Duck bore the scars of more than a few knife fights from his past. Three black lines stained his broad flat face, accenting his high cheekbones. His young wife, a short woman with small eyes, a low forehead, and a large broad chin was his partner during the trapping season. Her name was Bëghąnıch'ërë, but the French traders called her 'Boni Cheri,' which was how her name sounded in the Dene tongue. Betrothed to Little Duck from her childhood, she lived with her parents on the small lake where they trapped and fished to survive on the harsh Barrens. For six months of the year, the temperature fell below freezing on the tundra. She wanted to travel with her husband and the other traders; however, she was expecting her second child in only a few weeks and her parents discouraged her from going on the trip.

The sole trappers of beaver and other furs in the hinterland of the Barrens for the Hudson's Bay Company were the Chipewyan. Any decrease in the Indian population would have a significant effect on the returns at the Hudson's Bay trading posts. The Bay traders treated the natives with respect for they depended on their ability to trap and bring in the pelts.

Little Duck's people were prodigious travellers and, unlike the Cree who tended to dwell close to the HBC forts along the shores of Hudson Bay, the Chipewyan seemed to thrive in paddling hundreds of miles inland. One of their people, Matonabbee, became famous among the Company men for bringing in the most furs to the HBC post at Fort Prince of Wales and for being a great leader among his people in the late eighteenth century.

Little Duck was a distant relative of Matonabbee and he wanted to prove that he, too, could be a great leader. More than that, he wanted to trade furs for one of the new blankets that the white men had brought in 1780. It was striped green, red, yellow, and indigo on a white background. It soon became famous all over the continent, appearing as far south as the Spanish territories. The Hudson's Bay Company had been selling woolen blankets since its inception in 1670 but the new 'point blankets' became very popular among the aboriginal people as a sign of distinction. The coveted blankets also kept one warm and the colourfast dyes prevented the colours from running when the blankets got wet. They became one of the primary European trade items sought by the native peoples from the Bay traders. These colourful blankets were so desired partly because of the wool's capacity to hold heat even when wet and because they were easier to repair than deer or bison skins. As with many of his people, the colourful blanket also served as a badge of honour for Little Duck.

Matonabbee had learned English during his time with Samuel Hearne, the famous English explorer who travelled inland to discover the Coppermine River in 1770. As his status as a leader increased, so did the number of his wives. Eight of Matonabbee's wives acted as beasts of burden on that epic voyage, each hauling sledges, cooking, and carrying loads. If one of his wives became pregnant, she would simply deliver her baby in the woods and then catch up to the rest of the group later. Women in this culture were treated as slaves. The rigours of their work aged them prematurely so that, by the time they were thirty years old, they were already wrinkled and back-broken old women.

Little Duck recalled how Matonabbee had convinced him to become a paddler for the Bay men. Matonabbee collected furs from those Indians who were reluctant to undergo the arduous trip to the Bay to trade their furs. Little Duck respected the Chipewyan leader who organized groups to transport the furs to York Factory. He remembered the times when Matonabbee brought back trade goods that he distributed among the Indians. For this, Matonabbee became a leader among his people. Little Duck believed that he could follow and work with a man such as this and with the white Bay traders.

Little Duck also learned to speak English from his time spent with Matonabbee. It was the English language that the Chipewyan used to speak to the Bay men and to the Swampy Cree near the fort. The two native languages had no resemblance to one another at all. Cree was an Algonquin language whereas Chipewyan or Dene was an Athapaskan language and Little Duck had no idea what the Cree people were talking about when they spoke. Most of the 500 Indian dialects in North America were so different that sign language was necessary throughout most of the continent.

In 1771, an account written about a group of English people who stayed with an Indian tribe for two years in the south stated that they 'conversed in their pantomimes with them.' It was almost as if the confusion of tongues, which took place in the Tower of Babel story in the Old Testament, had occurred in North America rather than in ancient Mesopotamia. Matonabbee and his Chipewyan guides often resorted to English to communicate with the Cree people who lived near the fort. Likewise, Little Duck learned to speak English during the long inland journeys to York Factory and during his time at the fort with the Bay men.

Before Little Duck's group set out for the forty-day canoe trip to York Factory, he traded with a group of natives who came from villages along the Upper Missouri where the Sioux and Cheyenne people traded. Little Duck learned that several of these people had become ill. A few days earlier, he'd helped carry a bundle of blankets that had arrived with these people; he kept one for himself to sleep on during the trip. It was a buff blanket with four coloured stripes, which he greatly admired. He was unaware that it was a Hudson's Bay point blanket. He just knew that it was a white trader's blanket and he liked the colours.

Little Duck gave another blanket from the Cheyenne traders to his friend 'Crooked Legs' who accompanied him as a paddler on the trip. Crooked Legs had other reasons for enlisting on the voyage to York Factory that year. A week earlier, in a wanton act of violence fed by rum supplied by the Bay traders, he had murdered his cousin Mishenwashence. The enraged family of Mishenwashence vowed revenge on Crooked Legs. Crooked Legs reasoned that, by accompanying Little Duck and the Bay traders, he might escape almost certain torture and death.

"We have to leave soon, Little Duck. I'm very afraid and I can't stay here any longer. These people are threatening to kill me. I don't even remember what happened." Crooked Legs knew his days were numbered should he stay anywhere near the village. For him, the sooner they left the better.

"Then bring your wives to help cook and set up camp for us. Tell them to pack now so we can leave early tomorrow morning. You can sleep in my tent tonight." Little Duck was aware of the rigours of the trip and he knew they would need all the help they could get. He could depend on Crooked Legs' wives to make life easier on the trip.

"You must tell the women to load all the furs from the village onto the white man's wooden boats. They are much heavier than our canoes and they can carry many more pelts than the canoes. And the river flows down to the Bay, which will make paddling easier." Little Duck knew what to expect on the trip, thanks to what he had learned from Matonabbee and, like him, he enjoyed giving orders to others. One of his orders was to put the folded striped blankets in the bottom of his canoe.

Chapter 2

Duncan Farquharson

Running face sickness

The white man's wooden boat that Little Duck described was the famous York boat, named after York Factory. The York boat had been around for over thirty years and would continue to be the chief mode of transportation for the Hudson's Bay Company for another 150 years. These wooden boats were fourteen metres long and could carry more than six tonnes of cargo. In rough water, they were safer than birch bark canoes. They could carry considerably more cargo due to their heavy wooden construction, which enabled them to bounce off rocks or ice without fear of puncture or breaking apart.

The York boat, however, was difficult to portage any great distance due to its enormous weight. Traders had to cut swaths through the woods using poplar logs as rollers in order to transport the boat. This was back-breaking work especially around one set of rapids on the Hayes River that extended for almost three kilometres. According to Sir John Franklin, crewing a York boat was arduous work and the paddlers experienced a life of 'unending toil broken only by the terror of storms.'

One of the Bay traders who supervised this journey on the York Boat was an Orkney man named Duncan Farquharson. Farquharson had suffered smallpox as a child, which left him severely scarred for life. His pockmarked face was frightening to the Indians who had never seen anything like this before.

"It looks like he was shot by one of the white man's rifles with birdshot," joked Crooked Legs in the Dene language. "Maybe he was aiming the gun backwards!" Little Duck smiled at this and remarked that not even a bear would attack such a man as this.

"Maybe we should teach him how to use a bow and arrow!" Crooked Legs smirked as he said this, unaware that Farquharson understood the Dene language. Farquharson knew they were mocking him in their canoes but he remained silent. His fellow Bay men never commented on his disfiguring appearance, knowing the reason behind it, but the natives were always intrigued. Several of them were taken aback, while others made jests and mocked him as they were doing now.

Farquharson directed one of the York boats. He kept to himself, knowing the Chipewyan did not need much supervision as they worked and certainly none as they hunted for game along their route to the Bay. Six canoes loaded to the gunwales with furs accompanied them. They set out on Tuesday, May 28, 1782, on a rainy morning. Farquharson estimated it would take about thirty-five days to travel the hundreds of miles downstream to York Factory.

The temperatures during the first week of their journey were so warm that Little Duck placed the folded blankets under some beaver pelts to keep them dry. On June 6, a cold front moved in and both Little Duck and Crooked Legs remembered the stowed blankets they'd received from the southern traders. That night they wrapped themselves in the blankets and used them every night thereafter. On June 20, Crooked Legs complained of fatigue and a headache. The next day, he had a fever and felt generally unwell with back pain and nausea. He was unable to paddle more than a few miles. The next day, a rash emerged: small red spots on his face and arms like pimples. By the full moon, a generalized rash erupted, covering his entire torso. Many of the spots had transformed into small blisters filled with clear fluid. Crooked Legs could do nothing but shiver in the bottom of one of the accompanying canoes and cover himself with the blanket that Little Duck had given him. After a few days, the pustules began to rupture and emit a putrid odour so foul that even his wives refused to attend to him.

By the thirtieth day of the journey, Crooked Legs could barely eat anything as his mouth and throat were also filling up with sores and even swallowing water was painful. Duncan Farquharson, having suffered this same malady in his youth, knew what Crooked Legs needed. He made a broth with herbs that eased the fiery pain in his throat. The sores on his face and trunk became raw and coalesced into a massive cobblestoned appearance of red pustules; scabs then began to form and fall off. It was this horrid phase of the disease that prompted the Lakota Indians, sixty years later, to call smallpox the 'running face sickness.' By the time they arrived at York Factory on July 2, 1782, Crooked Legs was moribund. In spite of the excellent care he received there, within ten days Crooked Legs, together with one of his wives and a third paddler, succumbed to the infection within the confines of a quarantined tent upriver from the depot.

Unfortunately, Little Duck also became infected with smallpox. He somehow managed to survive, thanks to the care of the Bay men at the fort, including Duncan Farquharson who took a special interest in him. It took the better part of a month before Little Duck could walk again because of the painful sores on the bottom of his feet.

Within that time, three more natives died at the fort. Shortly after their arrival, the Hudson's Bay factor placed York Factory under quarantine to limit the spread of smallpox to the surrounding Cree. This single act proved to be lifesaving for the various tribes in the area.

Following his recovery from smallpox, Little Duck befriended Farquharson and travelled extensively with him, trading in the Barrens for many years. He improved his English, albeit with a Scottish accent. The two traders now shared similar pockmarked faces and the Chipewyan trader understood what Farquharson must have suffered as a youth. Somehow, the kindness shown towards his good friend Crooked Legs endeared Little Duck to this laconic Scotsman. He regretted that he had once secretly mocked him for his scars.

No one really knows exactly where and when the smallpox epidemic of 1781 to 1782 began. Like an ember glowing quietly in one small area in the vastness of the North American continent, the epidemic soon began to flicker and brighten, consuming enormous swaths of human habitation on the east coast. It then exploded into a conflagration that the country had never seen before, nor since. It was the first complete continental infectious disease epidemic in North America. Tens of thousands died, mostly Indians of every tribe. It seemed that there was little difference whether one was a Cherokee in Georgia, a Pueblo in the Spanish territories of New Mexico or a Chipewyan in Alaska; smallpox exacted a heavy toll on the indigenous people. Mortality rates exceeded fifty per cent in some regions and, according to several historians, even up to eighty per cent in others. As one researcher commented in 1945, 'Smallpox killed more Indians in the early centuries than did any other single disease.'

Another smallpox epidemic on the Great Plains from 1836 to 1840 also claimed thousands of lives. Again, many Indians died and an entire Mandan village was annihilated. The epidemic of 1781 to 1782, however, would go down in history as the 'Great Smallpox

Epidemic.' It seemed to coincide with the American Revolutionary War, devastating armies on both sides. In fact, it so debilitated a Revolutionary army besieging Quebec that the Americans had to turn around and head home. Some historians believe that, from that notable incident, smallpox may have saved Canada from the Americans. It did not save any Indians, however. Instead, it decimated them. Without natural immunity to smallpox, Native Americans died in vast numbers. Historian David Brion Davis describes this as 'The greatest genocide in the history of man. Yet it is increasingly clear that most of the carnage had nothing to do with European barbarism. The worst of the suffering was caused not by swords nor guns but by germs.'

The destructive and desolating power of this particular virus continued to have ramifications for centuries for the people of the First Nations of the North American continent.

In July 1782, a group of young Scottish Hudson's Bay Company recruits at York Factory was unaware of the effect smallpox would have on their lives.

Chapter 3

York Factory: the Premonition

Boreas domus, mare amicus

In the summer of 1782, six canoes and a York boat paddled by Chipewyan Indians brought their tribe's furs to York Factory, a major trading post on the Hayes River as it entered Hudson Bay. Three of the Indians from the western Barrens were sick upon their arrival on July 2. By July 11, these three Chipewyan had succumbed to smallpox and died at the fort. The responsibility of burying them in the cemetery fell to young William Stewart, one of the new recruits at the fort.

Stewart was not a swarthy lad as some of his comrades at the York Factory post were. Rather, he was an ungainly, pimply-faced adolescent of nineteen with rusty-coloured hair. Having a late growth spurt, he seemed to be all ankles and wrists. As a Hudson's Bay Company recruit, he had enlisted for five years but had been at York Factory for only a month. He was already homesick for his family and had never seen a dead body before, so this was indeed a daunting order. He had been assigned to this gruesome task by the factor at the trading post, Matthew Cocking.

Cocking was an amiable thirty-eight-year-old writer who had made several inland journeys into the territory where the Bay men now traded. This year he was assigned the role of chief factor, supervising a slew of young Scottish recruits from the Orkney Isles, one of whom was William Stewart.

It was not from malevolence that Cocking appointed Stewart to this difficult assignment; rather, he had a fondness for the lad who was rather serious and studious. Stewart, however, had a tendency to avoid tasks that required any physical exertion since his arrival at York Factory in June. Cocking felt that Stewart needed to do this type of work to help him develop into more of a man. Besides, Stewart was the newest recruit with the lowest seniority and he had to pay his dues like the rest.

Cocking likewise once had to pay his dues. He spent years canoeing and hiking overland with Indian guides to several posts in the interior where he transcribed Company correspondence and post journals. In fact, the year before he had straightened out some bad accounting at Cumberland House and successfully balanced the financial records there. Cocking's intelligence and diligence contributed to his promotion to assistant factor at York Factory in 1770. In 1781, the Company promoted Cocking to factor of this famous Hudson's Bay Company trading post, where he earned fifty pounds a year. Although he was an Englishman, he enjoyed the company of the Scots from the northern isles and treated them fairly.

Since its inception in 1670, the Hudson's Bay Company recruited young men and even boys from the Orkneys Isles, a fertile archipelago off the northern tip of Scotland. They were hired to work at the remote trading posts of the Canadian Shield territory for several reasons. Not only were they inured to nasty weather and hardships of the north, but they also proved reliable and capable of withstanding the environmental and social deprivation peculiar to life in the outposts of the Canadian Shield.

Unlike other traders, the Orcadians could survive for prolonged periods in extreme isolation without losing their sanity. Several of them married natives and had families as Matthew Cocking himself had done. To this day, many native families of northern Manitoba have Scottish surnames which originated in the Orkney Isles. Youthful Orcadians, with the promise of adventure and a guaranteed income, left the port of Stromness in droves during the eighteenth and nineteenth centuries to join the Hudson's Bay Company ships, destined for a new life in Canada. Young Orkney lads impressed the HBC recruiters so much, with their determination and prowess, that by 1800 over eighty per cent of the Company's overseas employees were Orcadians. William Stewart was one of these recruits. Many years layer the motto for the Orcadians was chosen as 'The North our home, the sea our friend' or *Boreas domus, mare amicus* in Latin. It was entirely appropriate for this hardened race of people.

After digging only a few inches, Stewart's shovel blade struck something hard. The ground seemed to resist any further efforts to penetrate it and digging a five-foot grave seemed impossible. He had never experienced anything like this in the fertile lowlands near Stromness in northern Scotland, where a shovel could sink several inches into the ground with mild exertion. On the bleak shores of Hudson Bay, however, the unyielding frozen earth made digging a simple grave almost a whole day's work. A crooked skein of Canada geese honked overhead as if to mock his feeble efforts in opening only a few inches of the frozen tundra.

Upon removing a thin layer of the surface peat, the ground felt cold and firm to Stewart's touch. Years later, the term 'permafrost' was coined to describe the continuous frozen nature of the great sub-arctic tundra. At the Hudson's Bay Company fort at York Factory, the frozen earth extended for a hundred miles south before one could dig into the ground without the jarring effort that Stewart was now exerting.

"I'm fair puckled," he muttered as he wiped the perspiration from his forehead. "I'll never finish this today without help!"

After an hour of grueling exertion, he clearly needed help to penetrate this stone-hard plot. Cocking warned him to get the bodies, wrapped in their blankets, into the ground as quickly as possible lest the disease spread. Cocking knew that the disease could be spread from corpses and that even a victim's clothing, blankets, towels and shrouds could retain contagious pus or scabs, which could be transmitted. Hence the urgency for a speedy burial.

Trudging back to the compound's depot building to seek help, Stewart gazed upward at the silent pewter skies that reminded him of northern Scotland. Scanning for polar bears midst the willows and blueberry bushes, he felt a wave of depression overwhelm him as he swatted the black flies from his face.

"'Tis a dreich day so it is!" Stewart exclaimed and continued walking towards the fort.

Stewart could not understand why so many Company men wanted to travel thousands of miles into the nethermost reaches of this inhospitable country just to bring back furs when they could remain in the comfort and safety of the fort. Suddenly overhead, the geese coalesced into an amorphous squadron and honked even louder as though they were now scolding him for his failure as a gravedigger. He paused and gazing upward at the geese, murmuring, "Why are they already heading south so early? It's still summer."

Some of the Chipewyan who arrived at the fort two weeks earlier had told Stewart and several of his friends that the early migration of the geese was an omen signifying something evil was imminent. The Chipewyan paddlers had prayed earnestly to the spirits that they would be spared whatever calamity this might portend. They were a superstitious lot and saw sorcery in any adversity that befell their people. Perhaps they were right, as smallpox had already claimed three of their tribe only a few days ago. Stewart, however, considered this superstitious nonsense. His strict Presbyterian upbringing caused him to bristle at such pagan ideas. Still, he felt a fearful apprehension as he walked past the three bodies and made his way towards the fort's enclosure under the dull gray skies. The giant HBC flag over the fort with its bright red cross fluttered ominously at half mast in the brisk north wind off the bay.

Inside the fort, Stewart met his companion and fellow Orcadian, John Ross, who was writing a letter to his family back home. Both Ross and Stewart had signed up for the usual five-year stint as apprentices with the Company for the meagre sum of six pounds a year. They were young and quick to adapt to the harsh climate and cramped quarters. Even the rigours of the northern wilderness presented a more favourable standard of living than a life of labour back home.

Ross was taller and more muscular than Stewart. He had dark hair and heavy eyebrows and, unlike his more sombre companion, Ross seemed to wear a perpetual smirk. This trait often resulted in irritating his schoolmasters back home. He had been caned more than once for the 'sin' of appearing too cheerful. Both Orcadians had known each other back in Stromness as schoolmates. They had sailed together to the fort on the same ship, the *King George* just two months ago.

"Have you finished digging already, William?" John Ross enquired. "You certainly work fast with a shovel, so you do!"

"Not really, I cannae delve the ground, so stony hard it is. You must come and help me or it will take me all day and those dead scabrous Chipewyan make me fearful."

"Of what?" Ross exclaimed. "Surely you're not superstitious about dead people?"

"I dinnae ken, but there is something strange and unsettling about 'em. The other Indians said that many of their people died and that the pox has spread northward from the south, from other tribes claiming many of their tribe." Stewart shivered as he said this.

"Are ye afraid of getting the pox yerself then? We had that special treatment back home that's supposed to protect us from getting it, don't ye remember?"

"You mean 'the scraping'? When we got our skin scraped from a pox victim? That was fearful don't ye think? Some people died from that." Stewart recalled what happened to one of his classmates who had the scraping treatment. "Don't ye remember wee Jamie McTavish? And they told his mother it would protect him from the pox, not gie it to him."

"Aye. He got scabs all over his body with a terrible fever while his poor mother watched him die. He even had the pox sores in his mouth and he could nae eat at all towards the end. But he's with the Lord now and ye mustn't fret yourself. After all we're still here," Ross feebly commiserated. "Dinnae fash yersel, laddie," he added in Gaelic.

At this point, Matthew Cocking entered the room to see how William was managing. "And have you dug those graves already, young Stewart?"

"No, sir. The ground seems to be frozen stiff and resists the spade to penetrate it. I was just asking John Ross to help me if ye don't mind, sir," Stewart said rather abashedly.

"That's quite all right. The ground even in July never thaws and can be difficult to dig. Ross, you be sure to help him will you?"

"Aye. I will be glad to do so. But sir, we were wondering about these Indians and how they got the pox and how does the scrapin' protect us?" Ross's enquiry was not unreasonable to the factor, who seemed to be quite knowledgeable regarding smallpox. In fact, his subordinates had great respect for his vast knowledge on most subjects.

"Well lads, the scraping, as you call it, is known as 'variolation' by the physicians and indeed it will protect you from smallpox for the rest of your days. You may recall the doctors rub some lymph from one of the sores of an infected patient into the scratch marks of your arm. It is not without risk though and some people will die from this procedure."

"If people die from it like wee Jamie did, then why do they do it?" asked Stewart trembling.

"Because if you get the disease by any other contact, one in three people will die. With variolation, only one in fifty will get sick and die. Many parents think it is worth the risk to protect their children. People have been travelling to Constantinople in Turkey for a century to get the scraping, as you call it. Variolation has probably saved thousands of lives."

Cocking sounded more like a doctor than an HBC factor in the wilderness of the north. He also knew that the near total immunity of Hudson's Bay employees resulted from acquiring natural resistance from extensive childhood exposure to the disease in the Orkney Isles. However, these two young men acquired their immunity by variolation.

"In fact, a British surgeon named Latham had scraped hundreds of people in Quebec after Wolfe's victory there in 1759. No one died from it, so variolation seems to be getting safer all the time. As you know, all Company men have been advised to undergo this procedure. It's unfortunate that these Chipewyan people weren't offered the same treatment or they would still be alive." Cocking was a fount of knowledge on smallpox. In subsequent weeks, this would prove to be of great benefit to the fort and the surrounding Cree people.

Cocking left the room and returned to the fort, leaving the two young recruits to resume their task of burying the dead Chipewyan.

"Well, I do need your help, Johnnie. I cannae dig that shovel into the frozen ground by myself and I dinnae ken what to do about it." Stewart sounded irritable and began to show his anxiety for failing to bury the three dead Chipewyan Indians. Besides, he believed that having Ross with him might dispel his awful sense of foreboding.

"Well, I have an idea, William. Why don't we start a fire near the place of interment and heat the blades? Maybe the frozen ground will yield to the shovels then." John Ross was always optimistic and agreeable, unlike his dour compatriot.

Stewart's face brightened at the idea. "Och! Yer a guid friend."

The two men returned to the cemetery, where a flock of ravens were circling the dead. A few were pecking away at the bodies. John Ross quickly chased them off while Stewart started a fire. Soon they had a blazing fire near the grave with the shovel blades heating in the flames.

"That's what we call a conspiracy of ravens back home, William. Ghastly birds they are. Always up to no good," Ross said as he pushed the shovel blades into the fire.

"Aye, but ye mustn't burn the handle, John, or we'll have naught to dig with!" Stewart warned.

"Right then. They look hot enough to me. Let's dig, William!" Ross's enthusiasm was soon met with success as the permafrost yielded readily with the hot shovel blades. After several hours, they managed to dig a five-foot trench sufficient for one body.

"William, we must bury them deep or the bears will dig them up."

"Aye, dig to five feet," Stewart tersely responded. This was an arduous task, taking the men most of the day.

After the completion of the grave digging, which eventually required both pick and shovel, the young men were exhausted. In the process of lifting the last of the corpses into its icy tomb, the body slipped from their grasp and slid roughly into the grave. In an instant, the covering blanket slipped off the body, revealing a most hideous sight. The native's face, covered in festering sores and scabs, emanated a fetid odour that made Stewart retch. They quickly threw several shovelfuls of soil into the pit to cover the body.

Suddenly a dagger belonging to the dead Chipewyan fell out of the blanket that Ross held, striking the shovel with a metallic clang. The knife was familiar to the two men as being a 'trade dag' that was primarily produced by the Hudson's Bay Company in Sheffield, England, to be used for trading with the natives. It was a seven-and-a-half-inch Beaver Tail dag. The Chipewyan used knives of this sort to skin animals.

"That dagger belongs to whoever was wrapped in that blanket!" Ross exclaimed. "We must bury it with him or we will bring evil upon ourselves!"

The two young recruits looked at each other in horror and quickly threw both the blanket and the dagger into the grave over the thin layer of soil they had just shovelled. It took them only twenty minutes to fill the hole with the frozen soil and peat that had taken them hours to dig. After filling all the graves and tamping them down, John Ross felt it necessary to say a few words on behalf of the deceased. He recited the twenty-third Psalm from memory. They then beat a hasty retreat to the fort, exhausted, hungry, and somewhat depressed.

On the way back to the fort, they met Matthew Cocking, who was just coming to check on their progress. They informed the factor that all three bodies with their blankets had finally been interred to a depth of about five feet. They did not mention to Cocking that they had unceremoniously dropped one of the Chipewyan into his final resting place, thereby exposing his pox-ridden corpse. As the three men walked back to the fort, a few gulls wheeled around the Company flag, seeming mysteriously to float in mid-air like white pieces of paper fluttering, wafting upwards in the onshore breeze.

Noticing Stewart's pallor, Cocking must have suspected that something had gone wrong. He asked them, "Are ye all right then? William looks rather pale. Perhaps I expected too much of you today?"

"Quite all right, sir, just hungry I expect. I'll be fine, thank you, sir," Stewart feebly responded. At this point, food was the last thing on his mind. Ross remained silent, only his smirk betrayed Stewart's unease.

"Well, you might want to wash up and pour yourself a mug of ale in the dining hall. The ale should bring back your colour. Dinner is in an hour and I believe old Angus Cameron will be joining us today. He is quite an interesting storyteller and he should take your mind off this difficult task. Well done, lads!"

After Cocking departed, it took a while for their stomachs to settle. They washed and cleaned up, and their spirits improved now that the horrid bodies were finally buried. The ale soon rejuvenated their spirits, their flagging energy and their appetites. They were to be in for a pleasant surprise in the dining hall later that evening.

Chapter 4

The Great Smallpox Epidemic of 1781 to 1782

Angelus mortis

The three unfortunate Indian guides buried on July 3, 1782, represented the first victims of smallpox in York Factory's long history. This was a unique communicable disease in that it had arrived from the interior and not by ship or from the fort itself. Even though the fort was located eleven kilometres inland from the bay, several diseases had managed to arrive via the boat brigades. These included measles, influenza and scarlet fever, but not smallpox. In 1781, however, the first great epidemic of smallpox struck the western part of North America, having arrived via native traders along the Missouri River. The disease spread northward like a prairie wildfire, devastating and dislocating many tribes of native people who seemed especially susceptible to the virus.

The inland posts of the Hudson's Bay Company were severely affected by this epidemic. Hudson's Bay Company factors at both Cumberland House and Hudson House give modern historians a fair idea of what it was like from their journal entries describing the epidemic. For example, on January 22, 1781, the board of the Hudson's Bay Company wrote: '[We] notice with deep regret the fearful mortality which has taken place among the Indians and half-breeds throughout the country from the scourge of smallpox.'

Sadly, smallpox affected nearly every tribe on the North American continent, including the northwestern coast natives. While rapidly scything its way through a multitude of tribes, it took another year and a half for the deadly disease to reach York Factory. The outbreak of 1781 to 1782 reduced much of the Chipewyan and Cree population around Hudson Bay. Mortality rates of fifty per cent have been estimated; almost double that of people of European descent.

What the two young recruits witnessed this July day in 1782, was the easternmost spread of this vile and most lethal scourge. In spite of their exposure to the stricken native guides and their infested blankets, both Stewart and Ross were immune to the disease thanks to the variolation procedure they received in their native Scotland a few years earlier.

Unfortunately, it would take another fifteen years before any Indian tribes were offered variolation in Canada. The first native groups in Canada given this procedure were the Mohawks near Kingston in 1796. Variolation was eventually offered to many more Indians in the British colony. This procedure continued for fifty years in Canada, long after Jenner's inoculation with vaccinia or 'vaccination,' as it became commonly known. Cocking was correct in his belief that the Indians should be protected by this procedure. He was painfully aware of their peculiar susceptibility to this most dreaded disease.

Nevertheless, for Stewart and Ross at York Factory, these deaths were an ominous thing indeed. They had heard about the European epidemics of smallpox. However, in this remote place? Surely, the vastness and remoteness of the Canadian Shield would not allow smallpox to find York Factory. The scabs they had seen on the three corpses could not be erased from their minds, however, giving stark evidence to the contrary. Stewart's feelings of impending doom that gray day at the fort were borne out a few weeks later with the deaths of three more infected natives on August 6.

That same month, Factor Matthew Cocking wrote to his superiors in London: 'I believe never a Letter in Hudson's Bay conveyed more doleful Tidings than this. Much the greatest part of the Indians whose Furrs have been formerly & hitherto brought to this Place are now no more, having been carried off by that cruel disorder the Small Pox. ... the whole tribe of U'Basquiou Indians ... are extinct except one Child.'

As the young recruits returned to the fort that late summer afternoon after burying Crooked Legs and the other two natives, a lone, blanketed Indian standing on the nearby riverbank quietly looked down on them rather disdainfully. Little Duck had just witnessed the burial of his closest friend in the frozen ground. Little Duck was unaware that he, too, would become sick in only a matter of days.

Chapter 5

The Highlander
Tandem triumphans

Stewart's unease and trepidation soon dissipated as he and Ross enjoyed a hearty meal at the fort that evening. They dined with Matthew Cocking and a senior clerk at the post, an older Scotsman named Angus Cameron, a Highlander. Cameron had often entertained them with stories from the past, especially those relating to the famous Battle of Culloden near Inverness, Scotland. Tonight they dined on roast venison with turnips, which they washed down with some full-bodied Scottish ale from the Belhaven Brewery in Dunbar.

For the next hour or so, they discussed their work that day with Cocking, Cameron and several other recruits at table, young men also from the Orkney Isles. Initially the younger recruits avoided sitting near them after learning what Ross and Stewart had done that day. However, the old Scot paid no attention, having survived smallpox as a youth. The recruits wanted to ask him about smallpox but he paid them no heed.

"Och. Smallpox! I was in bed for three weeks when I was twelve. Horrible disease! Dinna let it bother ye, laddies. Ye'll get over it," Cameron said.

Cameron, a colourful character, had a flat, straight nose and intense Scottish eyes with an immense set of side-whiskers that merged into a full gray beard. He wore his plaid tam o'shanter with the colours of his clan at a jaunty angle. His high savant's dome suggested a superior intelligence and, with his delightful accent, he was a captivating raconteur. He was determined to entertain the younger men that evening with the story of the Battle of Culloden.

Soon after Cameron began his narrative, Cocking interjected, "The Battle of Culloden, lads, was the last battle to be fought on British soil just outside Inverness. For the Scots, it was their last chance to put the Stuarts back on the throne. For the English, it was 'do or die' to keep George the Second as King of England. So you see, lads, there was a lot at stake for both sides. And many of your fellow Orcadians were staunch Jacobites, supporting the rebellion."

And so the animated dinner conversation focused on the Scotsman's elaborate tale of Culloden and the Jacobite's inglorious defeat.

At first, Cameron began in the *auld* language: Gaelic. He regaled the young men with the story of the great battle of April 1746 in which he managed to barely escape with a few of his clansmen after the English had taken the field. He began slowly, solemnly at first in *sotto voce* as he described the clans arrayed on the field outside Inverness. He then reverted to English as his narrative of the battle heated up.

"Ye should hae seen them in the glory of their plaids, standing there with the braying of the bagpipes as they prepared to strike down the redcoats. I tell ye, lads, it was a sight to behold!"

At this point, he had the undivided attention of the young recruits, especially Ross and Stewart, who had heard this story many times before but never tired of hearing it. Spellbound, they gathered around the silver-haired Scot on the wooden benches in the great hall as they nursed their ales, listening intently as the Highlander's nostalgic eloquence increased in volume. John Ross knew that he had ancestors who fought on both sides of this famous battle and he became transfixed by Cameron's telling of it.

"We had the Frasers and the Mackintoshes and the MacDonalds of Glencoe. Ah, it was a beautiful sight with all the colours lined up for sure! The Frasers and the Stuarts in their bra' red tartans, and their broadswords gleaming and the sweet sound of the pipers spurring them on. And 600 Camerons, cottars and farmers and crofters with their banners waving high over the moor. All of them yelling *'Tandem triumphans!'* as they charged."

Cocking interjected briefly here to explain the meaning of the Jacobite motto for the fascinated recruits. "*Tandem triumphans* ironically means 'triumphant at last.'"

"Och! We had whipped 'em at Prestonpans, we whipped 'em at Falkirk and we knew we could whip 'em at Culloden."

Cameron wiped some spittle from the corner of his mouth as he tried to imitate the sounds of the pipes. In describing the headlong rush of the clans into the field, he let out a bloodcurdling battle cry with tears streaming down his red cheeks and disappearing into his bushy side-whiskers.

"The Highlanders charged 'em with their swords and their Lochaber axes. They wielded their claymores, their scythes and pitchforks too. But alas, we were no match against the English muskets and artillery with their three pounders firing round iron and canister. It was a bloodbath. My cousin Alexander Cameron had his head blown off by a cannonball only a few feet from me. We were droppin' like bloody flies on the moor! In an hour it was all over."

At this point Cameron paused dramatically to quaff some Belhaven Ale. Letting out a resonant belch, he then resumed his grandiloquent tale to describe the devastating denouement of the battle. Matthew Cocking smiled and nodded knowingly.

"But it was a disaster of tragic proportions, an ungodly end for Bonnie Prince Charlie and the Jacobites on that fateful day. The British slaughtered the prisoners and took away the clans, the kilts and the pipes from the Highlands. Och! Will the Scots ever recover from this tragedy?" Cameron pounded the oaken table, which made them all startle and the dishes rattle.

Taking advantage of the awkward silence, Cocking added, "For ye see, boys, the British and the Duke of Cumberland in particular were determined to quash this rebellion once and for all. Moreover, they were brutal about it too. They killed the wounded, tracked down most of the escapees and burned the houses of anyone who harboured a Jacobite. They devastated the clans, and the whole system of clan rule fell apart for the Highlanders after Culloden. Entire communities were pillaged and sent packing for no other reason than that they could not speak English. The British destroyed the entire Scottish Highland culture in retribution. For many Scots, it was a major calamity. Others, however, felt it was for the greater good since it ended the clan system of government that could not continue the way the world was heading. For better or for worse, the battle at Culloden and the failure of the Stuart restoration put an end to all that, you see."

Cameron shook his head solemnly and poured himself another draft. Then he slowly lit his pipe and for the remainder of the evening sat frowning in quiet contemplation, shaking his head dramatically from time to time.

The young recruits also remained silent, some holding back tears as they remembered having lost great uncles and grandfathers in that famous battle. For Stewart and Ross, this exciting story momentarily took their minds off the depressing events of the day. The three dead Chipewyan paddlers who had succumbed to smallpox were still foremost in their minds after dinner that evening. Their aching muscles from digging into the frozen ground would remind them of their difficult task for several days. Nevertheless, the sentimental old Scot and his colourful narrative created an exciting diversion for the dinner hour and for a brief time at least, the young recruits forgot about smallpox and its gruesome victims.

Chapter 6

The Fulfilment

Kyrie eleison

Later that evening, William Stewart pulled Matthew Cocking aside and asked him, "Sir, just how did these Chipewyan people in this remote country ever get this European illness when none of us have it ourselves and no one on the ship was sick?"

"Aye, that's a good question, William. The truth is nobody seems to know for sure. For you see, the vast expanse of the Barren Lands and indeed the whole continent would seem to preclude the spread of disease of any kind to such an extent as this. One might think that distance alone would protect the natives from smallpox. However, such is the contagious nature of the fur trade. And of course, where there's money and furs, there will be sickness."

Stewart thought about this for a moment. Cocking, for his years, seemed to be wise. Realizing how quickly the disease could spread, he established a quarantine for the Cree Indians who resided six miles upstream from York Factory. He later sent Stewart, Ross and several other recruits to administer food and medicine to those in quarantine. He also delivered a dispatch to the local Cree tribes, which instructed them to stay away from the fort. These measures seemed to work since only three more smallpox deaths were recorded at York Factory that century. The natives at other Hudson's Bay Company forts sadly were not as fortunate.

At Cumberland House on the Saskatchewan River, some forty days' paddling from York Factory, Factor William Tomison and his men showed great compassion to the dying natives. They brought them into their own very cramped quarters, fed them and administered medicine to them and then, finally, buried all those who died of the disease in the deeply frozen ground. Matthew Cocking's journal entry on July 2, 1782, stated: 'Not one in fifty of those tribes in La Pas area is still living.'

In an effort to limit the spread of the smallpox epidemic of 1781 to 1782 in the bay area, Matthew Cocking's last recorded official act involved sending urgent dispatches to other HBC posts at Fort Severn, Fort Albany and Moose Factory in August 1782, advising the other factors of the smallpox cases and to effect similar quarantines.

That night, William Stewart slept fitfully, waking frequently, feeling his face for scabs and quietly uttering the Lord's Prayer at intervals to himself. The images of the grotesque facial sores on the corpses wrapped in blankets he buried that day would not leave him. He even resorted to mumbling a prayer from his childhood, "Matthew, Mark, Luke and John, bless the bed that I lie on." He eventually cried himself to sleep.

The next day, Cocking, sensing their discomfiture, ordered the two young recruits to hike north to the shore of Hudson Bay for some fresh air and a change of scenery. Carrying a musket, they followed the river for several miles to the estuary, where clusters of tepees pitched close to the white gravel beach stood and where stands of black spruce and low bush blueberries grew. Cree Indians were catching wild trout as they entered the bay, smoking them for their winter food supply. Unlike the Chipewyan from the Barrens, these people lived on the edge of an expansive boreal forest, a wild frontier where, eons ago, glaciers sculpted innumerable lakes and massive herds of caribou roamed for millennia. In fact, tens of thousands of calves had been born on the surrounding tundra since early June and, by the end of July, they would be led across the rivers with their herd on their annual migration.

Despite its reputation for being a cold and inhospitable place, the shore of Hudson Bay was alive on this summer's day with thousands of shorebirds. The two men were overwhelmed by the myriad of Arctic terns, Hudsonian godwits and white-rumped sandpipers, all twisting, diving and soaring against the azure sky. The sheltered waters of the estuary also attracted beluga whales and their calves. Ross and Stewart had never experienced anything like this. They both realized that this was, indeed, a great land, a 'rough-hewn Eden of the north' as Cocking had put it.

Their visit to the shore took their minds off the events of the previous day. For over an hour, they threw rocks high into the air along the shoreline. With the tide out, the heavy thuds of the rocks landing on the soft mud flats sent several pecking gulls and terns scurrying. They both kept a sharp eye out for polar bears and Ross was never more than a few feet from his Brown Bess musket. Stewart seemed to have forgotten the feelings of foreboding that disturbed him so much the day before. The Orcadians enthusiastically competed with each other to see who could throw the farthest rock and who could make the loudest splat sound in the mud. After an hour of their high-spirited game, they headed back to the fort.

However, Stewart's earlier premonitions of imminent disaster that July day soon became a reality. Only a few weeks after burying the Chipewyan smallpox victims, three French warships under the able naval commander Jean-François de Galaup, Comte de Lapérouse, sacked and burned York Factory's palisades on the new moon, August 8, 1782.

The French sailors commandeered the fort without a single shot being fired. The French, in support of the American Revolution, were ransacking British possessions in Hudson Bay and along the coast. Cocking wisely knew they did not stand a chance with only sixty men against 600 Frenchmen. One of the ships was a seventy-four-gun man of war and most of the labourers and Company recruits had no knowledge of how to fire their own cannons in any event.

Just before Lapérouse captured York Factory, Matthew Cocking cleverly managed to load the *King George* with a rich cargo of furs. Successfully eluding capture, he escaped to England with all the furs from the fort, much to the French admiral's chagrin. For this act, Matthew Cocking earned an official 'Approbation' from the Company. To this day, his excellent documents continue to provide historians with a source of information that has proven to be invaluable regarding the operations at the fort and the management of the smallpox victims.

The Indians did not fare well however, following this debacle. The Hudson's Bay Company had suffered irreparable damage in their trading relationships with them. The Chipewyan suffered severely from the lack of provisions that had been destroyed in the raid and from the ongoing epidemic of smallpox, which had been ravaging the various tribes in North America. By the time winter was upon them, half of their people were dead.

Both William Stewart and John Ross spent four more years at York Factory, assisting in its reconstruction after the French laid waste to it. Following their five-year tenure, they took administrative jobs with the Company in London as clerks, a lifestyle that eminently suited them after the rigours of the tundra. They both married and remained lifelong friends in spite of their different personalities. Nevertheless, that bleak July day back in 1782 continued to haunt them whenever anyone discussed the dreaded pox. Both men ensured that their wives and children received Dr. Jenner's new vaccine against the pox in 1798.

The Hudson's Bay Company fort at York Factory eventually recovered from this disaster and remained active for another century, long after the smallpox epidemic of 1781 to 1782. The fort was rebuilt twice more to maintain the lucrative fur trade for the Hudson's Bay Company. By 1860 the complex comprised some fifty buildings, which stood conspicuously on the immense wasteland of the implacable Pre-Cambrian shield on the eroding shores of the Hayes River. Surrounded by a myriad of lakes that spangled the tundra, York Factory remained the most important trading post for the HBC; all goods entering the West and all the furs from the interior had to pass through York Factory at that time.

After almost two centuries of service as the principal headquarters or *entrepôt* of the north for the Hudson's Bay Company, York Factory finally ceased operations in 1957. In 1936, the federal government declared York Factory a National Historic Site. It was eventually turned over to Parks Canada.

Over the years, archaeological explorations revealed the remains of several of the original buildings with over 200,000 artifacts collected, many now residing in the Manitoba Museum in Winnipeg. The graves of fort officials, hunters, servants and First Nations people are still contained within an old cemetery at York Factory. The erosion caused by the nearby Hayes River has prompted scientists over the years to examine the cemetery to determine whether any bodies have been released from the permafrost. The Hayes River, in fact, has reclaimed sixty metres of the fort's waterfront, including many old buildings. Only the main depot and a smaller storage building remain today.

After 1782, no further smallpox victims ever arrived at York Factory. The only smallpox at the fort was now encased in five feet of permafrost in the Sloop Creek cemetery. The Hudson's Bay recruits had struggled to excavate the graves from the iron-hard ground. Shovelling the frozen earth back into the pits, they then painstakingly covered the bodies. The accumulation of insulating peat over the years on top of the gravesites assured their frozen state. The pox-infested blankets covering the bodies eventually froze solidly into the permafrost. They were never again exposed to thawing temperatures, even in the brief warm summers that York Factory annually enjoyed.

Chapter 7

The Arctic Institute of North America (AINA), September 2017

Turning left onto 24th Avenue Northwest to avoid the traffic on University Drive, Rachel Thompson headed east towards the Crowchild Trail, one of Calgary's major expressways. The traffic was ridiculous as usual and she became trapped in the gridlock from the exodus of university students and staff heading home after classes. *Why couldn't they have put the Arctic Institute somewhere other than the University of Calgary campus?* It had been raining all day and she just wanted to get home to her condominium in southwest Calgary, but the clogged Crowchild was unyielding.

After sitting in traffic for twenty minutes, Rachel felt herself becoming irritable with the incessant swish of the windshield wipers so she turned on the radio. A boring CBC commentary about punk rock in New York City was in full swing. Rolling her eyes, she reached over to change the station just as the traffic started to move. Suddenly a weird mix of electrical sounds with a rapid beat introduced a series of reverberating primal screams; it sounded as though someone was being tortured in an echo chamber.

"What on earth is this garbage?" Rachel uttered aloud to herself. Hesitating to switch stations after listening to this strange cacophony, she became intrigued as to what type of 'music' the CBC was playing.

After four minutes of broadcasting a mixture of electrical squawks and high-pitched squeals, the commentator announced, "That piece was *Forgotten* by the York Factory Complaint, a two-man punk rock group out of New York City. The group began in 2009 and in 2014 produced an album called *Lost in the Spectacle.* The group describes their album as being driven by a 'resistance to pacification,' whatever that means."

Reading from a review article, the announcer described the music as 'a discharge of revulsion, utilizing a factory-floor aesthetic and rendered through a repetitive, atonal, sonic sludge.'

"Yikes! That's terrible. Why, it's not even music. It's just a disgusting noise," she ranted. Rachel could not believe how anyone could find this group entertaining. "Sonic sludge, indeed!"

Then the announcer added something that intrigued her.

"The moniker 'York Factory Complaint' refers to a strange illness that afflicted workers at the Hudson's Bay fort at York Factory back in 1834 to 1836. It's a strange name for a strange group that considers itself to be musicians. Yet the genre of contemporary noise music has produced its own cult following," the announcer added.

Rachel had forgotten the traffic jam that held her back on 24th Avenue. After listening to the eerie sounds on the radio, she became oblivious to the traffic. She wondered how she had managed to turn onto the Crowchild Trail and suddenly realized she was almost halfway home. When the news came on the radio, she quickly switched it off, as she could not get the name of this strange punk rock group out of her mind. An astute archaeologist, Rachel's recollection of Canadian history was excellent. She was familiar with much of the Hudson's Bay Company history in the far north. *Didn't the Hudson's Bay Company start the fur trade in the seventeenth century at York Factory?* York Factory was a well-known fur trading post on Hudson Bay at the entrance to the Hayes River and, in the 1830s, many people got sick there, she recalled.

"Didn't the York Factory Complaint cause people to die?" she questioned aloud.

After arriving home, Rachel kicked her shoes off, poured herself a glass of wine and googled the unusual malady. She discovered an old medical reference regarding the 'Complaint' but the article failed to explain what caused it. She decided to phone Dr. Wojeich Jaworski, one of her colleagues at the Arctic Institute, about this unique historical illness. Jaworski was a forensic pathologist who worked at the Arctic Institute with Rachel and was familiar with diseases from the past. Rachel respected his encyclopedic knowledge of Canadian history and medicine.

"Yes, Rachel, I am familiar with the York Factory Complaint," he said. "It was always considered to be caused by lead poisoning, although there have been some problems with that diagnosis over the years. The symptom complex merely suggested lead poisoning but it was never actually confirmed by any laboratory testing."

"Why is that?"

"Well, because you can't simply make a diagnosis of a disease that occurred 180 years ago on clinical grounds alone. You need laboratory confirmation. Just like the sailors in the Franklin expedition. Until they were able to get bone and hair samples and measure the lead concentration in the 1980s, the diagnosis of lead poisoning was mere speculation. Making a diagnosis in retrospect can be shrouded with error."

"But why has no one done testing on any of the men buried at York Factory who died of the Complaint?"

"Good question. First, many who died of the Complaint were not even buried at the fort. Secondly, I don't think anyone has bothered to give it serious consideration until now," Jaworski replied.

Rachel's growing fascination with this illness brought on a wave of questions. "But, Wojeich, wouldn't that be a fairly easy thing to do if the bodies were buried in permafrost? Wouldn't they be preserved just as the Franklin sailors on Beechey Island were? And wouldn't that make a great research project?"

"Yes, yes and yes, Rachel. But getting the paperwork approved and permission from Parks Canada and the Arctic Institute and the Province of Manitoba would be overwhelming. Not to mention the First Nations who consider the old fort to be sacred. Many of the people buried there are Swampy Cree who lived their entire lives there. You would need to jump through a lot of hoops to pull off a project like that."

"Maybe so, but I need you to help with this, Wojeich. We need to get the Institute to do an archaeological dig of this kind as a research project. We could probably get several papers published if we finally discovered the true cause of the illness. You know what they say, 'Publish or perish.'"

"You know, you are right, Rachel. I'll talk to Gordon Dowling about this and see what he says about such a project. But why all this sudden interest in the York Factory Complaint? What brought this on might I ask?"

"You wouldn't believe me if I told you."

"Try me."

"Okay, so I was stuck in traffic coming out of the university and turned on the radio and suddenly this god-awful noise was being played on CBC. Intrigued, I listened for a while and they said it was by a punk rock group out of New York that called themselves the

York Factory Complaint. I can just imagine a couple of tattooed guys with burgundy-coloured hair playing this stuff with a synthesizer in their parents' garage. Where they came up with the name beats me. However, it got me thinking about the strange illness that they called a complaint. With our modern technology, all we would need to do would be to exhume one of the victims of this illness, do some hair and bone analysis, and come up with a definitive diagnosis."

"That simple?" Jaworski sarcastically replied.

"Well, yes, if we can get the funding and all the necessary approvals and get through the paperwork."

"Hmm. That is not so simple. Rachel, I think your idea has merit and I will start working on it. Gordon Dowling has managed to get difficult projects of this kind approved before. I'll give him a call."

"Thanks, Wojeich, and thanks for listening. I still cannot believe there is a punk rock group named after a mysterious ailment from the nineteenth century. I wonder what they were smoking to come up with that. Millennials. Hah!"

Rachel poured herself another glass of wine and began researching York Factory and its famous Complaint. She finally fell asleep on the couch with her laptop at her side.

The next morning, she met Dr. Gordon Dowling, one of the Arctic Institute's physical anthropologists, in the hall outside her office.

"I hear you have a complaint, Rachel. Did you wish to discuss that with me?" Dowling feigned a look of disapproval and concern.

"No, Gordon, everything's fine actually. I have no complaints. The people here are great to work with and I love my work. Why do you ask?" Rachel was now worried that someone had spoken ill of her.

"Well that's not what I heard. Jaworski tells me you have a big Complaint." Dowling broke into a smile and wagged his finger at her, laughing.

"Oh, Gordon, how dumb of me to fall for one of your nerdy puns. Yes, of course the York Factory Complaint. This fascinates me and I think we should apply to exhume one of the bodies at the cemetery at the fort, but we can't do this without your help. Think of the papers that a project of this kind could generate. In addition, we would be solving an age-old mystery. As a physical anthropologist, wouldn't that be right up your alley?" Rachel could be very persuasive at times.

"Yes, Rachel, it would be. I admire your enthusiasm. Jaworski and I have already spoken at length about the possibilities and we think if this proposal were approved, we just might undertake an exhumation by next July. The three of us should sit down and begin to make tentative plans for this project. We will need to submit our application within the month to the director."

Rachel was ecstatic when she realized that the eminent Dr. Gordon Dowling would support her with the application for her idea to the Arctic Institute. The Arctic Institute had celebrated its seventieth anniversary the previous year and had unveiled a new vision statement, 'Advancing Knowledge for a Changing North,' which was featured on a glossy brochure that Dowling plucked from his jacket pocket.

"Listen to this, Rachel, in case you have any doubts regarding the merits of your ideas about a project at York Factory. 'At AINA, we work in partnership with northern and Indigenous organizations, researchers, governmental and non-governmental institutions, and all others interested in Arctic issues from across Canada and around the world. Our parliamentary mandate is to advance the study of the North American and circumpolar Arctic through the natural and social sciences, the arts and humanities and to acquire, preserve and disseminate information on physical, environmental and social conditions in the North. We strive to meet that mandate through diverse multi- and interdisciplinary research activities. Blah, blah, blah," Dowling added.

Rachel took the brochure and turning it over asked Dowling, "I know all that stuff, Gordon. So what's your point?"

"My point is that when you submit your proposal for this project Rachel, try to incorporate some of the same phrases used in the mission statement. The directors love it when you baffle them with their own bullshit. Commit some of it to memory just in case you are interviewed. That always impresses them. And do your home-work on the history of the York Factory Complaint. Jaworski and I have decided to let you direct this project, subject to approval by the director, of course."

"Gordon, that's fantastic!" Rachel's enthusiasm for the project and her appreciation for Dowling's support were clearly visible. She leaned over and gave Dowling a hug, something she had never done before. Dowling's face in response turned beet red all the way up to his balding dome.

"Okay, but there's a lot of work to be done to complete our sub-mission. After that, it's up to the directors," Dowling advised. "You may want to tell your boyfriend that you will be gone for a month next summer with this dig if it gets approved."

Looking away, Rachel was clearly uncomfortable with this last bit of advice. "Right," she said softly. She had not told anyone about her recent breakup with her boyfriend of two years and she wasn't about to disclose anything regarding her personal life right now, especially to someone as senior as Gordon Dowling. She knew that a project of this nature would take her mind off her disappointment. As far as her ex-boyfriend was concerned, everything was about him.

Rarely had he shown any interest in Rachel's work and he seldom asked her about her research. What she needed now more than ever was a distraction and the anticipation of this project instantly lifted her spirits.

"Look, why don't we grab a coffee together later this morning with Jaworski and we can discuss your proposal informally?" Dowling suggested.

Rachel agreed to meet with her mentor later that morning at 10:00. She decided to give Wojeich Jaworski a call to see if he could join them to discuss the York Factory project. However, just thinking about her recent breakup still left her with a sinking feeling. *Screw him!* She was determined more than ever to focus on this project.

Two hours later, the three scientists huddled together in a corner of the cafeteria by themselves. They were being rather secretive lest their project should reach the director before their formal submission. Dowling wrote notes on a clipboard while Rachel used her tablet.

"So the way I see it, we need to obtain approval from the Arctic Institute first in order to proceed with any of the necessary paperwork. This should be fairly easy since this project could provide several articles from all branches of northern research. As you well know, the York Factory Complaint has presented itself as a mystery to the medical profession for years," Jaworski advised.

"Yes, you being the lone physician on our team know about that more than anyone, Wojeich. By the way, we will have to dig through permafrost, which is a considerable challenge. We will need all sorts of equipment, such as propane heaters, electric shovels and gas powered generators," Dowling added. He had published several papers on the recession of the permafrost in conjunction with climate change and was booked to present a paper the following summer in Russia on the effects of climate change on permafrost.

"There will no doubt be some artifacts buried with the body, such as clothing or personal items. These would potentially provide another research paper. They might provide a window into life in the early nineteenth century," Rachel suggested. As a forensic archaeologist, this subject was an area of her expertise.

"Yes, there are lots of possibilities here. One of the things we need to work on as soon as possible is to get the director to talk with Parks Canada. We also need to inform the RCMP," Dowling advised.

"Why the RCMP, Gordon?" Rachel was intrigued.

"Because we are digging up a dead body from a cemetery. Even though it has been buried for over 180 years, they might want to ensure there's no foul play. They will likely just rubber stamp this approval since it falls under the auspices of the Arctic Institute."

At this point, Jaworski interjected, "Perhaps we're getting ahead of ourselves. We have not even identified a body yet. How do we know if any victims of the York Factory Complaint are even buried there? Records show that at least thirty-two known people suffered from this disease, including the three people who succumbed to it in the winter of 1834/35. Historical records also suggest that there was a ten per cent mortality from the Complaint during the peak years. We need to identify the names of all thirty-two people and find out who died of the Complaint and whether they were buried in the York Factory cemetery. To my knowledge, there may be hundreds of people buried there from over the centuries. Finding a specific body there could prove to be tricky."

"Wojeich is right, Gordon. I was up late last night and I have already reviewed the names of all the Hudson's Bay employees who died of the Complaint. There is a man, however, named Joseph Charles buried in the Sloop Creek cemetery at York Factory. It is generally believed he died of the Complaint after suffering with it for more than a year. He first became ill in April 1835 and was sick for much of the year. Just as he was improving, he had a relapse in December and finally died on May 27, 1836," Rachel explained.

"Are we certain that he actually had the Complaint?" Dowling asked.

"Just listen to this report about his condition that I found in the archives," Rachel interjected. "'Joseph Charles, who first became ill in the late spring of 1835, was indisposed of, and after that he had a major relapse on 20 April 1836 and on 27 May expired at this place … from a severe attack of dyspepsia. The same disease which has prevailed here each spring since 1834, notwithstanding the assiduous care and attention of Dr. Whiffen, it increased until he grew more and more feeble, till at length it proved fatal.'"

"Where did you find that information, Rachel? That's fascinating!" Dowling exclaimed.

"From a medical report from Dr. Charles G. Roland, who was a prolific writer and physician. Listen to how he ends his paper on the York Factory Complaint. 'A sustained and exhaustive archaeological survey of York Factory has not yet been made; when it is, possibly the final piece of this puzzle will be set in place.'"

Rachel closed her tablet, looked at her two colleagues rather seriously and in dramatic fashion pronounced, "Gentlemen, we are going to have to dig this guy up in order to find this missing piece of this puzzle. I believe the exhumation of Joseph Charles is necessary to solve the mystery of the York Factory Complaint."

Chapter 8

The Seminar: Medical College University of Manitoba, October 2017

And to these children God gave knowledge
– Daniel 1:17

On a blustery autumn afternoon in Winnipeg, three first-year medical residents in the Infectious Disease program met in the Medical School library to discuss their joint presentation to be given the following week. The team had appointed Sarah Goldman to do the PowerPoint presentation while classmates Frederick Allan and Lisa Richardson would do the bulk of the research. The ambitious trio of medical residents in Infectious Diseases was scheduled to present to other residents, medical students and medical staff at Grand Rounds.

The subject of their paper was "Communicable diseases – how are they spread?" Dr. Frank Emberley, their mentor, had been assigned to review their presentation and he was running late. Goldman was an attractive and intelligent brunette with a master's degree in science, while Richardson and Allan both had bachelor's degrees in chemistry and biology.

Frederick Allan also had a degree in Canadian history. He was interested in medical history and those infectious diseases prevalent during the time of the explorers and fur traders. He seemed out of place in a medical library, with his lanky six-foot-four frame and his dry humour.

"So I hear this guy, Emberley, is a real stickler about handwashing. He apparently wants to make sure we get this point across in our presentation," Allan commented.

"Yes, although you might think this is sort of like motherhood and apple pie for Infectious Disease residents. I mean who doesn't wash their hands these days anyway?" replied Goldman.

"Lots of people don't wash their hands," Richardson interjected. "And especially doctors. That's why we have so many nosocomial infections lately." Lisa Richardson was a vivacious and articulate blonde with a diamond stud in her nose and penetrating green eyes; she had a tendency to be outspoken because of her keen sense of justice.

"Noso-who? What are you talking about, Lisa?" Allan asked sheepishly.

"A nosocomial infection is an infection you get when you are in the hospital for another unrelated illness. You are not supposed to get sicker in the hospital. That's why Emberley wants us to belabour this point. He wants us to emphasize the importance of handwashing for all doctors. They get so busy they often forget to wash after seeing a patient," Richardson explained.

"Ah! So what we're presenting in this talk is basically an info-mercial for handwashing? Well, that's great, but what will change doctors' behaviour to make them more inclined to wash their hands?" Goldman enquired.

At that moment, Dr. Frank Emberley, Professor and Head of Infectious Diseases, Department of Medicine at the University of Manitoba, strode into the room, having caught the tail end of their discussion. He was wearing a white lab coat with his stethoscope draped around his neck. He clutched a cell phone in one hand and a bottle of disinfectant in the other. His head was shaved and he wore a navy blue polka dot bow tie.

"Good afternoon, ladies and gentleman! Sorry I'm late, but yes, you have raised a very good point. How do we change people's behaviour regarding hygiene, especially doctors in a hospital setting?"

"By using charts and graphs describing rates of hospital-acquired infections?" asked Lisa Richardson.

"That's a good start, Lisa, but might I suggest that your presentation include a discussion on fomites?" Emberley added. He had written a paper on 'The Epidemiological Evidence of Viral Transmission via Fomites in a Hospital Setting' and he wanted to make sure his students were familiar with the subject.

"What are fomites exactly?" Allan enquired.

"I am surprised that you have not come across this term in your research," the professor scolded. "Fomites are any object or material upon which microbes can reside and be transmitted to humans. It is the main reason why we wash our hands and why I am carrying this bottle of disinfectant. My cell phone has the potential to be a fomite for infection, as does your laptop, and the doorknobs and countertops in the hospitals. Even our stethoscopes can spread disease. Physician's neckties have been cultured and shown to harbour a host of bacteria. That's why I wear a bowtie. You will recall that we have a cleaning staff using disinfectants daily on counters and desks and doorjambs because they too are fomites. If you've ever been on a cruise ship, you'll see the crew ensuring you clean your hands before you enter the dining room."

"A cruise ship! We should be so lucky. I would wash four times a day if I could go on a cruise!" exclaimed Sarah Goldman. Emberley frowned.

"So, was it the famous Louis Pasteur who discovered fomites?" asked Allan. "How long has medical science known about this?"

"Actually we've known about fomites for hundreds of years, but doctors have chosen to ignore the fact that germs can be spread by unwashed hands and fomites. And no, it was not Pasteur but rather an Austrian physician named Ignaz Semmelweis. Back in the 1840s, Semmelweis first recognized that puerperal fever was killing women who had just given birth. He traced the disease to those doctors who, after working in the pathology lab, examined their patients without washing their hands. He proposed the practice of handwashing after making the astute observation that puerperal fever was three times higher in those wards where physicians performed deliveries than those serviced by midwives. Obviously, some contaminant from corpses in the path lab was being transmitted to women after their babies had been born."

Lisa interjected, "That's disgusting! Why would they do that?"

"Because it became a political issue for doctors. They were an arrogant lot. They did not want an upstart contemporary telling them what to do. You know the saying, 'But we've always done it this way.' Sometimes change comes painfully slow."

"Well, it's a good thing doctors aren't arrogant nowadays!" Allan wryly remarked. "Anyway, what happened to Dr. Semmelweis? Did he win the Nobel Prize in Medicine?"

"No. Sadly, he became a pariah among his peers. He became profoundly depressed and then died in ignominy in an insane asylum. Today he may well have won the Nobel Prize but he was ahead of his time. However, he is considered a pioneer in the use of antiseptics." Emberley was turning this prep session into a full history lecture and all three students were captivated by this fascinating information.

"In fact, the willful ignorance of his contemporaries is referred to as 'the Semmelweis Reflex,' which describes the reflexive rejection of new information simply because it contradicts entrenched beliefs. His ideas were rejected by some very bright people at the time."

"They don't sound too bright to me. Talk about bigots in science," muttered Allan.

"Yes they were but, to get back to your question, fomites were recognized back in 1763 when the British military sent blankets that were infested with smallpox to Indians, who contracted the disease from the blankets, many dying from the ensuing epidemic. Therefore, it is reasonable to say that Britain was the first nation to incorporate smallpox as a biological weapon to kill its enemies. Sadly, it was the beginning of biological warfare in the dark annals of history."

"They really did that? That's terrible! Who would do a thing like that?" exclaimed Lisa.

"Well, the British government did. It was an undertaking to control and limit the number of First Nations during the early period of colonization by the British. An officer named Lord Jeffrey Amherst planned and supervised the transfer of infected blankets to the Indians under Chief Pontiac in the summer of 1863 during the siege of Fort Pitt. He was the commanding general of the British forces in North America during the battles of the French and Indian wars. He really hated the First Nations people and his goal was to wipe them out entirely with smallpox by the use of blankets as fomites, and it almost happened. Hundreds died as a result of this cruel and racist policy."

"So they knew back then that disease could spread by touching contaminated objects and yet the doctors in Austria over a hundred years later still refused to wash their hands. They were wilfully ignorant!" Lisa Richardson at this point was quite incensed.

"Yes, they were, but the point is that, even today, germs are spread from touching inanimate objects. The British had knowledge of this aspect of infectious diseases over 200 years ago."

Emberley was familiar with this bit of medical trivia; in his lectures, he would often quote from historians who described the siege of Fort Pitt, which is now Pittsburgh. It was a well-known fact that British military authorities approved of attempts to spread smallpox among the enemy. It was a deliberate policy of the British authorities in the colonies to infect the Indians with smallpox.

At this point Frederick Allan became animated in the discussion. "I hate to get off subject, Professor Emberley, but if smallpox were still around today, could it be spread from an infected blanket or a handkerchief?"

"Absolutely. In fact, smallpox outbreaks were once traced to cotton that was imported back in 1908. That's when medical science started to pay closer attention to the transmissibility of infection by fomites. Fortunately, smallpox has been eradicated globally and the last recorded case was in Somalia in 1977. Shortly after that, public vaccinations ceased. But it has been estimated that smallpox over the centuries has killed a billion people."

"Yikes. So if smallpox were to return now, we might all get sick?" asked Lisa Richardson.

"Yes you would and so would all those baby boomers who were vaccinated before 1979. The smallpox vaccine only protects people for eight to ten years at best so virtually everyone on the entire planet would be susceptible if the dreaded orthopoxvirus were ever to be released."

"What if that happened?" Sarah blurted out. "Shouldn't we all get vaccinated then?"

"Well, no. There is always a risk with any type of vaccination and since scientists feel the disease has been virtually eradicated, why put people at risk? Besides, the 'anti-vaxxers' would jump all over this one since the vaccinia vaccine carries a long list of contraindications and side effects. There have been no cases of smallpox in forty years, which more or less proves that the disease has virtually disappeared from the face of the earth."

"Why do you say 'more or less' professor? You seem to have some doubts about the complete eradication of smallpox?" Frederick Allan decided to play the devil's advocate at this point.

"Well, because smallpox still exists in the freezers of two labs in the world – one in Novosibirsk, Russia and the other in the CDC in Atlanta – I suppose it is always possible that a lab error or leak could unleash the virus onto mankind again." Emberley tried to be reassuring.

"Does the National Virology Laboratory in Winnipeg have smallpox? What if it somehow got out?" Allan asked.

"No, Canada's National Microbiology Lab does not have small-pox in its freezers. Only the two labs I mentioned earlier house the smallpox virus. Besides, Winnipeg's level four lab is probably the safest lab in the world right now. However, we are getting off track for your presentation next week. This is fascinating stuff but it's all theoretical, don't you see?" The professor tried to steer them back to their presentation on transmissibility of viruses in hospitals.

"Whoa! Wait a minute!" Lisa Richardson was clearly exercised about this discussion. "Why couldn't smallpox get out of the freezer and cause a massive epidemic? Wouldn't it be better to destroy those viruses that are in Atlanta and Novo-whatever?"

"Novosibirsk, Russia. Called the Vector Institute; it's basically the CDC of Russia. It houses research facilities for all levels of biological hazards and is very secure. It's located in a secluded area with an entire regiment of soldiers protecting it ever since its construction.

And no, why would the Russians destroy their smallpox samples as long as the Americans have theirs? And vice versa?" Professor Emberley seemed well informed about the status of other level four labs in the world.

"So, this is a case of 'microbiological détente' between the two most powerful nations on earth. Am I right?" asked Allan. "And what about the Chinese or the North Koreans? Do they have smallpox in their level four labs?"

At this point, Emberley realized that the subject of smallpox had somehow hijacked his seminar topic and the students could not focus on the subject at hand. Not wishing to quash the spirit of scientific enquiry in this small cadre of keen medical students, he went with the flow and announced to them, "Okay guys, enough about smallpox for now, but next week, each of you in a twenty-minute presentation will discuss the smallpox virus from a different perspective. Richardson, you will discuss the history of viruses in general as they pertain to laboratory accidents and leaks. Allan, you will present the possibility of the resurgence of the virus via fomites and, Goldman, I want you to discuss smallpox as an agent of bioterrorism. Got it?"

All three nodded enthusiastically in agreement. Emberley felt a twang of guilt over having his students research a disease that no longer existed. It was information of no practical value, sort of like discussing sheep-raising in Australia to the Inuit. *What the heck? It will keep them busy and they might gain invaluable information regarding the principles of viral transmission, which is what this course is all about.* Being an expert on smallpox was sort of like owning a Studebaker.

Chapter 9

Lab Accidents and Fomites

Good judgment comes from experience; experience comes from bad judgment

The following week, Frank Emberley moved his seminar to a larger classroom. He had invited interns and residents to attend for the main purpose of teaching them basic principles in infectious diseases using his three new residents. The subject of smallpox as the focus of the discussion also aroused the interest of several members of the medical staff, many of whom were in other services and departments.

"I wish to welcome everyone to today's seminar on infectious diseases. We will have three short presentations to demonstrate some basic I.D. principles followed by a question and answer period. Dr. Lisa Richardson will begin with the subject of 'Level Four Labs – Just how safe are they anyway?' Lisa?"

Lisa began her presentation by showing several dramatic headlines on the screen with articles from various scientific journals and newspapers. From the prestigious journal *Science* in 2004: 'Infectious diseases. Mounting lab accidents raise SARS fears.' The next slide was also from *Science*, July 2014: 'CDC Closes Anthrax and Flu Labs after Accidents.'

Then glaring headlines from the *Guardian* in England appeared on the overhead screen: 'Revealed: one hundred safety breaches at UK labs handling potentially deadly diseases. Blunders led to live anthrax being posted from one lab and holes being found in isolation suits at a facility handling Ebola-infected animals.'

After showing these headlines, Lisa discussed the risks of working in microbiology labs, with a cover slide that stated: 'Lab Accidents Do Happen.'

"An estimated 500,000 laboratory workers are employed in various laboratories in the United States," she said. "These people are annually exposed to a variety of pathogens that put them at risk of infection."

She paused for effect before going on to describe other lab accidents involving the transmission of lethal viruses to workers, including the release of the Marburg virus in Germany in 1967, which infected thirty-one lab workers and killed seven.

"And another example of a deadly lab accident includes the 2004 Ebola lab accident in Russia which killed a female scientist after she pricked herself with a syringe."

She then went on to discuss other data, including anecdotal case reports and some newsworthy breaches, which had taken place at the CDC in Atlanta in the past, citing lax security, inadequate inventory methods and complacency as the main reasons for these accidents.

Several physicians in the audience, however, looked skeptical. During the question-and-answer period, one medical resident asked, "But isn't the level four lab in Winnipeg one of the safest labs in the world?"

Lisa Richardson had anticipated this question. "Well, that is an excellent question," she said. "There are only around fifty facilities in the world with level-four containment for the world's deadliest bacteria and viruses. The CDC lab in Atlanta is one, the National Microbiology Lab in Winnipeg is another and the Vector Institute in Novosibirsk, Russia is a third level-four facility. However, let me remind you that there have been problems with all these labs and I quote:

"'Shortly after the official opening of the National Microbiology Lab in Winnipeg, in 1999, the building had a leak in which waste water made its way into the city system. This was something that was not supposed to happen but did again in 2000. More serious was a collision that took place in 2005 with a FedEx vehicle. It was soon learned that the courier was transporting deadly pathogens, including flu, tuberculosis and anthrax. Streets surrounding the accident were immediately closed as the intact containers from the collision were gathered. In 2008, around thirty lab staff had to be given antibiotics after being exposed to anthrax.'"

Lisa left the headlines from the *Winnipeg Free Press* on the screen for added effect as she described the story. "If I might add one more headline from the CBC from February 2018. 'Forty-five incident reports between January 2015 and October 2016 shed light on risks at the National Microbiology Lab in Winnipeg.'"

At this point, someone at the back of the room emitted a low whistle.

"Yes, more than a dozen employees may have been exposed to potentially dangerous pathogens in incidents at Winnipeg's National Microbiology Laboratory over a twenty-two month period. The anecdotes cited above involving both the Centers for Disease Control and Prevention, and the National Microbiology Lab in Winnipeg clearly demonstrate the need for ongoing safety reviews and security analyses. Each year deadly pathogens transported to major labs around the world involve a multitude of handlers and labs. We need to be more vigilant than ever since 9/11." Lisa Richardson reached for her water bottle and paused for a moment.

"In July 2014 at the U.S. National Institute of Health in Maryland, several glass ampoules from the 1950s containing viable smallpox were discovered in a refrigerator belonging to the FDA. They were eventually flown by helicopter to the CDC in Atlanta where they were destroyed in February 2015 in the presence of a WHO team. Neither the scientists at the NIH nor the CDC believed that these ampoules could contain viable smallpox, but they did. The point is, imagine if that helicopter were to crash? Perhaps, in retrospect a Brinks truck might have been safer to transport these vials. Just because researchers have a PhD doesn't mean they always use common sense."

Several heads nodded in the audience. Most of this information was new to the medical people in attendance. These stories seemed to keep many in the audience spellbound.

"Oh, and one last anecdote: The last case of smallpox on planet earth was in 1978 and it was not the case from Somalia. It occurred in the United Kingdom in which a woman named Janet Parker contracted the disease because of a laboratory accident. Ms. Parker had been employed as a photographer working in a darkroom on the floor above a research lab that housed the smallpox virus at the University of Birmingham. So, she wasn't even a lab worker. The virus somehow made its way through the ductwork to where she worked. In spite of having been vaccinated only twelve years earlier, she died of smallpox.

"So yes. Lab accidents do happen and they can be very danger-ous. It is not *if* smallpox will be released by a laboratory accident, but *when*. Thank you for your attention."

At this last pronouncement, a few heads turned and Lisa Richardson sat down to save time for her colleague, Frederick Allan to discuss fomites.

After a brief introduction by Emberley, Allan began a somewhat tedious lecture on a subject they had all heard before. Frederick

Allan then surprised everyone by throwing in what Emberley had hoped would not be mentioned: "The historical use of fomites in the spread of smallpox."

He then went on to reiterate details from Dr. Emberley's lecture from the week before, describing the role of the British during the Indian Wars when fomites were intentionally used to infect natives. Describing this historical incident as the first recorded instance of bioterrorism in North America, Allan went on to say something that aroused considerable attention from his audience.

"There are probably hundreds of smallpox-bearing fomites buried in the northern tundra in permafrost today such as clothing, shrouds, blankets and even the corpses themselves. Should these ever be disturbed, it is entirely possible that smallpox could be accidentally released into an immunologically naïve population and once again become a plague of colossal proportions. If the smallpox virus has been kept viable in the freezers of the CDC in Atlanta and at the Vector Institute in Novosibirsk, Russia, then it stands to reason that it could be viable in the permafrost of the subarctic regions as well."

At this pronouncement, several hands went up and numerous questions were asked at the same time similar to a press conference:

"How could a virus possibly stay viable for that long in the permafrost?"

"When were the last victims of smallpox buried in the permafrost in northern Canada?"

"Wouldn't the virus become attenuated after so many years and lose its viability and its lethality? Wouldn't the DNA disintegrate with time?"

At this point Frank Emberley stood up to quiet the audience and bring some semblance of order to the seminar. Frederick Allan, unable to answer all the questions, recognized he was out of his depth and quickly sat down.

"This is all theoretical," Emberley reassured the audience, "and no one has ever made any archaeological excavations where victims of smallpox have been buried. Just because there may be smallpox victims buried in permafrost doesn't make them contagious."

"But what about the Franklin bodies buried on Beechey Island up north? Weren't those bodies intact when they were exhumed? And couldn't any pathogens on those bodies, whether bacterial or viral, likewise remain intact and therefore be contagious?"

This last enquiry came from one of his own staff who was familiar with the Franklin Expedition and the famous archaeological dig back in 1984. Three sailors of the famous Arctic exploration, buried in permafrost, were finally exhumed in that project and their bodies were preserved. The sailors had tragically died during the disastrous and ill-fated expedition in the nineteenth century.

"Yes, all these things are theoretically possible but we need to move on to our last speaker of the day," advised Emberley. He had not anticipated such a heated discussion on something that had long ago become extinct. He tried to steer the discussion away from the possibility of the re-emergence of smallpox by introducing his next speaker, Dr. Sarah Goldman.

"Ladies and gentlemen, Dr. Goldman will now address us on the subject of smallpox and bioterrorism." Emberley sat down wondering what Sarah might have added to her presentation.

Chapter 10

Smallpox and Bioterrorism

Variola as the ultimate WMD

"Thank you, Dr. Emberley. Could smallpox make a comeback? Is it lurking somewhere awaiting the right opportunity to once again cause a global pandemic?" Dr. Sarah Goldman began her presentation in a rather dramatic fashion. Looking over her glasses and pushing aside her dark hair, she paused for effect. The audience was spellbound.

"The previous speaker alluded to the great frozen repository of the northern permafrost in Canada. One must not ignore the vastness of Siberia in which hundreds of bodies afflicted with smallpox over the centuries have likewise been buried. Now, with global warming, the permafrost is melting and some of the bodies are resurfacing. Russian scientists fear that the deadly smallpox virus will eventually be resurrected by climate change. In addition, they believe that it is just a matter of time. In fact, they have already discovered corpses from the last century with smallpox lesions. Using hazmat suits, scientists from the Vector Institute have discovered fragments of the smallpox DNA on these bodies although they did not find the virus itself." Sarah then displayed the source of these findings on screen.

"So the threat of bioterrorism may not come from a level four lab in the United States or Russia, but from the ground itself in which smallpox is released into the environment. From earlier presentations today, one can see that the smallpox virus makes an ideal agent of bioterrorism. It is highly contagious with a high mortality rate and few people have been vaccinated against it. And lastly, there is no known cure."

Dr. Emberley felt this last statement might have been a little too dramatic. He squirmed in his seat and checked his cell phone for messages. Sarah continued to discuss the controversy over why neither the CDC nor the Vector labs were willing to destroy whatever stockpiles of smallpox they kept in their freezers.

"Endless ethical and political questions abound regarding the destruction of these viruses, as you can well imagine. After the attacks of 9/11, the concern regarding bioterrorism has been elevated, in particular the use of smallpox as a biological weapon. Let me quote a line or two from the *New England Journal of Medicine* April 25, 2002, by Dr. Jeffrey Drazen regarding these concerns:

"'Unfortunately, even if we all become well acquainted with the clinical presentation of smallpox, by the time the disease is recognizable, it will probably be too late to prevent hundreds or thousands of deaths. Thus, the most pressing question is whether we need a pre-emptive vaccination campaign against smallpox. The decision on such a plan depends on the likelihood that terrorists will use smallpox as a weapon. A year ago, it seemed unthinkable. Recent events, however, have raised the possibility that such an attack could conceivably occur.'"

Goldman continued with another slide. "After almost sixteen years since 9/11, we have yet to see any major acts of bioterrorism on the North American continent. A few isolated cases of anthrax poisoning in 2001 occurred in which there were five deaths. One successful attack with salmonella was reported in Oregon in 1984 with no fatalities. But the big shoe of smallpox has yet to fall." She paused for a drink of water.

"The reality simply stated is that one of the most lethal viruses known to man remains hidden in two freezers. These lethal frozen stocks of variola are guarded and monitored by the governments of Russia and the United States. Even though the disease has been extinguished in the wild, it still exists in the lab. If rogue laboratory workers or terrorists were to gain access to these remaining smallpox repositories, the results would be catastrophic for the entire world.

"One of the more frightening revelations comes from a Soviet defector, who in 1992 advised that he had overseen an extensive, illegal program to develop smallpox into a highly effective biological weapon. Now that was twenty-five years ago, but at present we have no idea what happened to any of that lethal material.

"Models of contagious infectious diseases such as influenza are being continually studied and there would be little difference if smallpox were the agent. With increasing international travel, once released, the virus would spread exponentially around the globe. Some uncertainty still exists whether or not any samples may have fallen into the wrong hands of government-supported terrorists."

At this point, several hands shot up in the audience.

"So Dr. Goldman, would you say the answer is mass vaccination? And if so, do we have sufficient vaccine to protect the North American continent?"

Sarah Goldman was prepared for this question. She showed a slide with the statistics of mass vaccination.

"Mass vaccination would not be without huge costs including the complication of vaccine-related adverse effects and deaths from vaccinia itself. The vaccinia vaccine is the most dangerous of all the live vaccinations that we currently have. Scientists in the *New England Journal of Medicine* article estimate upwards of two to three hundred deaths would accompany a pre-emptive mass vaccination program in the U.S. alone."

Another hand went up. "Dr. Goldman, it has been sixteen years since 9/11. Do you really feel the risk of bioterrorism with smallpox is a threat?"

Sarah once again deftly handled this question.

"Whereas the probability of such an attack seems less likely with the passage of time, the possibility still exists as long as the virus exists in level four lab freezers. Furthermore, since the breakup of the Soviet Union, we have no idea if defectors have permitted the release of previously protected hordes of biological weapons such as smallpox to rogue states.

"In fact, the director of the State Research Center of Virology and Biotechnology (Vector) in Russia has issued a warning to all labs. His concern was that terrorist organizations could lure former underpaid Soviet researchers to smuggle variola samples to be used as biological weapons. I will quote him directly. 'All you need is a sick fanatic to get to a populated place. The world health system is completely unprepared for this.'"

The next question came from one of the internists in the audience.

"Dr. Goldman, do you know of any countries or groups that currently administer the vaccine for smallpox?"

Her quick response was well researched. "We believe the Israeli army and a good proportion of its health care workers have been vaccinated after 9/11. All U.S. military and health care workers such as those at the CDC and USAMRIID in Maryland have also been vaccinated, as well as any virologists that might encounter smallpox at NIH labs such as the one that was found to have sixty-year-old ampoules containing viable smallpox in 2014. Dr. Richardson, you will recall, alluded to this in her presentation earlier. And there are mandatory five-year boosters for all these groups.

"In closing, allow me to quote from Dr. Donald Ainslie Henderson, the CDC epidemiologist who was responsible for the smallpox eradication program in the 1970s. He said, 'The greatest threat in bioterrorism is the use of the smallpox virus.'"

The lecture ended with a prolonged question-and-answer period, which returned to the controversial issues of pre-emptive mass inoculation and whether the United States and Russia should destroy their stocks of the smallpox virus. Dr. Frank Emberley was pleased with the participation but quietly wondered if his star residents may have been overreaching in some of their answers. Nevertheless, he had to admit that they had done their homework. He closed the afternoon seminar by acknowledging his three speakers, saying, "The decision regarding vaccination will best be accomplished on a factual and rational basis and not on the basis of fear. Physicians will have a major role to play should the unlikely event of a smallpox release ever occur. I wish to thank you for your attention and participation today."

Many of the attendees stayed to discuss the smallpox questions with the presenters. After a lengthy and invigorated discussion, they were finally forced to leave the lecture theatre when the cleaning staff showed up.

Chapter 11

Franklin Expedition 1845

They that go down to the sea in ships
— Psalm 107:23

The two oldest Hartnell brothers had always done things together while growing up in South East England where their father had been a shipbuilder in Chatham on the River Medway. They lived with their parents and a younger brother, Charles. A cousin, Francis Pocock, lived not far away and the four boys were inseparable growing up. Together they frequently accompanied their father when he visited the mile-long shipyards. They watched the hundreds of shipwrights, block makers, riggers, and rope makers at work, while they scampered over the many docks and piers of the massive construction site.

John Hartnell was twenty-four with a shock of dark brown hair and brown eyes. His younger brothers, Thomas and Charles, were fair like their mother. Sarah Hartnell doted on her three sons and observed with concern their increasing fascination with ships as they visited their father's shipbuilding yards and talked to the sailors and several of the midshipmen of the Royal Navy about life on the seas.

The majority of people in their town had some connection to shipbuilding or sailing and the Hartnell family was no exception. When news of the Franklin Expedition became known, the two brothers signed up and soon found themselves serving on the 372-ton HMS *Erebus* in the spring of 1845 with their cousin Frank Pocock. The three men served as 'able bodied seamen' on the *Erebus*. On the morning of May 19, 1845, the *Erebus* and the 325-ton HMS *Terror* set sail from Greenhithe, England, with a crew of twenty-four officers and 110 men. Franklin's goal was to discover the elusive Northwest Passage. After 300 years of polar exploration during the great age of Arctic discovery, the Northwest Passage still remained undiscovered.

"Why do you suppose Pa won't let Charles come with us, John?" asked Thomas as the brothers leaned on the taffrails of the stern deck, watching the davits lower crates of supplies into the hold. The smell of fresh paint permeated the air. "And what did he mean about not putting all his eggs in one basket?"

"Well, he doesn't think it's a good idea for all of us to sail on the same ship in case something might happen to us for one thing," John explained. "And besides, he wants Charles to stay with Ma and finish his schooling."

"But, John, this is the best equipped ship in the world. It even has a steam engine in the hold and our Captain is James Fitzjames! The *Erebus* has two mortars and ten guns and it has already proven its worth with Captain Ross in the Arctic expedition for four years. It has even been equipped with armour plating for protection from the ice. What can possibly happen?"

Young Thomas Hartnell already missed his younger brother, Charles, and could not understand his father's decision to keep him home. His assessment of the ship was correct: no Arctic expedition had been so lavishly equipped with all the technological advances of the day.

"Pa seems to have his doubts, Thomas. And besides, when we get back, the three of us can take the next trip together." John was optimistic about this trip too, but he could also see his father's point of view. As the ships departed, Francis Pocock joined the brothers at the taffrails. Suddenly a dove flew down, landing on the foremast of the *Terror* in almost Biblical fashion. Everyone on shore saw this as a good omen and Franklin's daughter later wrote in her diary that this was 'the providential blessing of the hand of God.'

In August of 1845, a British whaler saw the two ships for the last time as they entered Baffin Bay. The weather abruptly turned sour and the west winds grew stronger as they passed through the monotonous Arctic landscape of Lancaster Sound. The crews struggled to tack day after day without gaining much headway. As the Arctic autumn bore down upon them, a weariness besieged both ships and the elation of the crew dissipated as they fought the waves and the ice-cold rain. Even the massive pinnacled icebergs and rock-strewn shores with their melancholic grandeur could not lift their spirits.

"I am not well, Thomas," John confided to his younger brother after five months at sea. "I don't know if I can go on." The older Hartnell brother had been losing both his strength and his appetite for several weeks. Now his gums began to bleed and small hemorrhages appeared in both eyes. His teeth were loosening and he found it impossible to chew meat.

"Have you seen the ship's physician about this?" asked Thomas.

"Aye. He seems to think I might have scurvy but I have been eating tinned fruits and vegetables as much as I can," he moaned.

Neither Hartnell nor the ship's physician were aware of the fact that despite the abundance of canned food, the process of boiling and canning removed any anti-scorbutic effects of the meats and vegetables on board. In fact, the entire crew was beginning to suffer from similar symptoms including lethargy, fatigue, and muscle aches and pains since even the vitamin C in the canned food had lost its potency over time. Even the daily allotment of lime juice was insufficient in providing enough vitamin C to stave off the 'sailor's scourge' for the men of the expedition. Skeletal studies 150 years later, eventually confirmed that scurvy was a major factor in the decline of the health of the crews.

By September, the two ships were locked in ice at Beechey Island where they set up camp on shore for the next seven months. On November 9, 1845, the sun disappeared and did not appear again until February 9, 1846. The prolonged Arctic winter with its depressing darkness had an enervating effect upon the men both mentally and physically.

"You need to be in sickbay, John, not working on the stores," cautioned Thomas who was becoming very concerned with the bleeding and bruising now quite evident on his brother's skin.

That week John Hartnell slipped on a chunk of deck ice and fell, severely damaging his right eye on the rigging. Following this accident, he was confined to sickbay and the doctor feared he might lose his sight. Despite being placed on a diet of tinned meat and vegetables, he continued to deteriorate.

By Christmas, he was comatose and on January 4, 1846, John Hartnell was dead. The crew buried him with much difficulty in the permafrost on Beechey Island. His epitaph recorded a sombre Bible verse that sounded foreboding: 'Thus saith the Lord of Hosts, consider your ways. Haggai 1 verse 7'

Young Thomas Hartnell painfully watched his crewmates lower his brother into five feet of permafrost; he was devastated and wept for days. Francis Pocock tried his best to comfort him, but he too grieved the unexpected loss of his childhood friend and fellow seaman. The ships spent the winter harboured in the bay by Beechey Island and tents were set up on the island.

The ships remained locked in ice until June 1846, when they finally escaped the icy grasp of Erebus Bay and departed into open water. Heading west through Peel Sound, they were soon blocked by ice and were forced to head south in the hopes of finding a passage west through Victoria Strait.

Unfortunately, they never made it. They sailed right into a lethal trap: the Beaufort Ice Stream, a continuous grinding flow of pack ice from the northwest that often kept the channel closed during the short summers now blocked their progress. Just north of King William Island, the two ships found themselves again beset in ice in September 1846. This proved to be merely the beginning of a sea of troubles.

Chapter 12

The Breakaway

Hidden in wonder and snow, or sudden with summer,
This land stares at the sun in a huge silence
Endlessly repeating something we cannot hear.
Inarticulate, arctic,
Not written on by history, empty as paper,
It leans away from the world with songs in its lakes
Older than love, and lost in the miles.

— F.R. Scott

For the next two years, the men endured environmental deprivation with long cold nights, boredom and scurvy. At mid-winter in the Arctic, the sun was so low that twilight appeared at mid-day. To make matters worse, Sir John Franklin had unexpectedly died on June 11, 1847. By that date, another fifteen men and nine officers had also succumbed to the debilitating effects of scurvy. The men greatly admired Franklin. His death demoralized the surviving crews. Men became depressed and desperate. As Thomas Hartnell mournfully said, quoting from John Bunyan, "'We are sinking now in the Slough of Despond.'"

By January 1848, the remaining men realized that the window of opportunity for escape from the Arctic was rapidly closing on them and they had to do something. Caught in the relentless thrall of Arctic ice, the captains recognized the men were in danger and ordered them to sleep in their clothes in the event that they were to break up from the pressure of the ice. It was unnerving for the surviving crews to hear the pounding and grinding of the floes against the hulls of the two ships each night.

One evening, the floes cradled the *Terror* and lifted it up several feet in the air with menacing tentacles of ice reaching up along the sides to the taffrails. After several frightening hours, the ice floe finally released its firm grasp and the ship was suddenly plunged back into the sea with a prolonged crunching and groaning and splashing of water, which quickly froze around it.

The next day the *Erebus* began listing at forty-five degrees. A discussion and a vote among the remaining officers of both ships ensued. On April 22, after a severe shudder shook the *Erebus* that night, over one hundred fearful men abandoned the dubious safety of both ships and set out towards King William Island. After a short stay at Victory Point on the northern tip of the island, they headed south, pulling a 1,400-pound sledge over the icy wasteland in an effort to seek an overland escape. They hauled tools, silverware, curtain rods, scented soap, books and writing desks with them, impracticably weighed down with the detritus of their culture.

After reaching the southernmost point of King William Island, they headed southeast through Simpson Strait in the hope of finding the mouth of Back's Great Fish River. Franklin had explored this region by land on an earlier overland expedition after George Back discovered it in 1834. Years later, Inuit people told stories about seeing white men drop like flies and many bodies had been left where they fell, unburied.

"Frank, why are we taking all that equipment with us?" Thomas Hartnell asked Francis Pocock. "How far do they expect us to go? And why are we now heading east? Is this not madness?"

"Aye, it is indeed madness, Thomas. We know not where we are going and we are overburdened wi' equipment and stores. We need to find some Esquimaux people who live here and ask them to help us find a way south to one of the inland trading posts. Captain Fitzjames said there is a Hudson's Bay trading post 600 miles to the south. Blimey, we should be 'eading sou'west where we saw the Esquimaux people last week. Or else go back to the ships."

Pocock had been giving their desperate situation considerable thought over the long months of their Arctic imprisonment. He had always been the adventurous type, a risk taker, and he realized that, now more than ever, extreme risks were necessary for survival.

"Six hundred miles over ice and snow? How is that possible, Frank? The ice never melts or blows away with the winds. The ice cracks around our ship constantly and, surely, it will crush the hull any day now! We cannot return to the ships. But 600 bloody miles? Egad, we will never make it!" Hartnell cried.

His lips quivered and he thought of his brother John buried in the permafrost hundreds of miles to the north. He had never been so frightened or miserable in his life. He could not sleep for thinking of home and what a fool he was to have come to this dark, cold, foreboding land.

"If only we could carry our food and drink and find some natives to teach us to hunt in order to survive on a southward expedition, it would be easier. Pulling this sledge with all of the equipment is exhausting us. We need to set out on our own. We would have a far better chance with a smaller group than with the main body of the crews pulling that infernal sledge." Pocock was starting to make sense but he needed to convince his friend.

"But that would be mutiny, Francis! Besides, we would need at least two more men to go with us. Who would you trust?" Hartnell was not convinced.

Francis Pocock thought for a moment and brightened, exclaiming, "Aye! Mutiny indeed, but who would bother to come after us in this icy wasteland? We should ask Robert Sinclair, captain of the foretop, or Richard Aylmore, the gunroom steward. They are about the same age as we are and have become good friends since we left England. They both still seem healthy enough to travel. Aylmore is good with a gun and can bring a musket for hunting. And to protect us from polar bears."

"Aye. I was thinking of those two, myself. Any others will hinder us." Hartnell was beginning to see some merit in this plan.

And so, one early morning in June 1848 before the rest of the crew had awakened, the four men left their icy camp and headed southwest across the frozen Queen Maud Gulf. Robert Sinclair was a blond rakish twenty-five-year-old Scotsman, who was agile and quick and excelled in his work on the foretopmasts of the *Erebus*. Richard Aylmore was short, squat and very strong from his work with the ship's cannons and mortars. These two men also felt that hauling the massive sledges hundreds of miles was a futile endeavour; they were quite willing to join their friends and find Inuit people who might be willing to help four men, but not seventy or eighty. Though no longer trapped on the ships, they recognized their hold on survival was tenuous if they stayed with the main group.

They travelled with a light wooden sledge, which they had hastily constructed from boards and ropes. They loaded a sack of flour, a musket, gunpowder and canned food onto the sledge and headed southwest across Queen Maud Gulf, taking advantage of the midnight sun. The weather was mild for this latitude and they travelled about twelve miles that first day, continuously looking for signs of open water and polar bears. Their skin and tongues began to turn black from the effects of scurvy and soon they collapsed from exhaustion. After the second day, because of the severity of their debility and extreme fatigue, they managed to cover only eight miles.

On the third day, they saw two Inuit hunters hauling a ringed seal behind them. The hunters had speared this seal for their families. The four sailors hailed the Inuit to ask how far the mainland was and if they had seen any open water. However, their gaunt and bearded visages frightened the two hunters away. Thinking that the men were ghosts or evil spirits, the Inuit hunters left the seal behind crying, "Kabloona! Kabloona!"

"Look chaps. We have our dinner for at least a week!" Pocock exclaimed.

"But Frank, I can't eat raw meat. It's disgusting," Hartnell moaned.

"We have no choice, Thomas. The Esquimaux eat their food raw and they seem to survive in this god-forsaken land. Besides, we have no fuel for a fire anyway out here on the frozen sea."

This unexpected gift sustained the four men for the next week or so. By eating the seal's raw liver and marrow, their vitamin deficiencies soon began to correct themselves. The general lassitude that had weighed upon them lifted and they trudged on, heading south, mile after mile, sleeping at intervals. Their compass was not reliable this far north; like most sailors, they knew their direction by following the stars at night. During the day, they marched on, keeping the sun on their right side, using the sailor's ancient art of 'dead reckoning.' They hiked laboriously under the winter sky plodding, one foot in front of the other, often losing track of the horizon against the monochromatic palette of gray.

A snowstorm incarcerated the men for three days in their make-shift tents, with the sound of the howling winds through the impenetrable whiteness adding to their sense of abject desolation.

The same ice pack that immobilized the ships that cold year also provided access across the Simpson Strait to the mainland. Over the next month of early summer, the men eventually made it to the northern shore of the continent and managed to hunt as they travelled, killing snowshoe hares and ptarmigans. Aylmore shot a snowy owl on one occasion. At times, they were reduced to scraping lichens from the rocks and boiling it for a tea, which tasted awful and provided little nourishment, but they continued on, hoping to find a trading post. During a five-day stretch, they subsided on an austere diet of water, cranberries, scraps of leather and some burnt bones. The men looked much alike, with lined faces and sunken cheeks, stooped over, looking down as they walked and at times overcome with feelings of impotence and despair.

Heading further inland in a southerly direction, they met a group of twenty-three Inuit who, although wary at first, soon welcomed them and fed them muskox, which they had killed earlier that week. The Inuit survived in the Arctic by eating the contents of a caribou's stomach and the testicles of a muskox, both powerful antidotes to scurvy. The sailors stayed with these people several weeks, regaining their energy on muskox and seal. The blackness of their mouth and face rapidly resolved with the Inuit diet.

They managed to communicate with each other by using sign language and drawing pictures in the snow. They learned that *kabloona* meant foreigner or 'white man' but the seamen were unable to understand what the Inuit were saying when they kept repeating the word *tuktu* with an excited expression. One day an elder whom they named 'Albert' after the Queen's consort in England drew a picture in the snow with his spear that soon revealed what looked like a deer with very large antlers.

"They want us to hunt with them and kill a deer! Tuktu must mean deer!" said Aylmore, the gunroom steward, smiling for the first time in months.

"Yes, yes, tuktu, tuktu!"

Aylmore then showed them their Brown Bess musket, which had not been fired for several months. The next day these four English sailors were among the first white men to witness a natural phenomenon still seen by very few today.

Chapter 13

Tuktu

Aurora borealis

The word *tuktu*, which Albert the Inuit had tried to explain to the sailors meant the Barrens caribou, which at this time of the year were calving on the Barrens tundra. They were part of the great Beverley herd whose range extends from Queen Maud Gulf, south across the tundra to what is now Manitoba and Saskatchewan. Recent surveys show their numbers to be as high as 275,000. In 1848, however, the caribou herds in the area exceeded half a million.

Migrating over 1,200 kilometres in a season, the females would drop their calves in the tundra of the Barrens in June of each year. Hunting them during this vulnerable time in their life cycle was greatly enhanced with the prolonged hours of the summer solstice during which the sun shines for twenty-one hours with a few hours of twilight just before midnight. The herds provided survival in a harsh land for the Inuit, but first the caribou had to come to them. When the caribou arrived, the Inuit were ready and prepared for them. All they had to do was sharpen their spears and wait, fighting the irritating swarms of insects.

Still thinking they were hunting deer with the Inuit, the Englishmen had no idea what they were about to encounter. On a bright afternoon in late June 1848, while hunting with their Inuit companions, they received the surprise of their life.

The late spring migration of tens of thousands of Barren caribou suddenly and thunderously came upon them. Vegetation, so meagre in the tundra, meant that the herd had to keep constantly on the move, grazing whatever foliage the Barrens provided. The ground shook as hundreds of the great antlered beasts engulfed the sailors. After recovering from their initial shock, they shot three caribou with their musket that day. At first, some of the Inuit ran away having never heard gunfire before. The sailors quickly called them back with warm smiles and cheers.

The Inuit hunters knew what to do and pursued a few males with their spears. Leaving the females with their calves ensured the survival of next year's herd; the Inuit tried to explain this to the kabloonas. That day the group took down eight more caribou and spent the next three days dressing them and smoking the meat that would sustain them for several months. The women scraped the hides for clothing and footwear; the antlers provided them with tools such as their *ulu* knives. Little of the animal was wasted.

Francis Pocock exulted to his friend, "That was truly unbelievable, Thomas. I had no idea this desolate land could sustain so many animals. We will have enough food to keep us alive for months. I have never seen so many animals in my life!"

While the other men were rejoicing in the success of the hunt and the promise for survival that it meant, Robert Sinclair was paying attention to one of the younger women of the Inuit family. When it came time to move on later that summer, Sinclair surprised them by stating he wanted to stay behind with this friendly tribe. He felt accepted by the small group and was falling in love with a young

Inuit girl who found the kabloona fascinating. Her name was Osha, which meant 'daughter of the sun.'

"I can't say I blame him, Thomas. Osha is a fair wench indeed and there is still no guarantee that we can ever make it out of here anyway. We should leave him here, wish him well and move on. At least he will be happy."

Francis Pocock was getting anxious to continue their trek with the hope of finding a trading post or an Indian settlement that would eventually take him back to England and to his family in Chatham.

Unbeknownst to these four survivors, the British Admiralty had ordered a massive search, which was now underway to the north. Several search vessels had been dispatched to discover the whereabouts of the Franklin ships that same year. A 20,000 pound reward offered by the Admiralty spurred the most extensive naval search in history. Tragically, only five months after the two ships were abandoned, James Clark Ross reached the area with two rescue ships and had come within 200 miles of the missing ships. So near, yet so far.

By 1850, some thirteen search ships including two American vessels scoured the northern waters for any sign of the *Erebus* and the *Terror*. However, the crews of the Franklin ships, instead of heading north where they might have been rescued, continued relentlessly southeast, hoping for some sign of civilization. This unfortunate decision was to seal their fate.

The four young sailors meanwhile had headed southwest and survived, whereas the rest of the crew died at a remote place that became known as Starvation Cove at the top of the Adelaide Peninsula. Dr. John Rae, the intrepid explorer and Hudson's Bay Company surgeon, discovered thirty-five to forty skeletons there in 1854. The cove was truly a desolate place in the winter, yet ironically in the summer, salmon and caribou abounded by the thousands. It is difficult to believe that such a beautiful place, teeming with wildlife, could be the repository for the ill-fated expedition where men finally indulged in a last desperate act of cannibalism. Hence, the tragic name, Starvation Cove.

Leaving their friend Sinclair behind with the Inuit tribe, Hartnell, Pocock and Aylmore tramped on south by southwest. Hiking became easier as the snow melted on the mainland and the weather warmed. They had regained their weight during their sojourn with the Inuit tribe. Their strength was likewise restored, which enabled them to cover greater distances each day and, like their Inuit hosts, they learned to live off the land. Yet, the 600 miles that Captain Fitzjames had promised barely introduced them to the vastness of the Barren Lands. In reality, the distance was more like 800 miles to any of the Hudson's Bay Company posts from where they had left King William Island in June.

As a precaution, the Admiralty had alerted the Hudson's Bay Company and its trading posts at Fort Good Hope and Fort Resolution before the ships had even left port. If trouble should arise, they were advised to offer support. Many of the native traders from the Barrens were likewise informed of the expedition and encouraged to watch out for them.

Fort Resolution, however, lay 700 miles to the southwest over the vast Barren Lands at the bottom of Great Slave Lake. Built in 1819 by the Hudson's Bay Company, it was the main fur trading post on Great Slave Lake.

"Francis, how will we ever find this fort?" Thomas Hartnell asked, discouraged and beset by fear. "Is it not much further south than Captain Fitzjames had told us? If only we could follow this Great Fish River, it might lead us to the fort."

"Aye, Thomas. Our only hope lies in finding some friendly Chipewyan people to sustain us for the winter. But we must march on to find this large river." Pocock as usual tried to remain optimistic.

After setting out again in a southwesterly direction in late July, they covered fifty miles in just over a week. They traversed the taiga, the skeletal forest that bordered the tundra. Passing marshes, lakes, bogs and streams, they resolutely plodded on, dreading another brutal winter in this great lonely land. All the rivers that emptied into Queen Maud Gulf from the Barrens came directly from the south. By following the banks of one river, they were able to catch fish as they travelled and trudged in the general direction southward. Makeshift rafts enabled smaller crossings but, with few trees in the Barrens, they struggled to find fords that allowed them to cross on foot.

An explosion of wild flowers brightened many of the fields as they traversed the open tundra. Overlaid with a patchy coverlet of bushes and stunted trees, the tundra provided them with nourishment from lichens and berries. Their short freedom from the yoke of ice and snow was soon ending, however, as huge flocks of Canada geese headed south in early September and the rich colours of ochre and crimson emerged dramatically from the thin layer of soil that covered the permafrost. As the autumn of 1848 approached, the men began once again to lose hope, as their southward march came to a halt at the formidable Back River, which the men called 'The Great Fish River.' They were still well above the tree line where it widened into a series of impassable lakes. The three men had no choice but to set up camp while they contemplated heading further west along the river's course. They had no way of crossing the river but the urgency of travelling further south weighed heavily upon them.

That night, they were entertained and awed by a majestic and scintillating display of the aurora borealis, which at this far northern geomagnetic latitude was breathtaking. The ethereal twirls of greens, pinks and violets dancing across the northern skies astonished the weary travellers. They had witnessed them several times over the past three years, but this night was outstanding for brightness and colour.

Shimmering curtains of lights, the aurora originated in the outer limits of the earth's atmosphere in an inspiring phantasmagorical display of nature.

"This surely is a good omen, gentleman!" exclaimed Pocock confidently. "These northern lights seem providential and it must be a sign from God. Perhaps our prayers will be answered after all. Do not 'the heavens declare the glory of God'?"

"Aye!" both Hartnell and Aylmore agreed in unison. "The glory of God, indeed."

Chapter 14

The Blonde Inuit

Variola arcticus

After three days of hunting and weighing their options, the sailors saw four large canoes with Indians paddling west along the north side of the river. These were Chipewyan Indians bringing their furs south to one of the inland trading posts of the Hudson's Bay Company.

Delighted to see other humans after many weeks, the three men hailed the startled Chipewyan who thought they were Bay fur traders and showed them the pelts in their canoes to sell. They took a particular interest in Aylmore's Brown Bess musket but, since it was the only thing that guaranteed their survival, the sailors demurred on using it as an item to barter. Instead, they offered them their knives and a hatchet in exchange for taking them upstream as far as they could go. The Indians willingly agreed and Pocock, Hartnell and Aylmore each settled into a canoe with the furs, greatly relieved to be rescued from their bleak situation.

Five days of paddling with the Chipewyan Indians brought them close to the source of the Back River. The trio had survived in the Arctic for several months, thanks to the benevolence of native groups and their own steely resolve. They had traversed over 400 miles since leaving the main body of explorers in June and were now well south of the Arctic Circle on the edge of the great northern boreal forest. Winter was their only formidable obstacle and already flakes of snow had fallen lightly. Their ability to live off the land had given them confidence although they knew that, without help, their remaining supply of gunpowder would not sustain them. They suddenly realized that they would not be making it to Fort Resolution this year.

They eventually arrived at a Chipewyan village where the women and children received them with considerable fanfare. The Chipewyan tried to relate to their white visitors that a group of Indians had arrived from the south to trade only a week earlier. Some of them had been ill just before they returned to their own village. The three English sailors were invited to sleep in a tent where the sick men had stayed and had left several woollen Hudson's Bay point blankets behind.

After dining on roasted rabbit and lichen tea, the three sailors soon fell asleep, covering themselves against the coolness of the evening with the Bay blankets. It was comforting to know that these blankets were made in England and that they had somehow arrived in the far north through Hudson's Bay traders. It was the closest feeling they experienced to being near civilization in over three years. They read the labels repeatedly and caressed the soft English wool. That night they slept soundly.

The next week the men hunted with their Chipewyan hosts, putting their musket to good use in shooting a deer and several rabbits. However, after twelve days with the Indians, Thomas Hartnell began to feel unwell. He complained to his two companions that his muscles ached and he had a headache and felt weak. Within a few days, he developed a fever and rash and very sore throat. About the same time, many of the Indians of this small village were likewise afflicted. Hartnell lost his appetite and barely managed to keep a few ounces of lichen tea down. His rash soon developed into a mass of blisters all over his body. His fever continued and he became delirious, crying out for his brother John. In spite of the best efforts of his good friends, Francis Pocock and Richard Aylmore, to care for him, Thomas Hartnell passed away, his body wracked in pain and his skin a confluent mass of sores, exactly two weeks to the day he fell ill.

"After all we have been through, I can't believe he has died of the pox, Richard!" wailed Pocock. "It's not fair to have travelled so far only to die like this. How did he ever contract this horrible disease in such a remote place as this?"

Richard Aylmore shook his head and covered Thomas Hartnell's face with the point blanket.

"Well, he is with his brother John now. There's nothing we can do except bury him and say a few words on his behalf, Francis," Aylmore consoled.

Within a day, three of the Indians had also died and several more had become sick. Some of them blamed the white men for bringing evil spirits to them. Others recalled that the visiting Chipewyan from the south had been ill before returning to their own village. The last thing the English sailors expected to find in this stark and remote land was smallpox and they wondered how a European disease had managed to arrive in this remote place.

By the time the snow had fallen, the village lay wasted with unburied bodies strewn in the tents, mainly children and old people. A few women had survived the smallpox infection but the entire village was virtually wiped out. Pocock and Aylmore escaped this plague, having suffered a mild form of it as children back in England. The following winter was brutal but the two sailors stayed with the surviving villagers, hunting and caring for their Indian hosts and at times surviving on lichens, moss and Arctic hare. They never made it to Fort Resolution. Living on the edge of the boreal forest, they hunted and took Indian wives, adapting to the rigours of subarctic life. They often talked about their fair-haired friend, Robert Sinclair, who had stayed behind with the Inuit people who cared for them that summer, and they prayed frequently for his safety.

In 1912, the *National Geographic* magazine published an article on 'The Origins of Stefansson's Blonde Eskimo.' The journals of Arctic explorer Vilhjalmur Stefansson recorded his observations of fair-haired Inuit people whom he referred to as the 'Copper Inuit' on the southwestern portion of Victoria Island. This was only 250 miles from where the men had left Robert Sinclair with his young Inuit wife, Osha. Although even earlier sightings of 'blonde Eskimos' had been documented, it was Stefansson's article that caught the attention of the public.

As for the unfortunate Thomas Hartnell, like a tragic hero, he succumbed not to the rigours and deprivations of the Arctic but rather to an age-old disease, which ironically had been introduced to the North American Indian by the careless and sometimes egregious actions of Europeans two centuries earlier. Now it had come full circle, ironically afflicting an innocent English explorer by his unwitting but benevolent Indian hosts. Thomas Hartnell was one of the last victims of the great smallpox epidemic of the 1840s – all because of a failed British Arctic exploration to find the Northwest Passage.

As for the fate of the Franklin Expedition, Viljhalmur Stefansson questioned how these men with muskets and shotguns could have 'contrived to the last man' to die of starvation in a land where, for centuries, the Inuit had survived using weapons from the Stone Age. Had they adopted even some of the ways of the Inuit, they might have survived, as did the four seamen who set out on their own towards the great Back River.

Chapter 15

The Graveyard, July 2018

Requiescat in pace

The Cessna flew northeast over Port Nelson on the west bank of the Nelson River. In the distance, the large inland sea of Hudson Bay formed a great grey horizon. The plane banked and headed east over York Factory towards a peninsula separating the Hayes and Nelson Rivers. The fort's white hexagonal cupola pointed skyward immediately beneath them. Numerous gunmetal lakes pocked the vast green tundra beyond the Hayes delta. Below, a pod of white beluga whales frolicked like sprinkled confetti in the estuary.

Rachel Thompson took several pictures as the Cessna descended over an island opposite the fort and approached a rough gravelled airstrip with scattered debris on either side. A team of workers from Gillam had recently restored the old runway. The spring thaw brought massive chunks of ice that gouged it severely every year. A bumpy landing followed and numerous large yellow storage drums sat at odd angles at the end of the runway. A Parks Canada guide met the group and transferred them and their equipment into a boat, which transported them across the Hayes; fighting a seven-knot current, they finally arrived at the wooden dock at the famous fort of York Factory. Normally the pilot would drop his passengers off and then immediately depart for other missions. This time, however, after securing the plane to some posts, he accompanied the three-member team so he could help unload the food and equipment.

After arriving at the fort, Rachel stumbled over the uneven ground, which had heaved earlier that spring from the permafrost. She was thirty-two years old and still single; she felt as though she had been a student all of her life. Rachel loved working outdoors and her chosen field of archaeology certainly provided many opportunities for this. Her postdoctoral project with the Arctic Research Institute of North America at York Factory was exciting; she had been planning and looking forward to it for eight months.

Rachel looked over the grounds of what had once been a thriving community. In the 1800s, York Factory flourished with over fifty buildings. All that remained now in the small clearing was an out-building and the large depot, which could be seen for miles across the flat Barrens. The Hudson's Bay Company trading post at York Factory had been the headquarters for most of the northern fur trade for almost two centuries. For an archaeologist such as Rachel Thompson, this place with its rich history was exhilarating. Earlier teams of archaeologists had uncovered the decomposing remains of eighteenth century structures, some of which were charred from the Battle of 1782 when the French under Comte de Lapérouse had burned the fort to the ground.

Other teams of archaeologists uncovered the remains of older structures and the abandoned campsite of the Swampy Cree First Nations who lived in the area prior to its permanent closure in 1957. The cemetery near the fort, however, was the object of this current investigation. Rachel Thompson and her colleagues from the Arctic Institute arrived at York Factory to undertake a forensic study on a body from the nineteenth century. They were prepared to exhume a corpse buried in the permafrost at the old Hudson's Bay Company trading post graveyard in an attempt to solve a 185-year-old mystery.

The team of three researchers flew from Calgary to Winnipeg and then on to Gillam, Manitoba, where they chartered a plane to York Factory on July 23, 2018. Two members of the team set up three tents near the depot building within a large chain-link fence enclosure to protect them from polar bears. With the help of the Parks Canada employee at the fort, they quickly unloaded their scientific equipment, tools, shovels, and a generator with several jerry cans of gasoline, which had been sent a week earlier by jet boat from Gillam, Manitoba, some 120 miles away via the Nelson River.

Roland Boudreau, the pilot for this expedition, was an affable forty-one-year-old Métis whose ancestors had been involved in the fur trade. After helping them unload their equipment, he began to take a keen interest in what this team of Arctic researchers was doing. Boudreau had studied history and Native studies at the University of Winnipeg and later obtained a desk job with the Department of Indian Affairs and Northern Development. The call of the north, however, led him to take up flying just as his father had done.

Boudreau was soft-spoken with jet-black hair and slight greying at the temples. He wore a small gold earring and sported a tattoo of an eagle on his right shoulder. He had been flying in the north for years, ferrying tourists to places like Churchill, where whale watching and polar bear sighting from tundra buggies was popular. After a brief meeting at the Gillam airport an hour earlier, he approached Rachel for a more formal introduction.

"Hi, I'm Rolly Boudreau. I understand you are the team leader here, right?"

"Yes, I'm Dr. Rachel Thompson. Thanks for flying us here and for giving us such a spectacular view of the bay. It was a smoother landing than I expected."

"Well, the landings can be very rough here even at the best of times with the north wind, but the weather gods were smiling on us today. So are you a medical doctor? Just what kind of research are you doing in this lonely, remote place for five days?" Boudreau's interest in the project was piqued when he discovered that the attractive Rachel Thompson was a doctor.

"Well actually, I'm a PhD archaeologist working for the Arctic Research Institute out of the University of Calgary and we're searching for artifacts that will tell us more about the history of this old trading post. But one of the other team members is a medical doctor." Rachel gave a polite but guarded response, as she did not want to reveal the exact nature of what her research team was looking for.

Boudreau's response was enthusiastic. "Wow. Over the years, I've brought tourists and university types here many times but this is the first time I have flown a research team to York Factory. You know, I cannot imagine anyone living here for years as they once did in the old days. It's such a lonely and remote spot. I recall coming here many years ago. We clambered down the steep river bank each morning finding what artifacts had been uncovered by the tide. We found so many neat things – pieces of clay pipe and blue plates, musket balls, old tin cans, knives, triangular-headed nails, plus colourful scallop shells. I remember that at the one-metre depth near the top of the bank, erosion exposed a number of cannonballs." Boudreau definitely had more than a cursory knowledge of the fort for someone who was a bush pilot.

"And just exactly what does the Arctic research Institute do?" he asked Rachel pointedly.

"Well, the Arctic Institute of North America was created by an Act of Parliament in 1945 as a non-profit tax-exempt research and educational organization. It was then transferred to the University of Calgary in 1976 from McGill University in Montreal. What we do is study and advance the knowledge of the Arctic, and acquire and disseminate information on just about every aspect of life in the north. Everything from permafrost to Inuit culture, polar bears and the effects of global warming." Rachel was almost quoting verbatim the official mandate of her organization as she had memorized the mission statement a few months earlier when she submitted her proposal.

"Interesting," Boudreau said, although at this point he was becoming more interested in the blonde-haired, blue-eyed Dr. Rachel Thompson than he was in some university-based research organization. "And the other doctors?"

"Dr. Wojeich Jaworski is a pathologist and Dr. Gordon Dowling is a forensic anthropologist. Both work at the University of Calgary. As you can guess from these occupations, we will be looking at one of the gravesites here."

"Well, you have lots to choose from, doctor. Have you been to the cemetery yet?" Boudreau asked.

"Please, call me Rachel. Would you mind showing me where the cemetery is located? We plan to begin our research by examining where they buried the dead at the fort. What can you tell me about it?"

"Certainly. Even though I come here many times over the years my last visit to the York Factory cemetery was several years ago, but from my recollection the graveyard is just north of that small outbuilding over there, which would be down river from here. I have no idea just how many graves there are, but it must have numbered in the many hundreds because the cemetery was used from the late 1600s to the mid-1900s. I don't recall many headstones that are still standing. Many of them have fallen over and become covered by peat and moss over the centuries. Much of the original graveyard has been eroded by the Hayes River over the years and Mother Nature has almost swallowed up the rest of the area with trees. Come on and I'll show you."

Boudreau was quite willing to help the younger researcher and they both walked towards the cemetery over a wooden sidewalk. They walked down a series of splintered wooden steps across a small creek known as Sloop Creek. Numerous trees and saplings had overgrown what was once a clearing. Grey weather-beaten picket fence enclosures surrounded many of the ancient graves. Several boards were broken and only a few headstones were still standing. As Boudreau had described, a thicket of willows and poplar had taken over the graveyard and partially hid this unique historic site from view. Enthralled by an overwhelming sense of history, Rachel bent over to read some of the epitaphs on the tombstones.

"I just read somewhere that this entire complex was designated a National Historic Site of Canada in 1936. I can see why. Many of these people were buried in the 1800s. This is truly fascinating!" she exclaimed.

"Yes, there is lots of history here. When it was first built, the main depot was the largest building on the North American continent at that time. Philadelphia was founded only two years earlier in 1682. That's how old the place is." Boudreau had been thorough with his own research regarding this little known site. Rachel was impressed that a bush pilot would know so much about history. After a short walk, they arrived at the Sloop Creek cemetery where they immediately encountered crumbling stonewalls.

"What kind of building was that and why is it in the cemetery?" Rachel asked.

"That's the remains of the Powder Magazine or munitions depot. It was deliberately built in this area for safety reasons. They wanted it as far away as possible from the main depot in case of fire. Apparently, one of the factor's wives suggested this location. Keeping the gunpowder in a stone building away from the depot made good sense even if it was in the cemetery," Boudreau replied.

"I would imagine she slept better at nights knowing that," Rachel remarked.

"Probably. Be careful here. There are so many unmarked graves in this cemetery that it's difficult not to walk on them." Boudreau was painfully aware that a few of his ancestors were likely buried somewhere in this cemetery. Numerous small fenced enclosures indicated the graves of children. Several tombstones nearby were adorned with brightly coloured ribbons.

"Why do they have ribbons on those tombstones?" Rachel asked.

"These ribbons were placed by First Nations people who recently visited the cemetery. The ribbons are attached to the tombstones either to invoke good spirits or to keep away bad ones, I suppose. It's a way of honouring their ancestors and showing that they are not forgotten. This cemetery is unique as it includes Europeans and native people together, often side-by-side. The Hudson's Bay Company didn't believe in segregation," Boudreau explained.

They arrived at one headstone but could barely read the name as it was so weathered. At another plot, a headstone rested right beside a wooden cross, suggesting the interment of two bodies on the same site. Rachel immediately took notice of this anomaly.

"Why would they entomb two people so close together with all the vastness of space here at the fort? Why, they're almost on top of each other!"

"Good question. I suppose they were from different eras and the ground may have been softer over a pre-existing grave, making it easier to dig. Burying bodies in permafrost could not have been an easy task. Here is a touching epitaph of the wife of one of the factors. 'Sacred to the memory of Nancy, wife of Frederick McPherson who departed this life 15th March 1911, age 20 years.'"

"Boy, life was indeed nasty, brutish and short in the far north. Imagine, only twenty years old," Rachel remarked.

"Yes and it wasn't all that long ago. Here's a much larger grave marker almost covered by debris." Boudreau brushed off the moss and lichen in order to read the inscription. It was a Bible verse from the Psalms. "'Behold, thou hast made my days as an handbreadth; and mine age is as nothing before thee: verily every man at his best state is altogether vanity. Psalm 39:5.'"

"Here's another one from the Psalms!" Rachel exclaimed. "'Surely he shall deliver thee from the snare of the fowler and from the noisome pestilence. Psalm 91:3.'"

"How depressing, I wonder what kind of pestilence caused these deaths?" Boudreau questioned.

"My goodness, they loved to put lengthy and depressing Bible verses on headstones in those days didn't they?"

"Yes, people were much more religious in those days especially living in such an isolated place like this. I have often wondered how they managed to bury them in the permafrost. It must have taken a lot of work just to get down a few feet. Back at the fort, you will find an opening in the floor where you can feel the icy ground just under the foundation. Back in the 1830s the Hudson's Bay Company rebuilt the fort to accommodate the heaving permafrost. You should have a look at it so you know what you are going to be faced with when you start digging," Boudreau added.

"Yes, I would love to see that. This place is truly amazing!" Rachel exclaimed.

Rachel did not want to reveal the exact nature of the mission's purpose so she remained silent regarding the project; however, the shovels and picks they brought with them suggested that some digging had to take place. After their brief visit to the cemetery, they walked back to the depot building where a Parks Canada employee met them. His name was James Klassen. Both he, his wife and two daughters lived at the fort during the summer months where they showed visitors around and served as docents for the historical site.

"Hello and welcome to the York Factory depot building. We have been expecting you, and I understand I will be assisting you in your research over the next few days. But why don't you let me give you a 'cook's tour' of this grand old building. York Factory simply breathes history. Is there any part of it you would like to see first?" Klassen asked.

After introductions, Rolly Boudreau got right to the point. "We would like to see the permafrost hole."

"Certainly, come right this way." Klassen showed them a trap door in the next room where Parks Canada had created a two-foot-square opening in the floor to show tourists the icy ground beneath the building. A thin layer of icy water covered the ice.

"They could probably store beer in here except it would likely freeze in no time!" Boudreau exclaimed.

Rachel laughed aloud at the thought of eighteenth century fur traders drinking beer.

"Don't laugh! We have found dozens of old ale bottles from the last century here including one from the Belhaven Brewery in Dunbar from the eighteenth century. Most spirits were brought here in kegs though," Klassen explained. "But the permafrost beneath us probably explains why this building is cool even in the summer."

"So how did they bury the dead in permafrost at the fort over the centuries?" Rachel asked.

"Well mainly by brute force, pick and shovel, or else they waited until spring and shipped the bodies home to England."

"Where would they store them until a ship came in or spring arrived?" asked Rachel, becoming increasingly more intrigued with this ancient place.

"They would wrap the bodies in a sort of body bag and lay them on shelves in a cold storage room. I can take you there if you like. It's kind of creepy though," Klassen cautioned.

"Let's check it out!" Rachel exclaimed. "Creepy or not."

Chapter 16

The Depot Building

Kischewaskaheegan

Several moments later, the three found themselves in a large darkened room with only one window. It contained several wooden shelves where the dead bodies had been stored before they were either buried or shipped home. The musty smell, which permeated the room, reminded Rachel of mouldy old suitcases and sawdust. The room was cool compared to the temperature outside.

Rachel glanced around the room. *Klassen is right. This place does breathe history.*

"I wonder how many bodies have been stored in here over the years," Rachel said. Her research of York Factory had not prepared her for this room or its gloominess.

"It's impossible to say, Rachel, but probably dozens, keeping in mind the long cold winters. A person could die in September of one year and remain here in cold storage until the following June," Klassen answered.

"You're right, this room is rather creepy," said Boudreau. "I think the doctor might find some of the other rooms with artifacts more interesting and less depressing."

Following their guide, they entered the main room of the depot building where the traders may have eaten their meals or held banquets to celebrate the arrival of the ships each year.

"This entire building was actually designed and built by shipwrights," Klassen continued, "and you can appreciate the massive timbers used to support the floors above. The building we are standing in was constructed in 1831. It survived the upheaval of the permafrost over all this time thanks to clever engineering. The large columns and beams were constructed in such a way as to make allowance for heaving and settling from the frost. A series of drainage ditches had been dug under the fort to carry off surface water. However, with river erosion and climate change slowly thawing this place, the depot building may not be here in another fifteen years."

"That would be most unfortunate," Rachel said. "Think of the loss to history. I suppose climate change accounts for the new vegetation too. We saw how much the graveyard is overgrown with trees and bushes."

"I probably shouldn't say this, but Parks Canada needs to invest more into this historic fort. Funding, however, has not been available to maintain several of these great historic sites. We do what we can but, until a few years ago, this place had less than fifty visitors annually. But let's go upstairs and see where they stored the furs."

James Klassen was happy to explain the history of the trading post, as he had done many times for tourists in the past. With less than one hundred visitors a year, he was bored much of the time and seemed to relish showing the ancient depot building to the various tourists. Just the previous day he had the opportunity to guide a group of nine tourists and show them the old fort and the ancient cemetery. They had arrived by jet boat out of Gillam, a three-hour trip, and only stayed for a few hours before turning around to head back to Gillam, a hundred miles upstream.

The second floor contained several tables covered in artifacts, which included shards of blue and white pottery, square liquor bottles, cannon balls, sewing needles made from bone for mending nets, tiny glass medicine bottles, and a harmonica. Saw blades, coiled chains, and old cannons with dozens of rusted cannonballs covered much of the floor, piled against the wall. Clay pipes were scattered everywhere.

"Several other rooms contain shelves where thousands of animal pelts were once stacked ceiling high," Klassen said. "A fur press with a large screw on the main floor compressed the furs for easier storage and handling. Thousands of pelts of beaver, marten, lynx, fox, raccoon, and deerskins were compressed and stacked into large bales to save space when shipped. For your interest, I would like to read some old records from the year 1787 declaring an inventory of pelts exported from Canada to Europe so that you will appreciate the extent of the fur trade back then."

He read from a copy of an old Hudson's Bay journal. "'139,509 beaver skins as compared to 68,142 martens, 26,330 otters, 16,951 minks, 8,913 foxes, 17,109 bears, 102,656 deer, 140,346 raccoons, 9,816 elks, 9,687 wolves and 125 seals.'"

Rachel gasped. "That's incredible. It's a wonder there were any animals left in the country. No wonder they needed a place this huge to sort, compress and store them all. I had no idea so many furs could be traded in one year, at a time when Canada wasn't even a fledgling nation."

"Yes, but not all of those furs went through York Factory," Klassen explained further. "Many of the furs were shipped from other Hudson's Bay Company forts such as Moose Factory, Fort Albany and Fort Prince of Wales. Later on, huge shipments were transferred through Montreal in the southern fur trade via the Great Lakes and the St. Lawrence with the Northwest Company. However, most of the furs were transported through York Factory. The fact that this building has 18,000 square feet suggests it was a very busy place in its heyday. It is safe to say that the fur trade built this country."

At this point, Rolly Boudreau stood up, checked his watch and stretched as if to reach the ancient wooden ceiling announcing, "Well, I think it's time for me to fly back to Gillam and leave these scientists to their project. I never get tired of visiting this old place. Thanks for the tour, James. Always fascinating!"

Boudreau bid farewell and descended the ancient stairs. Rachel quickly applied her lip gloss and followed him down to the main floor.

"I'll walk with you to the dock if that's okay, Rolly. I'd like to ask you a few more questions."

"Sure, whatever you like," Boudreau responded enthusiastically.

They walked over the boardwalk beside an ancient ship's anchor that stood over six feet high surrounded by tall grass on the soggy tundra.

"What's on your mind, Rachel?" Boudreau asked.

"I'm curious to know how you know so much about this place. You seem to know more than the Parks Canada guide."

"Well, my mother was a full-blooded Swampy Cree who lived here until she was twelve and then her family was moved to York Landing in 1957 when the Company shut down York Factory. She met my dad who was also a bush pilot, so I am really a part of this place. Some of my ancestors are buried in that cemetery we saw today. The Cree called this place Kischewaskaheegan, which means 'the Big House.' So when I come here, it's not simply a historical visit but a return to my roots and to my family's village. The Cree people consider this place sacred."

"I didn't realize the association of the native people with this place until you explained the ribbons on the graves today."

"Oh, yeah. This place would not have been able to operate without the people of the First Nations who replaced the Scots and English workers after 1821. My grandparents lived and worked at the fort most of their lives."

"What would they do besides work? It must have been boring during the long cold winters without electricity at the fort." Being an archaeologist, Rachel wanted to know more about this unique trading post and the artifacts they had seen earlier. Rolly Boudreau was giving her a glimpse into its history through his own family connections. She found this fascinating.

"I don't think they got too bored. They kept busy with the fur trade and making repairs to the fort. They had regular church services, sometimes three times on Sunday. Christmas and New Year's were celebrated with parties with Cree from other parts of the country who came to visit. They played soccer, held dances, and tended animals. There were horses, a pigsty and even a bull that belonged to the minister. The Hudson's Bay Company even managed a school until the fort closed. No, the Cree loved it here and many were heartbroken when the fort finally closed in 1957. For years the displaced people would return to visit York Factory since it was their ancestral home. They still have reunions here, although most of the original people have passed on. Life was easier here for them and the Company treated them well. During the summer months, the Company fed the people and gave them credit to buy supplies for the following winter. So you can see why the place is considered special, even sacred to the Cree."

"Rolly, this is fascinating stuff. What kind of illnesses did they have? Did any medical doctors ever visit here?"

"No, not for many years. Several people died from epidemics like influenza back in the 1920s. A bad outbreak of scarlet fever here killed many of the Cree people. Later on, doctors and nurses were flown in once a week and things started to improve. However, the Cree people were tough and used herbs and roots from the tundra to make teas and traditional medicines for themselves. They ate off the land and walked hundreds of miles throughout the tundra to visit relatives at places like Shamattawa or Kaskatamagun. Stories from oral tradition tell of Indian hunters in the dead of winter returning empty-handed after hunting for a week on the tundra. Not many white men could do that except for maybe Samuel Hearne and John Rae."

"And here I always thought that York Factory was operated by the English and Scots. I guess I was wrong," Rachel said.

"The English managed the place and all the chief factors were Scots or English, but most of the employees were Cree. The English referred to them as the 'Home Guard.' By the way, you said your last name was Thompson. Well, guess what? David Thompson, the famous explorer, spent time here and wrote about York Factory and the Cree in his journals. In fact, he came here when he was only fifteen."

"This is all new to me. I had no idea how rich the history of this place is."

"So you see, Rachel, York Factory isn't so much a place about the Hudson's Bay Company as it is about the Swampy Cree people, the Muskego who really kept this place alive." Boudreau was getting a little emotional and he gazed upwards at the old depot building which bore a sign saying 'Hudson's Bay Company, Incorporated May 2nd, 1670.' It was likely just as it had been in 1833 when the fort was reconstructed for the third time. He wondered how many tens of thousands of animal pelts had been shipped across the

Atlantic to the auction houses of London from this particular post over the many years of operation. He turned to Rachel and felt a twinge of sadness at leaving. He was beginning to like this bright young woman.

"Rolly, you are a fount of knowledge about York Factory. I am sorry you have to leave so soon."

"Well thanks. It was a pleasure to meet you, Rachel, and I will look forward to picking you and the rest of your team up in five days when you call. Good luck with your project. Keep a sharp eye out for polar bears; make sure one of your team carries the rifle at all times. You can always run into the depot building if you see one although they haven't been seen around here for quite some time."

"Thanks, Rolly. Have a safe flight back. You have certainly been a big help with your explanation of this place. I did not appreciate the input of the First Nations people here over the centuries. Your own story is very touching and I can see why you have an interest in the history of York Factory."

They shook hands warmly and Roland Boudreau soon left in the boat with James Klassen, heading downstream and across the Hayes to the island landing strip. Before long, his plane flew over and buzzed the depot. As he headed south towards Gillam, he looked back and watched the lonely white sentinel of the depot building disappear over the vast horizon of green tundra with its myriad of pockmarked lakes. He felt a certain wistfulness and was not entirely certain whether it was for York Factory or the lovely Rachel Thompson.

Chapter 17

The Complaint

Saturnism at Hudson's Bay

Having stumbled earlier that day on the irregular ground, Rachel decided to walk back to the tents on the long, stable wooden boardwalk at York Factory. Her earlier visit to the graveyard with the knowledgeable bush pilot Roland Boudreau had rekindled her interest in the research project, which she and her two medical colleagues had been planning for months. Their goal was to obtain artifacts from one of the oldest graves in the fort's cemetery to help solve an age-old medical mystery. Deep in thought, she looked up to see Dr. Gordon Dowling hauling a generator, propane heaters, and other equipment to the cemetery. Gordon Dowling was a balding, overweight fifty-seven-year-old anthropologist who loved his job. Earlier archaeological explorations had unearthed what appeared to be several unmarked graves from the eighteenth century. Dowling chose one grave in particular to be the focus of their investigation for the next five days.

"How are things setting up?" Rachel asked him.

"Well, the last time we were here two years ago, we found the marker over the grave when we used proton magnetometers in the cemetery.

As you know, this technology is able to locate buried objects in the soil including any iron objects in the ground. It can also measure soil resistivity and is a very useful device in detecting grave pits, particularly if the graves have not been disturbed. We are confident that the body in question was interred around the time of the Complaint," he assured her.

Dowling had been utilizing proton magnetometers in other archaeological digs to find soil disturbances that showed evidence of several other burial sites. He had spent time at York Factory on an earlier project, two years earlier, locating some of the more peripheral graves in the permafrost with this sophisticated technology.

"What would you say if I told you we have two bodies in one plot?" he asked.

"Well, if it's what I saw earlier today with our pilot, then we might have a problem," Rachel responded.

"How so?"

"Well, for one thing, we don't have the paperwork for any more than one dig, nor do we have the time to exhume and separate two bodies frozen in the permafrost here. The bodies could be at different depths also." Rachel was sympathetic to Dowling's proposal but it had been difficult enough to get approval from Parks Canada, the Ministry of Natural Resources from the Province of Manitoba, and the RCMP to perform their investigation and autopsy. After her conversation with Boudreau, she also didn't want to disturb a grave that might belong to one of the natives or any of his ancestors.

"Yes, but we do have permission to dig one plot. If two bodies were to exist in the same plot, it would be irrelevant, wouldn't it?" Dowling coolly challenged.

"Yes, I agree. I suppose we could disinter two bodies if they are buried together in the same plot. Anyway, how can you tell all that with the device from just some soil disturbances?"

Rachel was an archaeologist whose scientific world differed from that of Dowling, a physical anthropologist, whose specialty required modern technology used in historic cemetery analysis.

Dowling paused from his work to enthusiastically explain, "Well, after clearing plant growth and debris from the surface soil to the permafrost level, we found a weathered tombstone that had fallen over with the dates in question from 1836. We then used two survey techniques, GPR (or ground penetrating radar) and proton magnetometry. Using a grid system, the results were compared and we are positive we've located a burial site, likely from the era of the Complaint. We are confident that this site holds permafrost-encased bodies that lie five or six feet deep, likely from the nineteenth century. We established the date to be in the 1830s, mainly because of its location within the main cemetery and from the crumbled tombstone and its disintegrating epitaph."

"Why don't we just rely on the tombstone and dispense with all the technology?" Rachel innocently asked.

"Because tombstones can get moved around or disappear over 172 years. Bodies don't. And keep in mind that proton magnetometers have been used for over fifty years to locate buried archaeological features by detecting anomalies in the soil. I should add, however, that ground penetrating radar is usually the best way to detect unmarked graves."

Rachel smiled and mused that the nerdy Gordon Dowling reminded her a little of Dan Aykroyd's character, Dr. Ray Stantz in the movie *Ghostbusters*, always so serious, always so technical. He seemed to revel in the use of gadgets and complex analysis with an almost childlike enthusiasm. She, on the other hand, was more of a pragmatist.

"So, are we going to be able to dig the body out within the time allotted?" Rachel asked.

"Well, Rachel, your idea back at the Institute to set up propane heaters with power from the generator should work. Jaworski is getting them in position as we speak. Then he will operate an electric digging spade to speed things up. After four to five feet, we'll dig by hand to avoid damaging the bodies unless they were interred in coffins. Wojeich has also set up some flood lamps so that we can work late and see what we are doing." Dowling added.

Just then, Jaworski appeared, carrying a long heavy-duty extension cord. He was a six-foot-three, lanky forensic pathologist who was obsessed with this project and worked in many capacities to prepare for the real work of doing an autopsy. Unlike many graveyard exhumations in which he had been involved, this one would be very different because of the permafrost, which totally preserved the body. At least he hoped so.

"I think we are all set, Rachel." Jaworski announced.

"Good job, guys. This should help solve the mystery of the Complaint once and for all."

"Who's complaining?" he asked with a faint hint of a Polish accent.

Rachel smiled at the hackneyed joke and quickly responded, "No one is complaining at all, Wojeich! I was just saying to Gordon that, with all this equipment and months of planning, we should be able to find the underlying cause of the York Factory Complaint of 1834."

"She's right," Dowling enthusiastically responded. "As long as we can dig through the permafrost with the equipment we have, we should find what we're looking for. That and perhaps some artifacts in the burial site may hopefully prove useful in determining what the Complaint was all about. That is where we expect you to contribute, Jaworski."

Wojeich Jaworski launched into a short but informative dissertation at this point, typical for pedantic physicians who are fascinated by unusual diseases. Even though they had all reviewed the history behind the mysterious illness, he couldn't help himself.

"The Complaint, as you know, was a phenomenon first recognized in the 1830s at the fort and was known specifically as the York Factory Complaint. It has intrigued physicians for years. Over the course of three winters from 1833 to 1836, an unusual epidemic ravaged the employees at the Hudson's Bay Company post at York Factory. In fact, a total of thirty-two people have been identified as suffering from the York Factory Complaint during that time – several died from it. Physicians have speculated for years about what caused the symptoms of abdominal pains, nervousness, weakness and weight loss. Some of those afflicted experienced convulsions and stupor prior to dying. But strangely, after 1836, the disease just simply disappeared."

Jaworski himself had speculated that lead poisoning explained the mysterious illness, which had also afflicted the sailors in the Franklin Expedition. He had been a student in the eighties when that historical excavation took place on Beechey Island in the Arctic. The archaeologists involved with that famous dig postulated that lead poisoning had contributed in part to the death of many of the Franklin sailors. The lead poisoning likewise affected the judgment of the officers. Instead of heading north to seek help, they set out in a southeasterly direction, which unfortunately spelled their doom.

"I brought an article for each of you by Charles G. Roland, called 'Saturnism at Hudson's Bay: The York Factory Complaint of 1833–1836.' You will recall, Rachel discovered this fascinating medical paper last year when researching this dig. I would encourage you both to review this paper since it is the basis for our investigation here and explains why we're exhuming a body tomorrow, providing the heaters work of course," Jaworski added.

"What an unusual expression, 'Saturnism.' It sounds so archaic or other worldly," joked Rachel.

"It's just an old English expression for lead poisoning," Jaworski replied. "It's the most logical explanation but it has never been confirmed. By obtaining hair samples as Owen Beattie did with the Franklin sailors on Beechey Island in 1984, we can finally establish what caused this strange malady. Several doctors also suffered from it in the winter of 1834. It's interesting to note that the higher incidence occurred among officers and factors and less frequently in the workers."

"But couldn't the Complaint be explained by something else? Like a viral encephalitis? Say, Powassan virus or perhaps Lyme disease?" Rachel had done her own research on the subject.

"I agree," Dowling chimed in. "There are a few oddities with the diagnosis of lead poisoning. For example, the investigating physician acquired the Complaint himself after being there for only one month. The other unusual feature is that everyone who survived seemed better by August of each year. After three winters, it mysteriously disappeared, although a few of those afflicted suffered relapses even years later. How do you explain that, Wojeich?"

At this point, Jaworski, the medical doctor in the group, felt compelled to continue his argument for lead poisoning as the cause of the malady.

"Look, we've hashed this out before and each time we come to the same conclusion of lead poisoning as the most likely diagnosis. Besides, an infectious disease this far north, especially when you consider that most of the victims got sick in the winter months would tend to eliminate a viral cause. No, Gordon, I would have to agree with the conclusion reached in the article by Dr. Roland. These people had to be drinking from some unknown source that contained too much lead or a similar toxic substance," Jaworski adamantly asserted.

"I agree with Wojeich," said Rachel. "There is also no mention of rash or fever, which dissuades one from buying into an infectious cause. Poisoning for sure. But exactly how? The soldered tin can was not available during this time as it was a few years later on the Franklin Expedition. However, there were many other potential sources of lead at the time that could have caused lead poisoning, such as lead paint. Lead was used in glazed pottery. The male employees at the fort would likely have used vessels such as these. Lead also lined containers used for food. Many of the men smoked from clay pipes, which certainly contained lead in the glazed varieties of clay pipes."

"Not to mention pewter," Jaworski added. "Nowadays modern pewter contains virtually no lead, but the older pewters with a higher lead content would tarnish faster and they could certainly be a factor in lead poisoning. Cups, plates and drinking vessels such as tankards made of pewter were commonly used at that time."

"Boy, you have a point there!" Dowling exclaimed. "All we have to do is get hair and tissue samples, and preferably bone fragments to prove once and for all that lead poisoning was the cause of the York Factory Complaint. Anyway, it's a good working hypothesis at this point."

"But what if, just suppose, we don't find elevated lead levels in our samples?" Rachel protested. "After all, I recall reading about a guy named Musgrove who went to the fort in 1837. He tested for copper and lead in all the utensils, and found no trace of either metal. He was adamant that no poison could possibly have been introduced and that the drinking water was 'pure and wholesome.' So what if he was right?"

"Well, then we will still publish a paper or two even if we are still in the dark as to the cause of the Complaint. An archaeological dig of this kind is a first for York Factory regardless of what we find," Dowling replied. "And who knows? We may find other artifacts in the dig especially with two bodies in one plot."

"Perhaps, but it's getting dark and we should get some sleep as we plan to start the dig early at seven tomorrow," Jaworski advised. "I'll leave the propane heaters on with fans overnight. I'll also check the generators before retiring and see you both in the morning."

"By the way, Rachel, you seemed to have spent a lot of time with our pilot today. Did you learn anything from him?" Dowling asked with a smirk.

"Only that some of his ancestors may have been buried in the cemetery. He said that at one time there were no less than seventy buildings here at the fort. Many were washed away in the spring floods over the years. He also said that there might be as many as 300 graves in this cemetery containing the bodies of traders and the Cree who once lived at the fort. He knew a lot about the history of this place and the history of First Nations people in general," Rachel replied.

"I was actually wondering if you learned anything else about him, like if he was married or not." The older and married Gordon Dowling seldom missed an opportunity to tease his young associate about being a single female.

"No comment as usual and, on that note, I wish you both goodnight." Rachel turned on her heels and headed towards her tent.

"Goodnight, Rachel. Sweet dreams," Dowling added with a mischievous grin.

That night the skies were clear with a new moon. Around midnight, powerful electromagnetic radiation rode on the solar wind, churning up the molecules of oxygen and nitrogen in the ionosphere, creating vast swirls of iridescent greens, reds and blues.

Rachel watched the dancing display of the aurora through the open flap of her tent. She was mesmerized at this astronomical phenomenon, wondering how many fur traders and First Nations people from centuries ago had witnessed these same northern lights from the confines of this fort. Surely, they must have felt comforted by these spectacular lights living on the stark lone tundra, she mused.

How *could you possibly feel alone out here with nightly shows such as this? No wonder the native people were so religious.*

Excited for the project the next day, she hoped that this cosmic exhibition bode well for the discoveries they were about to make. She was excited after the many months of planning and preparations and had difficulty falling asleep. When she finally did, her dreams were a strange mélange of beaver pelts and York boats, muskeg and bush pilots.

Chapter 18

The Dig

Habeas corpus

Following an early rise and a quick breakfast the next morning, the team got to work in the cemetery. The twilight of dawn with hundreds of birds coming alive on the shore of the Hayes River seemed to welcome the scientists to their project at the plot. Propane heaters with fans powered by generators overnight had helped melt a few inches of surface ice. The researchers removed the tombstone and carefully leaned it against a nearby tree. Its darkened and algae-covered face made it difficult to read, but after a few minutes with soapy water and a scouring pad the words emerged from the weathered granite headstone:

Sacred to the memory of Joseph Charles,
A Native of Hudson's Bay,
Who Departed This Life at York Factory on the 29th day of
May, 1836,
The 29th Year of his Agh.
Deeply regretted by his friends and associates

"Agh? What does that mean?" Rachel asked.

"It is probably a tombstone typo," Dowling explained. "I'm guessing they meant the '29th year of his life' but they ran out of room so they put 'age' instead but then spelled it wrong, You'll see a lot of engraving errors if you hang around old churchyards."

After pouring several gallons of hot water into the grave, the team managed to thaw only two feet of permafrost by late afternoon. They were running out of patience at the slowness of the thawing process. Fortunately, another generator belonging to Parks Canada was discovered on-site, which enabled the team to use one more hot air blower. When directed into the pit, this second blower helped to increase the thawing and sped up their progress considerably. Soon the frozen earth yielded more readily to their electric shovel. Drs. Rachel Thompson, Wojeich Jaworski and Gordon Dowling spent the entire day thawing and digging the frozen ground in this manner.

On the third day, they discovered two burial sites right next to each other in the same plot, both approximately five to six feet down. A rough-hewn wooden coffin rested beside a crumpled blanket together with several strewn artifacts made of wood and leather. Gradually they emerged from the frozen pit. Rachel was meandering among the tombstones when this discovery was made.

"Where's Rachel?" Jaworski asked. "She needs to see this."

A moment later Rachel reappeared with pen in hand. She had been writing epitaphs down in her notebook. "Listen to this one guys," she exclaimed. "This is so sad. A thirty-year-old woman died after she lost both of her children when she was only thirty years old. 'Jenny, beloved wife of Frederick Gray, departed this life September 7, 1927, age 30 years. Children Amy Elizabeth died January 1923, age three years. Charles died January 1925, age 11 months. Jesus said Suffer the Little Children to come unto me for such is the Kingdom of God.' What a sad epitaph. Imagine, children and babies are buried here too."

"Rachel, it looks like we finally have the coffin and there is a part of a blanket showing a few feet away presumably from a separate burial." Dowling said.

Solid ice slowly dissolved around the coffin on the right side of the pit. What appeared to be a Hudson's Bay point blanket revealed itself lower towards the left, approximately five feet into the pit. After donning masks and gloves, the three researchers knelt in a close circle, huddled over the pit, fascinated, as Hudson's Bay history slowly unfolded before them.

After a few hours of warming, a corner of the blanket became pliant. The thaw had exposed an edge, revealing the blanket's bright red, green, yellow and indigo coloured stripes. The blanket, however, remained frozen and firmly adherent to the underlying permafrost. Suddenly the scientists became eerily quiet when it became evident that they might have inadvertently travelled back in time to two different epochs at the fort. Two very separate eras, juxtaposed in the permafrost, accentuated the vast history of peoples that came and went from this fort over a 333-year period.

Rachel broke the silence. "This is unbelievable – that blanket is still in great condition. I read that the first order for the Hudson's Bay blanket was for only 500 blankets. They were all made in England in 1779. At first they were shipped to Fort Albany and then later to York Factory. The factors traded them to the Indians for furs and they have been around ever since. The traders, of course, were bringing blankets to trade as early as 1688, just not this type, which is called the point blanket. We have no idea just how old this particular blanket could be though."

"It certainly looks familiar," Jaworski remarked as he poured more hot water over the coffin and turned off the heaters.

"Well, that four-striped pattern has been adorned on travel mugs, snow boards, mittens, hats and even Swiss army knives. The pattern has endured over the centuries and is still very popular. Even the athletes at the 2010 Winter Olympics in Vancouver wore team coats with this distinctive pattern," Rachel expounded.

"The point blankets were highly favoured by the natives who traded with the Bay and transported them deep into Spanish territories now known as the southern United States. This blanket probably dates back to the early 1780s, according to historians."

"It seems every time we do a dig of this nature we are entering a time capsule. Only this time, it appears we may be entering more than one," Dowling remarked, wiping beads of perspiration from his forehead.

"I'm guessing this ice has preserved whoever lies in that coffin. Let's just hope it's from the era of the Complaint and let's also hope that the gravestones didn't get moved around," Dowling cautioned.

"Whoa! What's this?" Jaworski exclaimed.

The coffin lid soon revealed itself after intense digging and scraping by the two men. A small plaque with faint writing appeared on the coffin lid under ice and dirt. Three brass screws held it in place.

"So, if this name matches the name on the tombstone, we can be certain that we have reached the tomb of one Joseph Charles who first became ill from the Complaint in 1835. According to medical records at the time, he suffered a relapse the following year and, after a prolonged illness, died on the 29th of May, 1836." Rachel reviewed the information she had researched earlier.

"Which is exactly the same year that the York Factory Complaint finally came to an end. If this plaque has Charles' name on it, we are in luck. Hopefully the body hasn't decomposed after all these years and we can obtain tissue samples and discover the cause of this mysterious illness once and for all," Jaworski interjected.

After scraping more ice from the coffin lid and the metallic plaque, Rachel jumped into the pit to read the inscription.

"Bingo!" she exclaimed. "It's Joseph Charles all right! The plaque says, 'Joseph Charles, died May 29, 1836, York Factory. Rest in Peace.'"

"Great! However, we have a lot more thawing to do. The coffin appears to be caked in solid ice. And so is that blanket that you like so much, Rachel. There's still only a small corner sticking out. Are you still thinking of removing it? If it belongs to a second grave, we may not have permission to remove any artifact from it. We don't know anything about what lies beneath it, you know," Jaworski scolded.

Rachel indignantly responded, "Well, it is close enough to the coffin to be part of our authorized dig. We could even cut off part of the blanket and leave the rest. It could be a very old Bay blanket, a significant artifact from the past. Wouldn't that be a great find for the Institute, not to mention another scientific paper?"

With this argument, they turned the heaters back on and continued to pour warm water over the coffin and the blanket. The three scientists did not remove their masks and gloves in the event that any infections from the past such as anthrax may have been buried in the pit.

"It's no wonder trees here don't grow very tall. Their roots can't penetrate more than a few inches even in the height of summer," observed Jaworski.

"That's because the average annual temperature is below minus five degrees Celsius. Geologists estimate up to fifty per cent of Canada's land mass is permafrost. Incredible, eh?" Dowling asked.

If there was one subject Dowling knew about, it was permafrost. In fact, he was scheduled to give a lecture in Moscow in a week to the Russian Arctic and Antarctic Research Institute on the effect of climate change on permafrost in Canada's North.

"We still have a lot of thawing to do if we are ever going to open the lid on this coffin. I think we should call it a day and continue tomorrow," Jaworski said.

Finally, the next day, all three members of the team removed the coffin lid following the painstaking efforts of the preceding three days. Considerable thawing had taken place overnight. Rachel Thompson took one look into the coffin, turned white as a ghost and jumped out of the pit in a flash. Looking back with a horrified expression, she gasped.

Chapter 19

Joseph Charles

Rigor mortis

Like a pupa emerging from an icy cocoon, suddenly from the ancient coffin, a man appeared with half-open eyes and a fixed grimace glaring through a shield of ice. Three long days were spent striving against the first five feet of permafrost before the scientists acquired their first glimpse of the coffin. Now it was open. For the first time in almost 200 years, the frozen body of Joseph Charles was uncovered to the fresh air and the blue sky above. It seemed as though he was staring at the researchers through a thick frosted windowpane.

"Omigosh! He looks alive!" Rachel quickly caught her breath. "That's not what I expected at all!" She looked at her associates for their reaction. Both of the men were not overly surprised at the sight of the corpse. They were familiar with the work done in the 1980s at Beechey Island when three bodies from the Franklin Expedition had been exhumed. Those corpses were also lifelike and physically intact after 140 years in the permafrost. As expected, Joseph Charles' body was in exceptional condition because of the ice. Gordon Dowling shook his head with a grim look. An hour later, the face of Joseph Charles was finally thawed and released from its icy bondage.

"Here is the face of a Hudson's Bay employee who died of the York Factory Complaint. He has not seen the light of day for over 181 years. Except for slight dehydration, he looks exactly as he did when he was laid to rest in 1836," Dowling dramatically exclaimed.

"Amazing. It boggles the mind to think he was buried here a year before Queen Victoria came to the throne – locked in Mother Nature's freezer," Rachel added.

"Indeed. Well put, Rachel. Yes, it does look as if he could have been buried just last week. He certainly defies conventional concepts of immortality, doesn't he?" Jaworski enquired philosophically.

After looking into the grave for several minutes, transfixed by the vapid stare from the lifeless eyes, the team began the arduous task of melting the ice block that entombed the rest of Charles' body. The painful grimace was so unnerving that Rachel threw a rag over the face of Joseph Charles while they continued to work.

By late afternoon, the body, finally freed from the frozen coffin, was removed for dissection. In directing the heaters into the pit, the blanket also melted and Rachel slowly pried it away in a solid clump, revealing frozen soil beneath. She could not know that only a few inches of permafrost separated her from the blanket's owner, Crooked Legs, the Chipewyan paddler from 1782. The sight of his frozen body interred beneath the blanket and a thin layer of earth would have frightened her far more than seeing Joseph Charles' corpse. Crooked Legs still had the sores and facial sloughing from the illness that killed him so long ago. The permafrost had preserved his diseased body, replete with all the horrid manifestations of small-pox. Yet his body lay hidden under a thin layer of soil.

After thawing the crumbled blanket with warm water, Rachel carefully inserted it into a large heavy-duty plastic contractor bag, sealing the end tightly.

She was unaware of the fact that the original seven-and-a-half-inch Bay trader knife had been hastily tossed onto the crumpled blanket by the anxious recruits that fateful day in 1782. Stuck to one side of the semi-frozen blanket, the knife was presently innocuous within the confines of the plastic bag.

In spite of her apprehension with the exposed body of Joseph Charles, Rachel was grateful for this valuable artifact, the Hudson's Bay blanket, conveniently buried almost within the same plot.

"Don't you guys tell any of those bureaucrats from Parks Canada about this blanket, and especially James Klassen. They'd have a fit," Rachel announced.

"Where is Klassen, anyway? He's been hanging around here for the past three days and I haven't seen him for several hours," Jaworski observed.

"I think this last part of the dig made him a little queasy so he went back to the fort. I really doubt that he cares about the blanket, Rachel. Anyway, you have done all the paper work for this dig. Technically speaking, the blanket was in our dig," Dowling assured her.

The three researchers lifted the the partially frozen body of Joseph Charles onto a table that was set up next to the grave and Wojeich Jaworski closely examined it. He was getting ready to perform an autopsy on the body with the help of his two colleagues. This was just as it had been done with the Franklin sailors. A large plastic tent placed over the table kept away the myriad of insects, yet allowed sufficient light to enable them to do their work.

"This might be a bad time for Klassen to show up if he's squeamish. I'm ready to open him up!" Jaworski exclaimed.

"Yes, but he is very interested in what caused the Complaint too," Rachel said.

"Rachel, he has some visitors to attend to and he wants to keep them away from this archaeological site while we are working," Dowling explained.

Jaworski then peeled the corpse's upper lip back to reveal the gums and teeth.

"Well, I can tell you most assuredly without even doing an autopsy that Joseph Charles died of lead poisoning!" Jaworski triumphantly announced.

"How on earth can you be so sure, Wojeich?" Dowling questioned.

"Because he has classic Burton's lines which are pathognomonic of chronic lead poisoning or, as you prefer, Saturnism," Jaworski replied.

"In English please, doctor!" Rachel blurted.

"Well, when someone has ingested lead daily over a few years, the lead eventually deposits itself in long bone, hair and other tissues. One place to see it is in the gums of patients with 'plumbism' where it appears as a bluish coloured line. Look here. You can see a very thin dark line that runs along the margins of the gums. These lines are also known as 'lead lines' and were first described by Dr. Henry Burton in 1840, just a few years after our patient was buried here at the fort," Jaworski expounded.

"Perhaps if Burton's lines were recognized at the time of the York Factory Complaint, a diagnosis might have been reached earlier and something could have prevented this disorder," Rachel said.

"Nah, I doubt it. Back in those days, more patients died from physicians than from the disease," Jaworski scowled.

"How can you say that, Wojeich? You're a physician," Rachel stated adamantly.

"Right. Well, for starters, Rachel, don't forget that I am a forensic pathologist so I don't treat people as regular doctors do. All my patients are dead." Jaworski smirked under his mask.

"But why are you so critical of medical doctors who do treat people?" Rachel continued her question.

"Oh no. Doctors do help their patients nowadays. However, it was not always that way. In the old days, they did some terrible things. For example, doctors used to treat smallpox patients by setting them beside a roaring fire when they were already burning up with a fever. That doesn't make any sense – they were already dehydrated from the disease. They would either purge or bleed their patients even though there was blood loss internally from the gastrointestinal or urinary tracts. In fact, the letting of blood was quite popular and used to treat almost any disease. Then there were dozens of useless and dangerous potions used to treat a variety of ailments. Oh, and let us not forget the benefits of leeches!"

Jaworski was now on a roll with his contempt and ridicule of practitioners past.

"It's very likely that those same doctors would have tried the same nonsense on the victims of the Complaint, I'm sure," Jaworski exclaimed from behind his surgical mask.

"Well, that's not very reassuring," Rachel said, frowning.

Jaworski shrugged and began the autopsy, collecting hair, bone and tissue samples from the major organs in the body, dropping them into small, labelled bottles of formalin, which Dowling carefully placed in a metal storage container. The autopsy of Joseph Charles took much longer than usual because of the semi-frozen state of the body. Hot air blowers helped thaw the organs being dissected.

The two men had done many autopsies together over the years and they knew each other well enough to finish each other's sentences.

"Tissue is the issue, Wojeich," Dowling said.

"Yes, but only if the sample is ample," Jaworski deadpanned as he placed a piece of bone into a bottle of formalin passing it to Gordon Dowling.

Rachel laughed at their weird sense of humour but could not get over Jaworski's poor impression of medical doctors. "Were all physicians that bad, Wojeich?" she asked.

"No, not all. Louis Pasteur, for example, found a cure for rabies long before science knew what caused it. He was exceptional. However, it was often the case that physicians attending a patient did everything least likely to give any benefit. Did you know, Rachel, that sometime between 1900 and 1912 in this country, according to Dr. Lawrence Henderson, that a random patient, with a random disease, consulting a doctor chosen at random had, for the first time in the history of mankind, a better than fifty-fifty chance of profiting from the encounter? Therefore, it is only in the last century over the long protracted history of medicine that doctors have really been able to help patients. It's amazing when you think about it."

Jaworski continued his informal dissertation while performing the autopsy; both Gordon Dowling and Rachel Thompson were fascinated with his knowledge of medical history in spite of his cynical comments about doctors. As he methodically dissected the semi-frozen corpse of Joseph Charles, he continued his eloquent argument, punctuated with sarcasm and ridicule.

"What did Job call his comforters in the Bible? 'You are all physicians of no value.' Such was the case for most doctors right up until the time of the First World War, I'm afraid to say."

"So Wojeich, how do you explain lead poisoning as a cause for the Complaint if only some of the employees suffered from it? Wouldn't you expect everyone sooner or later to exhibit signs of lead poisoning if drinking vessels were the cause?" Rachel asked.

"Good question, Rachel. The fact is that most nineteenth century residents of England probably had lead poisoning to some degree even before they left its shores for the New World. The high burden of lead that these people carried worsened during their stay here at York Factory. For some individuals it did not take long before symptoms of lead poisoning appeared. Isotope analysis of many skeletons from that era confirm that lead poisoning was common in England since lead was ubiquitous back then."

"Will you be doing isotope studies on poor Mr. Charles for lead poisoning?" Rachel asked.

"Absolutely. Furthermore, if his Burton's lines are any indicator, I can almost promise you that his lead levels will be ten times the level of that found in local natives living outside the fort," Jaworski added.

Two hours later, the team carefully laid the corpse into the coffin and then packed up their equipment. All three members of the team solemnly shovelled earth back into the pit as if Joseph Charles was being laid to rest for the first time. The two men tamped the surface, replacing the fragile headstone and spreading peat to cover the signs of the exhumation that had taken place.

The three weary scientists returned to the tents and ate a hearty supper cooked on an old barbecue left at the site. They had just enough propane to cook a big pot of chili with a few slices of semi-stale bread. In her tent that night, Rachel could not erase the image of Joseph Charles' frightful grimace from her mind. She slept fitfully.

Chapter 20

The Departure

Ursus maritimus

On the fifth day of the scientific exploration at York Factory, Rachel Thompson left a message on her satellite phone requesting the charter airline company come and pick them up. A helicopter would have been much easier, but at 1,800 dollars an hour, an airplane was cheaper and could carry more of their equipment. The Cessna 180-G with 230 horsepower and a carrying capacity of 1,300 pounds was their only option. The pilot, Rolly Boudreau, had an excellent flying record; he was also an exceptional guide with his expansive knowledge of the north. He was looking forward to picking up the team at the fort and meeting Rachel Thompson once again.

Boudreau planned to land his plane on the peninsula across the Hayes River where he had landed five days earlier. James Klassen, the Parks Canada employee, agreed to pick him up once he arrived. He would then ferry him by boat across the Hayes where the two men planned to load the equipment onto the boat at the old fort.

Rachel heard the Cessna's drone in the distance. Looking up, she saw the leading edge of the wings glinting in the noonday sun, the plane poised in mid-air like some great bird of prey over the peninsula. She quickly finished packing her equipment, grabbed her camera and applied her makeup.

Rachel was excited about the project and the discoveries her team had made over the past few days at York Factory. She decided to run down the wooden walkway to the dock to greet Roland Boudreau as he arrived on the boat. She could see across the Hayes River where the plane had just landed; to her dismay, no boat was in sight. It was a clear day and the bright sun created a myriad of sparkles on the rapidly flowing river. Wild raspberries, Labrador tea, and blueberries lined the shoreline to her left. Across the river, a pod of seals frolicked midstream, playfully twisting and diving in the silt-laden water of the Hayes Estuary.

Suddenly, she saw something move out of the corner of her eye that paralyzed her with fear. Fifty feet away to her right, a 500-pound female polar bear and her cub ambled along the shore heading towards her. The bears were picking up clams and dead fish left behind by the receding tide, oblivious to her presence. Finding food on this cold and barren coast was a full time job for hungry polar bears. During the ice-free summer, polar bears hunted and scavenged along beaches and coastlines. This pair had been foraging since leaving the pack ice on Hudson Bay the previous month.

Rachel froze, unable to move from fear; her heart began beating rapidly and her armpits were soaked from the adrenaline rush. In her anticipation to meet Boudreau, she had forgotten to bring the shotgun.

The bears had not yet seen her. The female raised her enormous snout into the air, sniffing towards Rachel who stood immobilized at the end of the dock. The bear suddenly caught a faint whiff of something unusual.

Rachel reasoned that were she to run back to the depot building the bear might see her, give chase and most certainly outrun her. However, if she remained on the dock, the bear would soon cross right in front of her. Jumping into the frigid waters of the Hayes was no option either since polar bears are excellent swimmers. She slowly walked backwards, keeping her eyes fixed on this behemoth of a bear and her cub.

Suddenly the boat came into sight and she could see the two men coming towards her across the river. Would they see the bear in time? Fortunately, the cub turned downriver chasing an Arctic lyre crab along the shore. The sow turned to follow its cub, giving Rachel a temporary reprieve during which she was able to step back several feet along the creaky wooden dock. As the boat came closer and reached the middle of the river, the red flames of a flare shot upwards and a loud crack alerted both bears. Curious, they sat on their haunches staring out at the incoming boat.

The men in the boat obviously saw what was happening; Rachel took a few more steps back towards the rickety stairway. The drone of the outboard motor increased its pitch as the boat sped up towards the dock. She backed up another step but, in walking backwards, tripped over her backpack, falling down with a loud thud, alerting the bear to her presence on the dock.

The mother bear, now only thirty feet away, turned and started to approach Rachel. Her docile cub reluctantly followed. A loud huffing sound emanated from the mother bear, which now stood erect on her hind legs with her ears bent forward, her huge head swaying from side to side. Rachel did not even try to get up; she realized the bear was exhibiting protective instincts now rather than just curiosity. Rachel knew that polar bears can appear to be slow one moment but in a matter of seconds, they can be instantly upon you. She also knew that they were not afraid of humans. The mother bear slowly approached, sniffing the air, her small beady eyes focused on Rachel, who with trembling hands reached into her backpack, fumbling for her can of pepper spray. The bear snorted and growled.

When the bear got within fifteen feet from the dock, the bright orange streak of another flare suddenly spewed from the approaching boat and struck the mother square in its backside causing it to turn and run wildly into the water, the cub chasing her. Splashing and diving across the Hayes River, using its large forepaws for propulsion, the bear left a trail of feces in its wake. The cub made vain efforts to climb on top of its retreating mother. In a moment, the bears were well into the main current of the river, their yellowish fur bobbing at intervals as they swam downriver towards the bay.

Rachel breathed a sigh of relief and slowly struggled to get back on her feet. The boat arrived forcefully at the dock; the giant swell from the outboard pushed it several feet onto the gravelly shore. Roland Boudreau immediately jumped out onto the dock while James Klassen lifted the motor and secured the boat.

"Rachel! Are you all right? That was awfully close!" Boudreau cried.

As he approached her, she fell into his arms, trembling and holding back tears.

"I forgot to bring the shotgun and I had already packed the pepper spray. Some Arctic explorer I turned out to be!"

"That's okay, Rachel. How were you to know? I'm just thankful that Parks Canada had that flare gun on board," Boudreau commiserated.

After a minute, they slowly released their embrace, both looking awkwardly at each other, Rachel still visibly shaken.

"Thank you for coming to my rescue. I don't think I have ever been so frightened in my life!" she exclaimed. They both sat down on the edge of the dock holding hands while James Klassen ran up to see how she was managing after her terrifying experience.

"That was a heck of a shot, Rolly! Good one!" Klassen exulted. "Rachel, that was scary. Where's your gun?" he scolded.

"I guess I didn't expect to see a bear after five days with only birds here to keep us company. I know, I know. There's no excuse,"

Rachel answered sheepishly. "Anyway, let's get the equipment on the boat before the bear returns." She wiped a tear from her eye, smearing eyeliner onto her cheek. Helping Rachel with the equipment, James Klassen replied, "Well I don't think it will be back here any time soon. Rolly hit that sow right in the butt with a twelve-gauge flare from a Geco flare gun. That will burn for a while." Klassen was clearly more impressed with Boudreau's accuracy with a flare gun than Rachel's narrow escape or her feelings.

"By the way, you owe Parks Canada ten dollars for the two flares, Rolly," Klassen quipped with a smirk.

The three walked up to the depot building together where they collected the equipment and the artifacts from their dig. Jaworski and Dowling were waiting for them.

"What was all that about?" Jaworski asked abruptly. "The first of July was almost a month ago, in case you didn't know."

"Aww, we were just scaring off a polar bear and her cub with a flare gun. No big deal," Boudreau explained. "Let's load up the boat as I have to be back in Gillam by four."

Within half an hour, the empty jerry cans, heaters, tents, generators and the plastic bag containing the blanket were transferred into the boat. After two trips, everything was loaded onto the Cessna. The team bid farewell and thanked James Klassen and his wife at the airstrip for their assistance and hospitality.

After walking around the plane, going over his usual inspection, Boudreau examined the interior of the Cessna to ensure the equipment was evenly distributed. The black plastic bag holding the blanket bulged in the back seat as the sun shone through the rear window and heated the air within. To make more room Boudreau gave the bag a push towards the rear of the plane. He never heard the soft popping sound from the bag. The plane soon took off and headed towards Gillam.

Chapter 21

Variola Unleashed

To err is human

By pushing the plastic bag to the back of the plane, Rolly Boudreau, the pilot of the Cessna, inadvertently allowed the centuries-old Hudson's Bay trade dagger to puncture the surrounding blanket and the bag itself. Following a sudden pop, a slow hissing from the bag took place as the hole allowed the release of warm air into the plane's circulation. A deadly aerosol containing desiccated skin cells from the Chipewyan's blanket from 1782 suddenly escaped from the plastic bag, ventilating the entire cabin.

Along with the skin cells, several billion revitalized smallpox viruses that had remained dormant for 235 years were immediately liberated from their prolonged icy confinement in the fabric of the native's Bay blanket. Following its removal from the permafrost, the blanket became a deadly fomite, capable of transmitting one of history's most lethal pathogens.

After the plane lifted off towards Gillam, the three researchers congratulated each other, regaling the success of their project at York Factory. When the plane landed at Gillam, everyone bid Rolly Boudreau a fond farewell. The capable pilot once again helped unload the equipment from the York Factory archaeological project onto the tarmac.

"Thank you for all your help, Rolly. It's been a week I shall never forget and I want to again thank you for saving my life today." Rachel leaned forward and gave the affable pilot a peck on the cheek.

"Will I ever see you again, Rachel? I would really like to take you out for dinner some time to learn about the discoveries you and your crew made this past week. As you know, I have a fascination for history of the north." Boudreau was blushing now and felt awkward. He wondered if Rachel might be aware of his ulterior motive.

"That sounds wonderful, Rolly. However, we have a lot of work to do in the next two weeks. I'll give you my email if you like and we can connect after that. Do you ever fly to Calgary? Dinner might not be an easy thing to arrange. Where do you live, anyway?" she asked.

"I live in Gillam but I often stay with my sister in Winnipeg when I have some time off."

"Well, I will be attending some meetings in Winnipeg with Parks Canada and the RCMP to review our preliminary findings around the middle of August. Why don't we get together then?" Rachel suggested.

"Great! I will definitely look forward to that. Here, I'll give you my card. If you find out when you will be there, I can work my schedule around that. I often fly tourists from Winnipeg's Richardson Airport to Churchill and back." Boudreau was clearly excited to know that he would have a date with this lovely young scientist.

After the farewell at the airport, Dowling and Jaworski loaded the equipment, the bag and the box of tissue samples into their van. They drove to the railway station where they left everything to be loaded onto the next train to Winnipeg. After returning to the airport, they joined Rachel Thompson for drinks and lunch. Two hours later, they caught a flight to Winnipeg on a Calm Air ATR 42.

Over the next few days, Rachel flew to Calgary where she unpacked and attended a seminar at the University of Calgary on the weekend. A week later, the York Factory artifacts including the punctured blanket finally arrived in a sealed box from Winnipeg. After opening the box, Rachel noticed that someone had applied a piece of duct tape on the outside of the bag. She wondered whether it could have been damaged en route and whether that might be a cause for concern. She decided to email Wojeich Jaworski to ask him if he was aware of the possible puncture.

She recalled an article in *Time* magazine that had been published in October 2016 regarding a case of anthrax that had been released in Russia from a body exhumed from the permafrost.

"Where on earth did I put that article? My stuff is in such a mess," she mumbled to herself.

After frantically turning things upside down for half an hour, she found it under her coffee table. The *Time* magazine from October 19, 2016, with the headline, 'Smallpox and Anthrax Concerns Russia,' reported how a small town in eastern Russia had been afflicted with an outbreak of anthrax seventy-five years earlier. Just as she began to read further, the phone rang. It was Jaworski.

"I just got your email about the blanket and the duct tape. When it arrived in Winnipeg, one of our techs saw it and put the tape over the hole after donning a Tyvek suit and respirator. He saw the sharp point of a knife protruding and he thinks it may have been buried with the blanket. It likely was stuck to the blanket when it froze in the permafrost. I doubt it's a cause for concern but we took cultures for bacteria and anthrax just to be sure. I wouldn't worry, Rachel. This thing has been in the ground for well over 200 years!" Jaworski's enthusiasm always intensified the more he talked about his work.

"But, Wojeich, I just found an article in *Time* magazine that mentions Russian researchers in Siberia who are investigating several resurfaced bodies. Apparently, as Siberian temperatures rose with climate change, several bodies resurfaced. Russian scientists in the article stated that anthrax could remain dormant in permafrost. They have been studying several bodies in the Yamalo-Nenets region of Siberia."

"Yeah, I saw that article too. Typical scaremongering tactics of the media. So Rachel, do you acquire your scientific information from *Time* magazine? Or perhaps the *Reader's Digest* might be more credible?" Jaworski could sometimes be cruel with his sarcasm.

"But a child died of anthrax in that area and twenty-four others became infected. I don't think we can be so dismissive, Wojeich!" Rachel was clearly becoming upset. As a post-doc, Rachel often found herself in that odd space where older males still often disregarded her qualifications. As a female researcher in a field dominated by men, she was constantly aware of the doubts cast on her because of her gender. Even though she had completed her doctorate, she felt that she was still 'earning her chops' and struggled to establish herself among her older peers. Right now, contamination of the artifact with anthrax was her primary focus. Her colleague, however, was not sharing her concerns.

"Yes. But the anthrax came from a reindeer that was released from the frozen ground with the high temperatures there last summer. It didn't come from a frozen blanket. While I appreciate your concern, I really don't think you need to worry. That article was over a year ago and it was all speculation. 'Fake news,' as Trump would say." Jaworski chuckled at his own humour, unaware of his condescension towards his younger colleague.

"But we know that some pathogens can be transmitted by bedding or clothing. That's why we wore masks and gloves and that's why we put the blanket in the plastic bag to begin with!" Rachel exclaimed.

"Okay, okay. Just to be safe, spray the bag with disinfectant, put it in one of our lab freezers and lock it. When Dowling and I get there next week, we can decide what to do. In the meantime, I will speak to the people at the National Microbiology Lab here in Winnipeg about our little 'lab accident,'" Jaworski reassured.

"Why do we have to wait until next week?" she asked brusquely.

"Have you forgotten, Rachel? Gordon is presenting the paper on 'The Effect of Climate Change on Archaeological Exhumations from Permafrost' next Monday in Moscow. He leaves this weekend and won't be back for at least a week or so. You might as well go to Winnipeg and file your reports with the RCMP," Jaworski advised.

Rachel swore and hung up. She didn't like to be patronized. She was tired and had a headache. She took two Advil and went to bed.

Chapter 22

Caucasian Mujahideen

Koltsovo

Shamil Aysha and Sulim Yakhyta were first cousins. Both men were in their teens when they lost their fathers in 1994 when the Russians invaded Chechnya to suppress the rebellion. Chechnya, a small, predominately Muslim area in the region of the Caucasus lies between the Black Sea and the Caspian Sea near Georgia in Southern Russia. It had been the seat of separatist violence since the start of the First Chechen War in 1994 in which atrocities on both sides were committed. The goal of becoming a separate state, independent of Russia motivated Aysha and Yakhyta to do what they planned to do today in the 'Science town' of Koltsovo, home of the famous Vector Institute.

The two cousins were similar in appearance with full dark beards and intense eyes. They had grown up together in the capitol city of Grozny. In Russian *grozny* means fearsome or terrible, the same word as in Ivan Grozny or Ivan the Terrible. Shamil and Sulim wanted to inspire that kind of fear in their enemy. They were both angry and united in their hatred towards the Russian government. Their hero was a rebel leader named Dokka Umarov with whom they fought in both civil wars against the Russians.

Umarov had been a thorn in Putin's side and he became known as 'Russia's Osama bin Laden.' He eventually became Vladimir Putin's most wanted enemy, sought for crimes of terrorism, homicide, kidnapping and treason. After leaving the position as the Chechens' separatist leader, Umarov, in an act of hubris, appointed himself as the Emir of the North Caucasus and declared it an Islamic state ruled by Sharia law. After committing several acts of terrorism, the Chechen jihadi died in March 2014.

The irony of this situation was that most Chechens today do not want to secede from Russia. In fact, the majority of the people are strongly in favour of Putin. Many Chechen rebels gave up on the idea of an independent Chechnya years ago. Moscow had declared an end to its counterterrorism operations in Chechnya in 2009. Perhaps this was premature.

Shamil Aysha and Sulim Yakhyta were different, however. They and their small band of followers constituted a splinter group, calling themselves the 'Caucasian Mujahideen' after the area of their origins. In the spirit of the martyr Umarov, they were determined to make the Russians pay for their crimes against Chechnya.

Chechen separatists had fought for years against Russia; the long and bloody struggle for independence from Moscow had resulted in hundreds of deaths. What began as a bid for Chechen independence in 1994, ended in numerous acts of violence. The fight for Sharia law under Umarov likewise ended with lawlessness and numerous deaths. Today's attack in Koltsovo would be no different.

Both Aysha and Yakhyta were resolved to make Russia loosen its iron grip on their fledgling nation – if it could, in fact, be called a nation. Years of repressed anger against their oppressors brought them to this juncture. To help with the rebellion, they had enlisted six comrades and accumulated several weapons in their cause, including five Russian-made RPG-7s.

The simplicity and relative availability of the RPG-7, with its devastating effectiveness, made it popular with guerilla forces such as theirs. These weapons had been around since the sixties and were used in the Vietnamese War. They were also widely used in Afghanistan. The two cousins and their comrades were now 4,000 kilometres from their homeland and prepared to die if necessary. Acquiring Russian-made weapons including AK-47s was not that difficult for the band of rebels who had several contacts in the area. An estimated sixty to one hundred million AK-47 assault rifles are still around since a Red Army soldier named Mikhail Kalashnikov first developed it in 1947. Hence, it was relatively easy to obtain these weapons for what the Chechens planned to do today.

The rebels met in the newly established Science town of Koltsovo, which was located only twenty kilometres from the centre of the Novosibirsk metropolis. The State Research Center of Virology and Biotechnology, also known as the Vector Institute, specialized in the study of dangerous viruses. In fact, the Vector Institute housed the level four laboratory where significant research on vaccines and bio-terrorism had taken place since its construction.

The Institute had been expanding ever since it was established in 1975. It now occupied a massive complex employing more than 4,500 people. The United States invested heavily in the Vector Institute following the fall of the Soviet Union and, in a few years, it became a world-class facility. A reinforced concrete barrier sur-rounded the sprawling campus. High-tech fences, cameras and motion detectors added security to the fortress-like facility.

Prior to the collapse of the Soviet Union, however, the Vector Institute fell under the umbrella of the huge Biopreparat agency in Russia. This was the Soviet Union's major biological warfare program developed in 1973. Comprising a vast network of labora-tories, Biopreparat focused on the development of numerous deadly biological agents.

Employing over 50,000 scientists, technicians and civilian workers at fifty-two sites in Russia, Biopreparat produced several pathogenic viruses and bacteria. To this day, it is uncertain as to whether biological engineering of smallpox and other viruses made them more virulent than they already were. According to Soviet defectors who had been in the employ of the Biopreparat program, the production of smallpox, rabies and typhus as bioweapons was estimated at ninety to one hundred tons.

In the 1990s, the World Health Organization sent an evaluation team to assess the safety of Vector. After six days of inspection, the team concluded that no significant security risks existed at the Institute. Today, however, the Caucasian Mujahedeen were determined to challenge those findings with their lives.

Their plan was simple. They planned to set off a series of explosions using homemade bombs from pressure cookers and gunpowder as the 'Boston bombers' had done in 2013. These devices were devised to be detonated remotely using cell phones in order to act as a diversion and draw away many of the guards surrounding the Vector Institute. The chaos that would hopefully ensue would allow Aysha and Yakhyta with their men to make a frontal attack on the main building with the RPGs and then charge in with the AK-47s. Their goal was to breach the security zone and gain access to the labs.

The homemade bombs or IEDs had been popular with Chechen rebels during the First Chechen War with Russia from 1994 to 1996. Many Russians also died from these devices in the Second War of 1999 to 2008. Shamil Aysha studied the construction and use of these bombs and felt confident that they would draw away several of the soldiers protecting the Institute. He hoped the RPGs would do the rest and blow open the entrance to the Institute. Even if Aysha and his men failed to gain access, they might cause general panic in the area and make a statement to the Russian government. He and the others were willing to lay their lives on the line today or at to least do some physical damage to the Vector Institute, if not its reputation for security.

"We are at war with Russia. Russia is responsible not only for the occupation of the Caucasus, but also for heinous crimes against our fellow Muslims!" Shamil Aysha announced to his men before setting out in the morning.

"Do not forget comrades! There are one million Chechens and 150 million Russians. If each Chechen kills 150 Russians, we will win! *Allahu Akbar!*" exulted Aysha.

"If we make it into the Institute, you need to look for the elevators to the fourth floor where the level four labs are situated. Then look for 'Anthrax' or 'Smallpox' freezers. If we can manage to blow up even one of these labs we have won," Aysha explained to his men. Clearly, this was a suicide mission.

The rebels crouched together in a van with their equipment, clutching their weapons while reviewing a map of the complex. They planned their attack at 0700 hours, just prior to the shift change when the soldiers would be tired. This would enable them to drive the van as close as possible to the front entrance. The Chechens had disguised the van as a public works vehicle in order to avoid any attention.

The Chechens had not considered, however, exactly how they would transport anthrax in the event they were lucky enough to find it in one of the dozens of labs in the Vector Institute. Anthrax as a bioterrorist weapon is not as easily transferable, nor is it as frightening as smallpox. After 9/11, scientists argued that smallpox specimens remained as a potent agent for bioterrorism, especially when one considered the turmoil in the years following the breakup of the former Soviet Union.

Aysha, Yakhyta and their compatriots were aware that an attack incorporating smallpox would create an international emergency. The world would certainly blame Russia for its injustices towards Chechnya if they were successful today. The Chechens, however, were so bent on revenge that they failed to appreciate the potential havoc that anthrax or smallpox might wreak on their own people if unleashed.

On Saturday, July 28, 2018, at 0700 hours, the IEDs detonated and a series of muffled explosions could be heard in the distance behind the Institute. Sulim Yakhyta watched through a peephole lens on the side of the van to see what action the soldiers were taking. Surprisingly, there was little activity and the Russian soldiers guarding the entrance to the Institute failed to disperse with the explosions. Several workers, gardeners and deliverymen seemed busy with their duties and barely looked up at the sound of the explosions.

"Comrades, we must act soon before the next shift of guards arrive. We must move quickly and decisively. There will be several guards, so remember, every shot must count," Aysha admonished. "Our target is the main doors of the Institute." Aysha admonished. After a short prayer, the men armed to the teeth, covered their faces with masks, left the van and headed towards the front entrance of the Vector Institute.

Although the Chechens anticipated some opposition to their brazen attack, they were unaware that they had been under surveillance even before they arrived in Koltsovo.

Chapter 23

Vector

Live by the sword, die by the sword

Numerous security cameras surrounded the town, many disguised in artificial trees and telephone poles, cleverly hidden in plain view. An army of soldiers, many dressed as cleaners, gardeners and delivery-men, protected the Vector Institute. Soon after the van arrived in front of the main building, a dozen laser lights targeted the passenger side of the van. Just as the Chechens began leaving the van to charge across the street, they were immediately met with a heavy barrage of gunfire from the soldiers.

"It's a trap! Everyone get down!" yelled Aysha. But his words of warning were too late.

Within seconds, the van was riddled with fifty-calibre gunfire from ASh-12 assault rifles. At such a short distance, the 12.7 x 55 cartridge was armour-piercing, a veritable 'thumper' of firepower. The engine block of the vehicle was destroyed with a resonant thud within a matter of seconds. Several of the Chechens dropped before taking even a few steps; their plan foiled before it even began. However, Aysha and Yakhyta were able to dive behind the van after exiting from the driver's side. Aysha aimed his RPG-7 at the front entrance and launched it only seconds before he was struck down in a hail of bullets. The grenade met the front doors with a terrific concussion that threw several Russian soldiers to the ground, seriously injuring three of them. Glass, concrete and metal showered outwards to the street, reaching as far as the van itself from the power of the explosion.

Sulim Yakhyta then launched his RPG, but his aim was off because of a bullet that suddenly lodged in his left shoulder. His grenade struck a nearby delivery truck loaded with specimens from various other labs for delivery and testing at the Vector lab. The truck blew up dramatically in flames, driver and specimens immediately incinerated before the awestruck eyes of the defending Russian soldiers. The impact of this second explosion took out three more Russian soldiers. A few more bullets struck Yakhyta and then two fifty-calibre slugs removed much of his head. He collapsed to the ground in a heap.

After twenty seconds of explosions, with blood, fire and glass shards flying everywhere, it was all over. Within the hour, the Kremlin received messages from the security director at Vector that the Chechens had failed miserably and the Vector Institute, the most significant level four laboratory in Russia, was safe, having received only minor damage in the skirmish.

"The bodies of the fanatics will be photographed, fingerprinted, cross referenced and disposed of within twenty four hours," the head of security at Vector proudly announced. "These people were amateurs."

The Russian president received the news with equanimity. He shrugged, only a hint of a smirk betraying his reaction to the terrorists' failed attack; as usual, he refused to comment to the news media.

Nevertheless, damage had definitely been inflicted by the Chechen zealots. Six Russian soldiers were dead and three more were injured thanks to the RPGs and the few rounds that the downed Chechens managed to fire before they themselves succumbed. Two lab drivers were instantly killed in the attack and a lab truck, also known as a mobile lab, was dramatically incinerated. The lab truck had been utilized for in-country deployments and this one was bringing lab samples from nearby nursing homes where Legionella was suspected in the air conditioning systems. Several old people had died of pneumonia over several months in these institutions. It was anticipated that Vector would be able to solve this mystery. At least until today's tragic events.

The Russian officials, as expected, downplayed the damage and ensured that the name Vector did not appear in the press. The headlines the next day read, 'Chechen rebel attack foiled in Novosibirsk.' The attack, however, was not exactly foiled, neither did it take place in Novosibirsk. The mere mention of Koltsovo would alarm Russian citizens familiar with the famous Science town and its primary employer, the Vector Institute, where thousands of scientists and support staff worked. A low-key approach to the 'event,' as it was called, guaranteed second-page news.

However, several employees on their way to work that morning took hundreds of pictures on their cell phones and the story quickly went viral. A picture is worth a thousand words, it is said. Images of the main entrance of the Vector Institute blown to pieces with several fallen Russian soldiers, blood running in the street and a mobile lab shooting flames thirty feet in the air was worth ten thousand words.

CNN Europe picked up the story by noon and that evening viewers as far away as Winnipeg, Manitoba, were seeing pictures of the level four lab that was 'breached,' according to reports. The question of the loss of negative pressure necessary to ensure containment was brought up numerous times. The story received further impetus when it was announced that a mobile lab truck was damaged in the battle and that it was carrying dangerous pathogens. The fact that it had been completely destroyed in the conflagration along with its microbiological samples was not mentioned in the *Breaking News*. Nothing could survive this horrific explosion, yet CNN still introduced a panel of 'what if' specialists from around the country to speculate on the lethal pathogens that could have been liberated from the mobile lab truck.

It didn't take long before more panels of 'experts' in infectious diseases, bioterrorism and Russian–Chechen relations were postulating worst-case scenarios as a result of the attack. The Russians quickly repaired the front entrance, managing to maintain the negative pressure of the facility throughout, but when CNN reporters got a hold of the story, anthrax, Ebola, and smallpox as agents of bioterrorism were front and centre of their sensationalist *Breaking News*.

When CNN interviewed Dr. Frank Emberley, Professor of Medicine and Head of Infectious Diseases at the University of Manitoba, his answers were guarded. When asked whether infectious agents could have been released in the terrorist attack in Koltsovo, his answer was reasonable: "It's difficult to say, but there certainly was substantial damage levied to the facility. If the Russians built the Vector Lab similar to the National Virology Lab in Winnipeg, the walls would be at least a foot thick and perhaps armour-plated near the entrance. Most of the dangerous pathogens would definitely be housed upstairs in labs reinforced with thick concrete walls. At any rate, less than five per cent of the laboratory space would have been dedicated to level four research labs. I think it is highly unlikely that there was any breach because of this attack," Emberley categorically stated.

CNN News gave Emberley barely fifteen seconds and quickly moved on to experts from the United States, who painted a much darker picture, demanding a statement from the Russian Ministry of Health.

"This attack on the Vector Institute could be the start of a major epidemic thanks to the Chechen rebels. The Russians should have been better prepared for this!" one expert pronounced.

Another Infectious Disease specialist from the CDC in Atlanta, concerned about a breach, demanded confirmation of negative pressure testing at Vector. He went on to discuss the fact that the Vector site was once part of a directorate called Biopreparat, founded in 1973. He pointed out that this massive organization supervised the design and production of biological weapons for two decades.

"Perhaps our listeners are unaware that a production line to manufacture smallpox on an industrial scale was initiated at the Vector Institute in 1990. The Russians made literally tons of smallpox in the 1990s. Some strains of smallpox were genetically altered so we really don't know what we're dealing with here," the CNN panel expert cautioned. The next day, the *New York Times* headlines screamed, 'State Research Center of Virology and Biotechnology Vector attacked in Novosibirsk!'

Yet the Russian officials at the Vector lab were confident that the attack from the RPGs had not even come close to breaching even a level one lab. Within a matter of days, however, their confidence would be shattered.

Chapter 24

Arctic and Antarctic Research Institute Conference

Variola prodromus

Dr. Gordon Dowling was scheduled to arrive shortly in Moscow to attend the Arctic and Antarctic Research Institute (AARI) annual conference, where he would make a presentation on Canadian arctic permafrost on August 7, 2018. The institute is the largest and most comprehensive organization involving Russian Arctic and Antarctica research. Several of its delegates joked that the institute was 'bipolar' in view of the two areas of study. AARI itself is located in Saint Petersburg but, this year, the annual scientific sessions were being held in Moscow. During the ten-hour flight from JFK airport in New York City, Dowling reviewed his paper several times. Ten days earlier, Dowling had arrived in Winnipeg from Gillam, Manitoba, after spending five days working at York Factory on Hudson Bay with two other scientists.

Looking out the window, Dowling viewed the lights from the city of Helsinki far below on the right. Soon his plane would be landing in Moscow and he would try to adjust to the time change over the next few days. The forensic anthropologist smiled as he recalled the interesting project at the old fort with its fascinating history.

Dowling did not tolerate international travel as well as he did when he was younger. He knew his biological clock was slowing and he suffered from rheumatoid arthritis. Jet lag was his nemesis and he usually flew a day or two ahead of conferences like this to overcome the effects of the time difference. Due to time constraints this luxury was not afforded to him on this trip.

Although he was a forensic anthropologist, he also specialized in the subject of the effects of climate change on permafrost. Based on his research, it seemed bodies were popping up everywhere as areas of permafrost thawed. He knew this had presented problems in Siberia's far north but he was not aware of this being a problem in North America. At least, not yet.

Nevertheless, the potential for thawing permafrost to allow bodies that had been buried centuries ago to re-emerge was a frightening reality. The possibility of a vulnerable populace being exposed to an infectious disease was of particular concern for Dowling and his colleagues in Calgary at the Arctic Institute. Hence, his interest in climate change.

Anthropologists are frequently called upon to investigate the remains of dead bodies in forensic cases. The identification of the body and the cause of death from physical characteristics of the skeleton defines much of their work. Forensic anthropologists will likewise assist authorities such as the RCMP and other police agencies in criminal investigations. Archaeological and historical projects such as the York Factory project invariably require their involvement as well.

Forensic anthropologists work in conjunction with forensic pathologists to identify the remains of bodies that are frequently beyond recognition. Dowling had worked with Dr. Wojeich Jaworski on several projects over the years. The last one at York Factor gave him special satisfaction because of the historical value dating back to the early part of the nineteenth century and because of the pristine condition of the body, which they had exhumed. The two had collaborated on significant articles over the years, which were published in criminology journals, police reports and even a few legal periodicals.

With the recent investigation at York Factory, they also hoped to publish several articles for historical journals such as *The Canadian Journal of History/Annales Canadiennes d'Histoire* and the *Canadian Historical Review*.

Digging in permafrost, such as the Beechey Island project back in the 1980s with Owen Beattie when he was a student, fascinated Dowling because the bodies were perfectly preserved by the permafrost. Dowling envisioned many more frozen corpses buried in the northern tundra awaiting investigation similar to the recent York Factory project.

Dowling's concern regarding the effects of climate change on thawing Arctic permafrost prompted him to prepare a scientific paper for the Arctic Congress on this intriguing subject, only from a North American perspective. Following months of research, he was scheduled to present his paper today at the AARI annual meeting.

Dowling was aware that the Russians had probably acquired advanced knowledge regarding the effects of climate change by studying their own enormous area of permafrost. One of the researchers who presented at a similar conference last year noted that sixty per cent of Russia's land mass was occupied by permafrost. The researcher postulated that the warming, thawing, and degradation of Russian permafrost had taken place in recent years to a significant extent. This scientist using mathematical models predicted that, by the middle of the twenty-first century, the surface permafrost would shrink by up to thirty per cent. The implication of this was that enormous quantities of carbon trapped in the permafrost would be released into the atmosphere, thereby accelerating the cycle of climate change.

Dowling planned to present the Canadian Arctic perspective on this same problem. He disliked the expression 'global warming' as it was too politically charged. Instead, he decided to use the more benign expression 'climate change,' He found it difficult to accept that this phenomenon was man-made and questioned much of the 'science' that was proffered by many of the delegates. He preferred to believe that cycles of solar thermal activity were entirely responsible for the thawing permafrost. Dowling theorized it might take a decade or so before things would cool down to their former state. He was careful not to make his views on the subject known, lest he come under attack by the 'ideologues,' as he privately referred to them.

After landing in Moscow's Sheremetyevo International Airport, Dowling took a cab to the Moscow Marriott Grand Hotel where the Arctic conference was to be held the next day in the large main floor ballroom. Dowling settled into his room and, although he had been hungry earlier, suddenly he had lost his appetite. His throat was a little sore and he was thirsty. Opening a can of Klinskoye Svetloe beer, he did not appreciate its crisp and hoppy flavour. For some reason, it somehow had little or no taste. He retired early, exhausted from the long flight, jet lag and the busy week with the York Factory project.

He slept soundly for several hours but woke up in a soaking night sweat in the middle of the night. The sheets and his undershirt were wet with perspiration. He felt hot and wondered if he had a fever. Dowling checked the temperature on the thermostat and went back to bed. A few minutes later, he began to shiver with chills and could not seem to keep warm. A fitful sleep ensued until he woke up as tired as he had been the night before. He showered, shaved, dressed and checked his computer presentation once more.

Dowling went down for breakfast but could swallow only sips of coffee and juice. Sitting alone in the hotel restaurant, he realized that his symptoms of headache and fatigue coupled with fever and chills could not be attributed to jet lag alone. His back pain was severe.

"What a great time to be coming down with the flu," he said to himself. He went to the hotel gift shop to see if they sold ibuprofen. They did and he bought a bottle at an outrageous price. Taking a couple of tablets with water, he then proceeded to the Grand Ballroom for the opening of the AARI annual scientific proceedings. Dowling sat down and loosened his collar. Beads of perspiration appeared on his balding forehead. In an hour or so, he was scheduled to present his paper to the 200 delegates who were presently pouring into the ballroom. He felt absolutely dreadful.

Chapter 25

What lies beneath?

Ante mortem

'Poxviridae' constitutes a family of viruses. The natural hosts for these viruses include humans, vertebrates and arthropods (insects and crustaceans). Sixty-nine known species of this family are divided into two subfamilies, the most lethal of which is variola, commonly known as smallpox. It has been estimated that this virus has killed 300 million people just in the twentieth century alone.

Gordon Dowling had been exposed to a 237-year-old strain of variola major on July 27, 2018, on the plane ride from York Factory to Gillam. The lethal virus contained in an infested blanket was accidentally unearthed during an archaeological investigation in the fort's ancient cemetery. Eleven days had elapsed since he had inhaled the lethal virus in the Cessna airplane en route to Gillam. During this time, Dowling had been in what Infectious Disease specialists refer to as the 'smallpox incubation period.' Although the double stranded DNA virus was multiplying at an exponential rate within every organ in his body, he had not been contagious to others. In addition, he had no major symptoms. At least, not until today.

Once the smallpox virus was inhaled into Dowling's lungs, it entered a host cell and began to clone itself. Immediately DNA replication and transcription began within his respiratory alveolar cells at an alarming rate. Variola, a large brick-shaped virus, has the capacity to replicate within only twelve hours. As soon as the newly produced viruses are released, the host cell dies. Because the virus itself contains enzymes for replication and transcription, it does not need to rely on host cell enzymes. This biological feature of the smallpox virus enables the infective process to accelerate greatly. It is one of the reasons that the smallpox virus is so deadly.

Following a series of complex intracellular processes, the smallpox virus that infected Gordon Dowling reproduced on a massive scale. By the time the incubation period had terminated ten days later, billions of viral particles were entering the circulation every hour, infesting every aspect of Dowling's anatomy. Before disseminating, the virus reproduced itself in the small blood vessels of his skin and mouth. That explained why his throat was so painful.

After infecting the throat and respiratory mucosa, the virus migrated to regional lymph nodes and multiplied. Today the virus abounded in Dowling's bloodstream and infected cells were lysing, releasing more virons in massive numbers. His symptoms of fever, chills and night sweats reflected this viremia. Soon his spleen, bone marrow and all his lymph nodes would be engaged in a colossal but futile immunological battle. Over a trillion virons per day were released just from his lungs alone; he didn't stand a chance.

Nevertheless, Dowling made it to the lectern and while adjusting the microphone thanked the chair for introducing him.

"Thank you for the kind introduction and for inviting me to attend this great conference with the AARI." Dowling paused and reached for the glass of water that had been provided for him on the lectern. Even though he was dehydrated and very thirsty, sipping a little water felt as though he was swallowing razorblades.

"In an attempt to spice up my lecture today, I have titled it 'Permafrost – What Lies Beneath.' Other speakers have discussed the subject of permafrost. This morning, however, I would like to provide a Canadian perspective."

Clearing his throat, Dowling adjusted his glasses. He hoped the ibuprofen would soon kick in.

"As was discussed previously, because of increases in global average temperatures in recent years, permafrost has been thawing at an increased rate. Permafrost currently covers twenty per cent of the earth's surface. This value is predicted to shrink by ten to eighteen per cent in the next quarter of a century according to the head of Russia's ministry disaster monitoring department. Of course, this has major environmental implications. The zones where permafrost can be found year-round are retreating irrevocably northward. In Canada as in Russia, we are witnessing this phenomenon with grave concern."

Dowling tried a few more sips of water and silently wondered how the word 'grave' had slipped into his talk. He moved on to the next slide.

"As last year's speaker pointed out, this phenomenon is implicated in the resurfacing of bodies of humans and animals, exposing our northern populations to infectious agents that have long been quiescent.

Of greater significance is the fact that previously frozen bacteria are being reactivated. This in turn accelerates the decomposition of plant and animal remains that have been dormant for eons. The resulting release of carbon dioxide and methane from this process may be contributing further to the rise in temperatures, which have been observed since the 1980s."

Dowling stopped and wiped his brow, his face flushed. He noticed a few red dots on the back of his hands that physicians refer to as a maculopapular rash. At first, these lesions could represent a variety of viral illnesses, but with smallpox, they were ominous. Within a day, these flat red spots would become raised and rounded like tiny blisters or 'vesicles.' Within two days, they would cover his body completely and begin to enlarge and coalesce. After five days, if he survived, they would rupture and become pustules, leaking viral-infected serum.

Dowling soldiered on with his lecture, painfully sipping some more water.

"Rich in organic material, the Arctic soil starts to decay once thawing occurs. As it deteriorates, large quantities of methane and carbon dioxide are released into the atmosphere, contributing to an increase in greenhouse gases. Melting permafrost would result in a positive feedback loop wherein thawing leads to greater warming and warming leads to greater thawing."

Dowling paused and hesitated to continue his talk. Bloodshot, his eyes glazed over and he finished his presentation from memory.

"There is so much organic material in the permafrost that encircles the northern hemisphere that even a small amount of warming will release massive amounts of greenhouse gases into our atmosphere as to ensure the acceleration of climate change."

Dowling was now at the point where even if a diagnosis of smallpox could be made and a vaccination was available, it would be too late to prevent or halt further viral replication. He was at the pre-eruptive phase of his disease and had now become highly contagious through aerosolized droplets from his oropharynx and respiratory tract. A cough or a sneeze from Dowling now would be lethal to anyone around him.

Dowling continued his talk describing how satellite imaging and remote sensing equipment could accurately record alterations in the Greenland ice sheets. No technological advances had been made, however, to assess thawing of permafrost until recently. Ever the lover of gadgets and technology, Dowling described newer ground sensors installed in certain areas of the permafrost.

"The Global Terrestrial Network for Permafrost currently follows more than 1,000 sites where monitors have been set up. Each of these sites is equipped with instruments that track temperatures in the top eight to ten feet. It is this system that has documented the rise in permafrost temperatures over the past decade or so. With the increased number of instruments scattered over greater areas in the subarctic tundra, we envision a much clearer picture of the effects of climate change and the corresponding carbon release from Canada's permafrost. However, more studies will be required to understand the effects of the various environmental factors in our changing climate. Thank you for your attention."

A hand shot up and pointedly asked, "Dr. Dowling to what degree do you feel that global warming is man-made?"

Dowling knew this question had to have been planted in the audience by the ideologues who were aware of his skeptical views on the subject. Even though he was seriously ill, he could tell a 'green guru' when he heard one. A follower of Huxley, Dowling believed that skepticism was of the highest duty of a scientist and that adherence to blind faith was an unpardonable sin. At this point, he felt so tired and weakened that he mumbled to himself, "What the heck," and decided to close his lecture with a bombshell that would reverberate among the gurus of green for months.

"The origins of the climate change phenomenon, in fact, lie entirely with cyclical solar activity. Climate has always been changing. We just haven't had sufficient time to have studied it with any degree of confidence. The totality of science does not suggest a convincing link to human activity as a cause for climate change. I believe the evidence base for that theory has been weighed in the balances and is found wanting. And now with the vast carbon sink of permafrost being released, the equation shifts even more towards natural causes than purported man-made causes. The causes of global warming have not been settled, and the science is still emerging. In my opinion, having studied this question for most of my career, the conclusions are at best tentative."

A collective gasp arose from the audience. Amidst catcalls and booing from every corner of the auditorium, Dowling quickly retrieved his memory stick from the lectern computer and sat down. Feeling light headed and dizzy, he pumped his legs a few times and bent forward in his chair. Soon he regained his composure and made it to the elevators before collapsing.

Chapter 26

Moscow State University Teaching Hospital

Variola Canadensis

When Gordon Dowling awoke, he had an intravenous pouring normal saline at a rate of one hundred millilitres per hour into his left forearm. An oxygen line pumped five litres per minute through a facemask, and two masked and gowned nurses attended to his vital signs. His head throbbed more than any hangover he had ever experienced. He slowly lifted his hand to his face and noticed a pulse oximeter monitor on his index finger. A nurse gently placed his hand back on the bed.

As he regained consciousness, he recalled his last provocative statement in his lecture to the AARI and wondered if perhaps he should not have said what he did. Not being a medical doctor, he wondered just what kind of bug could be laying him so low. His throat was so raw he could barely speak, and even if he could speak, these Russian nurses did not understand a word of English.

"*Kak dela?*" one of the nurses asked. "You awake now?"

"Yes, I'm awake. Do you have any Advil?" Dowling croaked.

Before the nurse could respond, the curtains around his cubicle were brusquely shoved aside and an older distinguished looking physician with a well-trimmed grey beard entered, accompanied by an entourage of residents, interns and fourth year medical students all wearing lab coats and surgical masks.

"Welcome to the Moscow State University teaching hospital, Dr. Dowling. My name is Dr. Alexei Kulagin and I am professor of medicine, subspecialty infectious diseases. This is my chief resident, Viktor Markov. I am here to examine you at the request of your admitting doctor. It appears that you arrived by ambulance shortly before noon today and you were unconscious and febrile upon arrival. Let me state from the beginning that a grand entrance like that always captures our attention. I'm sure as a research scientist you will appreciate we like a good teaching case like you."

"Thanks, I think," mumbled Dowling.

"You are most welcome. Our University Faculty of Medicine was founded in 1992 and we consider ourselves one of Russia's more prestigious centres of higher learning. However, enough about the history of this institution. We wish to know more about your history, Dr. Dowling." Kulagin appeared to be a sincere and most affable physician, Dowling thought to himself.

"First of all you are Canadian, no? And a doctor?" Kulagin enquired.

Dowling offered a thin smile and nodded. "I am a forensic anthropologist. Most of my patients are skeletons."

Kulagin and some of his residents laughed. Dowling wondered to himself if this doctor was related to Boris Kulagin, the Russian hockey coach from the famous Summit Series in 1972. He decided he would not go there and would just cooperate as best as he could. Dr. Kulagin's English was excellent, with a pleasant Russian accent similar to that of Pavel Chekov of *Star Trek* fame.

"To begin with, Dr. Dowling, let me say that, no, I am not related to Boris Kulagin. It seems, whenever we have a Canadian patient, they always ask that question and remind me of the great hockey series and the fact that we lost. Markov here wasn't even born then," Kulagin chuckled.

"Anyway, the residents who have examined you today are a little baffled as to your diagnosis. Your temperature was 39.6 and your heart rate was 124 when you arrived in the emergency department earlier. Your respiratory rate was thirty-six and you were moderately hypoxic. A chest X-ray revealed some patchy infiltrates and you have a generalized maculopapular rash including sores in your mouth. In addition, your white blood cell count is over 30,000. Of course this all points to some type of infectious disease, most likely pneumonia, and that is why I am here to examine you."

Having earlier donned a large plastic surgical mask, gown and gloves, Kulagin gave Dowling a thorough exam and spent more than a few moments examining his throat and eyes, which were quite bloodshot. He listened carefully to his chest and frowned, looking somewhat perplexed.

"Well, doctor, your heart rate is down to ninety-six but your chest has some fluid build up. We are taking blood cultures and starting you on intravenous antibiotics. We are uncertain as to this rash, however. Can you give me a list of any medications you are taking, Dr. Dowling? Perhaps you have developed an allergy to one of them?"

"I take Crestor, thyroid pills and baby aspirin every day. I have also been giving myself adalimumab injections every two weeks for rheumatoid arthritis since last year. This morning I took some ibuprofen for my headache," he whispered.

"Well, it is possible you may have developed an allergy to the aspirin you have been taking. We will stop that today and administer some antihistamines. You also do not need the Crestor while you are sick, but we will continue with the thyroid replacement while you are here. We will also be moving you into an isolation room as a precaution. Okay?" Kulagin asked.

"But I have always taken the aspirin!" Dowling protested.

"Yes, but you can develop an allergy to a drug at any time even after taking it for years. Recent evidence suggests that most people don't need to take aspirin if they are healthy. I suspect you might have an aspirin allergy, which would explain your rash but certainly not your fever. That is something else entirely," Kulagin advised.

"Thank you, doctor," Dowling replied hoarsely.

After his examination of Dowling, Dr. Kulagin conferred with his chief resident. "Are you familiar with this drug he takes for his rheumatoid arthritis, Viktor?"

"Yes, it works wonders for suppressing the inflammation of rheumatoid arthritis but it also suppresses the immune system, which makes him less capable of fighting infection," Markov replied in Russian.

"Exactly, Viktor. This is of great concern for this fellow. Whatever bug he is fighting may take over without an intact immune system. We should be very aggressive in treating him," Kulagin advised.

Later that afternoon, Dowling was transferred to an isolation ward. Large doses of Cefuroxime and Levofloxacin were administered intravenously. Until the blood cultures returned in a day or two, this combination of agents was reasonable for a severe case of community-acquired pneumonia. Dowling fell asleep after taking liquid Tylenol. He was unable to swallow anything except fluids.

The next day, Dowling's temperature spiked despite the IV anti-biotics and more Tylenol. After peaking at forty degrees Celsius, Dowling became delirious. Nurses sponged him and placed two large fans near his body. Viktor Markov looked in on him frequently during the day. By the evening of August 8, Dowling's rash was more prominent and vesicles had appeared. His face became unrecognizable from the swelling and the developing sores. By the time Dr. Kulagin made his rounds the next morning, Dowling was comatose. Tea-coloured urine drained from a catheter into a bag hung at the foot of his bed, which Kulagin bent over to examine.

"My God, what have we here? Bloody urine?" Kulagin exclaimed. After taking one look at Dowling and his vital signs, he turned to his residents and angrily shouted for them to leave the room.

"Everyone out! And tell the nurses only people with hazmat suits allowed in here. We need viral cultures sent to Vector immediately. I want all adjacent rooms to be cleared out and we need to put the entire ward on lockdown. Get me the hospital administrator and the heads of Medicine and Surgery on the phone." Kulagin had never raised his voice to his residents before. His chief resident, Viktor Markov, was shocked.

"What do you think is happening, Dr. Kulagin?" he asked.

"I am almost afraid to tell you, Viktor. This is like seeing a ghost from the past. I once saw a few cases as a student in the 1960s in Siberia, but we have always believed that smallpox had been eradicated back in 1977."

"Smallpox!" Markov exclaimed. "But how is that possible?"

Chapter 27

Guarnieri Bodies

In extremis

Dr. Alexei Kulagin's sense of urgency was unnerving. "Viktor, I must confess that yesterday I was uncertain and dismissed the possibility of smallpox. I assumed Dowling had pneumonia with an allergic reaction to aspirin. However, today I have no doubt that this is variola major. You and I will be all right. We receive ongoing boosters as infectious disease specialists but those nurses and the staff and patients in Emergency are all unprotected. We need to call the airlines, his hotel and anyone he met at his scientific conference. Get all the residents to help you with this. And you must call the Vector Institute and get their epidemiologists out here in a hurry," he demanded. "And we will need at least 50,000 ampules of vaccine."

"Yes sir, I will get on it immediately. But why so many vials of vaccine?" Markov asked.

"You will soon understand. One vial will yield one hundred injections so we should start with at least five million doses. We may need even more to effect a ring vaccination in the heart of a city the size of Moscow. I want you to take pictures of this Dowling fellow and send them to the Vector Institute immediately. Oh, and quarantine everyone who has set foot in this room. No one leaves the hospital!" Kulagin's mind was racing at the myriad of things he had to do and he was suddenly struck by the enormity of this situation.

Unlike most other physicians of his specialty, Alexei Kulagin knew about this disease. He was one of the few physicians in the country who had actually seen a case of smallpox as a clinical entity before it became extinct when he was a young doctor back in the sixties.

"Where on earth did this infection come from?" he asked aloud. Dowling was unresponsive. Kulagin knew he had to save this man in order to determine the source of the infection. His mind raced and he thought of the only two places in the world where the variola virus was kept, the CDC in Atlanta and the Vector Institute near Novosibirsk. Then he remembered the Vector Institute attack that took place twelve days earlier. If there were a breach during that attack, the incubation period would be about right if that were the source of Dowling's infection. *But how would a Canadian who has only been in Russia a few days possibly contract this disease from the Vector incident?* Kulagin was perturbed.

Kulagin turned to his patient who was showing signs of respiratory distress as his lungs filled up with fluid. Dowling's rash was more florid and his lips were now dusky. His face took on a cobblestone appearance from the multiple pox lesions. He was showing signs of severe hypoxia and needed ventilation with a respirator.

Kulagin left the room and called anaesthesia to insert a breathing tube into Dowling's trachea. He advised them of the diagnosis and the precautions they should take. By this time, Dowling's vesicles had morphed into multiple pressurized iridescent pustules mainly on his face. He grabbed a scalpel and quickly biopsied one of Dowling's lesions without anaesthetic and prepared it for microscopy. Comatose, Dowling did not budge during the procedure.

Fortunately, a small histopathology lab with a microscope down the hall with was located. This meant he would not have to take the dangerous sample to another area in the hospital.

Kulagin knew that viral cultures were the gold standard in making the diagnosis of smallpox, but this would take precious time to confirm. *Way too much time!* He had to think fast. Even though electron microscopy could make a diagnosis of an orthopoxvirus infection, it would not confirm smallpox definitively. Other orthopox viruses looked identical under electron microscopy. Besides, it would take more time and likely contaminate the entire lab. A polymerase chain reaction analysis would also take several hours and expose lab technicians to the virus. While Kulagin considered his options, Viktor Markov ran down the hall masked and gowned.

"Dr. Kulagin, I called Vector and notified them about this case. They would not believe me until they saw the pictures. They are sending a team as we speak. They will take over the management of this outbreak after they receive laboratory confirmation. Our hospital administrator has ordered a quarantine of the entire building."

"Well done, Viktor. I can't say that I blame the Institute for wanting more information since the last recorded case of smallpox was forty years ago. We will give them that information shortly. Help me with this skin scraping will you?"

"Absolutely, sir. Just what are you making a slide of the patient's pustules for?" Markov asked.

Dr. Kulagin went on to explain to his protégé the details of the procedure.

"Under an ordinary microscope, cytoplasmic inclusions can be seen in the skin when stained with hematoxylin and eosin if it is truly smallpox. These inclusion bodies, which are called Guarnieri bodies, would confirm the diagnosis if it is present. I confess I have not done a stain of this sort for years so I might need your help, Viktor," Kulagin said.

A sheet of plasticized instructions for performing the stain was posted on the wall near a sink stained pink and purple. Both men sprayed their gloved hands from a bottle of Lysol after taking the specimen to the lab. Nurses, orderlies and medical residents were rushing around in a flurry of activity to remove patients from adjacent rooms. Kulagin was suddenly very thankful to have the intelligent young Viktor Markov with him today, as he did not want to expose anyone else on this floor. He felt that everything in the ward was most likely contaminated.

Leaning out of the lab door, he barked to the nurses, "Spray everything down in this hallway! Turn off all air conditioning and block all vents with anything. Use incontinent pads if you have to. We cannot have any air leaving this entire ward!"

Turning his attention to Dr. Markov, Kulagin explained, "The H and E stain will yield results faster than cultures or any other diagnostic procedure. This is of utmost importance and I will ask you to do the stain, Viktor." Kulagin's hands were trembling.

Markov was meticulous in his preparation of the slide as he realized the importance of obtaining a definitive diagnosis for the patient, the hospital and the entire world for that matter.

"You know, Viktor, Guarnieri bodies were first discovered by an Italian physician of the same name. They are found in all poxvirus infections including cowpox, but there was no way this could be disseminated cowpox. Their presence in Dowling's skin scraping will be diagnostic for smallpox."

"I must plead ignorance that I have never even heard of them," Markov announced.

"Well, why would you know about them? They have been just a medical curiosity for four decades. But today, their presence could be of utmost importance," Kulagin stated.

After several minutes of staining and drying the slides, Markov placed one on the deck of the microscope and moved over for Kulagin, who started scanning. At first, he couldn't see a thing and panicked. Then he realized, in his urgency, he hadn't turned the microscope light on. After what seemed to be several minutes, Kulagin found what he was looking for: oval-shaped cytoplasmic inclusion bodies, and lots of them. These were the sites of replication of the smallpox virus in the cell. To be able to visualize them under an ordinary light microscope meant there were billions of virus particles just on this slide alone.

"Have a look, Viktor. Those are Guarnieri bodies. Can you see those pink blobs? They are B-type inclusion bodies. See how the smallpox virus has commandeered the cytoplasm for the manufacture of more viruses. They are exiting the host cell as if they were coming off a production line by the billions."

"Yes, there are lots of pink blobs, as you say. Would this appear in a case of chickenpox, Dr. Kulagin?"

"No, that would be highly unlikely because smallpox replicates in the cytoplasm of the host cell and then forms these bodies. Chickenpox replicates in the nucleus as do herpes viruses so these inclusion bodies are specific for smallpox. It is a good way of distinguishing smallpox from chickenpox infections."

In fact, Kulagin had initially considered the possibility of disseminated chickenpox in Dowling's case because of the drug that he was taking for rheumatoid arthritis. However, Dowling's pustules were mainly on his face, which was typical for smallpox.

It suddenly occurred to Kulagin that there was another telltale sign that suggested Dowling was suffering from smallpox and not chickenpox.

"But that is an excellent question, Viktor. Do you remember seeing those lesions on the bottom of Dowling's feet when we examined the urine bag at the foot of the bed earlier?" Kulagin enquired.

"Yes, I do recall seeing them. He even had sores on the palms of his hands."

"Well there you go, Viktor. Exactly. Chickenpox usually spares the palms and the soles. Smallpox does not. But you raised a good point." Kulagin turned off the microscope light. "We have some work to do before the people from Koltsovo arrive. I wonder if the Americans should be informed since a lab breach could just as easily take place at the CDC as at Vector."

"I am certain the directors at the Vector Institute will make that decision for us. They will not want to cause panic, sir," Markov speculated.

"I am sure you are right. We need to attend to our patient. The anaesthesiologist will be intubating him shortly and placing him on a respirator. Then we need to identify and isolate everyone who was exposed to him. They should be okay once the vaccine arrives from the Institute."

"What else do we do?" Markov enquired.

"We also need to find out everything we can about this Dr. Gordon Dowling. Where he stayed in Moscow, which airline he took to get to Moscow and where he has been in the past two weeks. We need a complete travel history and identification of all contacts both in Russia and in his home country. In the meantime, we need to research how we can treat the patient."

Kulagin was still troubled about the origins of this disease in a Canadian on Russian soil. He wondered if perhaps the NML in Winnipeg might have housed smallpox and if there could have been a lab accident there. However, if that were the case there would likely be cases of smallpox in other Canadians. Kulagin decided to contact Canada's Public Health Agency at the NML in Winnipeg to see. He wondered how he might make a discreet enquiry without giving away the tragedy lying in front of him.

"Let's get some rest, Viktor. There are lots of empty beds on this ward now. We have a definitive diagnosis of smallpox. There is not much more we can do for Dowling now except supportive therapy. We will see him first thing in the morning and hopefully the Vector team will have arrived with cidofovir," Kulagin said.

"Very well, sir. I could use a few hours of sleep," Markov replied.

The next morning on August 10, Dowling's condition had deteriorated. Just as Kulagin and Markov were about to check on their patient's condition, a nurse shouted a Code Red emergency from Dowling's isolation room.

Chapter 28

Investigation and Containment
Status epilepticus

Rushing to Dowling's hospital room, Kulagin feared the worst. The nurse was suctioning Dowling, who was bleeding profusely from his mouth around the endotracheal tube that had been inserted by the anaesthesiologist. Dowling was seizuring violently and his skin was turning black. Kulagin immediately recognized that this could be hemorrhagic smallpox, one of the most deadly variants. Viktor Markov put his stethoscope on Dowling's chest and simultaneously felt for a pulse. His pulse was barely palpable.

"Diazepam five milligram IV stat!" he shouted and soon the clear yellowish fluid was slowly injected into Dowling's veins through the intravenous, bringing his seizures to a halt. However, the patient's face was blue beneath the multitude of pox lesions and he truly looked morbid. Markov drew a vial of blood from Dowling's radial artery for blood gases and gave them to one of the nurses.

"What about trying intravenous Valacyclovir, Dr. Kulagin?" Markov enquired of his mentor.

"There is no evidence for this drug in treating smallpox, but we have nothing to lose. Let's start with Valacyclovir and then try other antivirals after that. We have no cidofovir in stock so your suggestion is reasonable. There is no known treatment for this virus so we are strictly in an experimental mode here. Antiviral medications have never been tried for smallpox. As the Americans say, 'we fly by the seat of our pants.'"

Kulagin knew they were out of their depth with this case. He needed the experts from Vector to get here as soon as possible.

"Hopefully, they will bring some vials of intravenous cidofovir to the hospital, Viktor. Perhaps you might call them just in case."

"Yes, Dr. Kulagin. Cidofovir. I have heard of it but have never used it. I'm afraid I will have to look that one up too," Markov replied.

Dowling's colour improved following his seizure but his glazed eyes reminded Kulagin of those of a fish packed in ice. Lifeless, vacant and bloodshot eyes that suggested Dowling was terminal.

After checking the internet for any other forms of treatment for smallpox, Markov received a text message from the lab informing him of Dowling's blood gas results.

"His blood gases during the seizure are terrible, Dr. Kulagin. We are running one hundred per cent oxygen now and I'm afraid he has pulmonary edema with ARDS," Markov lamented.

ARDS or acute respiratory distress syndrome occurs when a variety of biochemical abnormalities from infection or injury take place in the alveoli of the lungs. With the buildup of fluid, gas exchange is impaired and the lungs can no longer do their job in transferring oxygen. Hence, the need to have Dowling intubated and placed on a respirator with one hundred per cent oxygen.

"The Vector people also want us to perform a polymerase chain reaction on Dowling's blood. It seems they are still skeptical about our diagnosis, Dr. Kulagin," Markov advised.

"I agree. We need every corroborative diagnostic test available. Just caution the lab regarding the situation we are dealing with here before they draw any blood. We need to treat Dowling's room like a level four lab. On second thought, Markov, you draw the blood," Kulagin ordered. "We don't need any more people than is absolutely necessary on this ward right now."

"Yes, sir. Right away!" Markov realized that this case would be one he would always remember. He had barely slept during the night but was unconcerned. He did not want to miss any part of what was happening. After all, medical history was unfolding before them.

The polymerase chain reaction or PCR assay was a simple but sensitive diagnostic test that could be done quickly and reliably. The polymerase chain reaction had been developed in 1983. It is able to identify an infectious agent by reproducing sections of its DNA to be analyzed. It amplifies the DNA in the serum in order to identify it. Whereas this process once required weeks, it could now be done in a matter of two to three hours with greater specificity. Detection and identification of infectious diseases has been revolutionized with real-time amplicon detection PCR. The specialists at Vector would definitely require a positive PCR test for variola before issuing a countrywide warning in spite of Kulagin's clever discovery of Guarnieri bodies.

Immediately after Markov drew the blood for the PCR test, Kulagin advised him that it would need to be taken downstairs and outside the hospital to a waiting laboratory.

"Whatever for, Dr. Kulagin? I thought we were trying to contain this virus if it is what we think it is." Markov was incredulous.

"Yes, Viktor, but I just got a call from the Institute telling us to use the brand new mobile epidemiology lab by Sechenov First Moscow State Medical University. It's downstairs on the street as we speak," said Kulagin.

The Russian Ministry of Health had equipped several vehicles designed to monitor the outbreaks of epidemics and unusual parasitic diseases. Markov requested that a technician in a hazmat suit take the specimens down to the lab where another tech in a similar suit would receive the specimens. A third technician sprayed the first tech with antiseptic spray before he was allowed to return to the hospital. The bus was equipped with a PCR lab and modern molecular, biological and microscopic workstations. Patented in 2015, the mobile epidemiology lab by Sechenov First MSMU was ideal for the current emergency situation at the Moscow State University Hospital. It would not take long to confirm Dowling's diagnosis with real-time polymerase chain reaction technology. This was crucial in making a definitive diagnosis. Three hours later Kulagin was getting impatient and began pacing.

"Viktor, call that mobile Sechenov lab and ask them if they have any confirmation for us with the PCR will you? I am afraid we are losing our Canadian anthropologist and we are running out of ideas," Kulagin's voice quavered, revealing his desperation and hopelessness.

Twenty minutes later, Kulagin had his confirmation of the diagnosis of smallpox from the mobile lab. Shortly afterwards, the team from Vector arrived only to discover that Dr. Gordon Dowling had suddenly died of hypoxia while receiving one hundred per cent oxygen and being on a respirator. Any pulmonary gas exchange was no longer possible with the fluid build-up in his lungs. In spite of his caregiver's valiant efforts, the fifty-nine-year-old anthropologist succumbed to the deadly effects of the virus on his already compromised immune system. Both Kulagin and Markov were devastated.

"Sir, we did our best. I don't think that diagnosing Dr. Dowling any earlier would have changed the outcome. This is a highly virulent type of smallpox we were dealing with," Markov consoled.

"Yes, Viktor, we did do our best. The drug used to treat his rheumatoid arthritis may well have been a determining factor for the rapid deterioration that we have witnessed. It is almost as if Dowling succumbed to 'hemorrhagic smallpox,' a highly fatal variant with a mortality rate of almost one hundred per cent. The drug he was taking for his arthritis no doubt contributed to this serious complication and bleeding. At any rate, the team from the Institute is now cleaning up and trying to find out more about our mysterious anthropologist from Canada. Of course, an autopsy will be done later today. I doubt the body will be sent back to Canada. I suspect it will be cremated very carefully and very soon. What have you learned from the Vector people about this case?"

"The hotel is now gathering information on him. The Vector people naturally think this is a case of bioterrorism and are vaccinating everyone in Moscow now. They have resorted to diluting existing vaccine supplies to effect greater coverage," Markov answered.

"Hopefully they won't run out before new vaccines can be manufactured. Viktor, I want you to document everything thoroughly. There will be numerous questions about how we managed this case," Kulagin advised.

"Yes, Dr. Kulagin. But shouldn't we be informing the CDC or the National Microbiology Laboratory in Canada, considering our patient is a Canadian?" Markov asked.

"You are absolutely right, Viktor, but that is not for us to decide. The Vector Institute and the Russian Ministry of Health and the President himself will decide that. In the meantime, we have work to do and it looks like you could use some sleep."

Kulagin felt uncomfortable lying to his chief resident, but he mistrusted the Russian Ministry of Health to inform the Public Health Agency in Canada. That evening he made another call to Winnipeg.

Chapter 29

Roland Boudreau

Diagnostic dilemma

Just thinking about Dr. Rachel Thompson brought a smile to Rolly Boudreau. He could not get the lovely young archaeologist out of his mind since they bid farewell to each other ten days ago at the Gillam airport. She was such a warm and intelligent woman whom he found quite attractive with her blond hair and penetrating blue eyes. He recalled her soft and sincere kiss at the airport, thanking him for saving her from the polar bear at York Factory. Like a teenager who was grounded for the weekend, he let out a long mournful sigh. Although, he was ten years older than Rachel he silently wondered if that might be a problem for her. It certainly wasn't a problem for him.

Boudreau had been lonely since his wife passed away three years ago. His friends kept telling him to find someone and start his life over again. Instead, he flung himself into his work, flying as many hours as his company would allow.

After leaving the team of researchers at Gillam with all their equipment, he flew to Winnipeg the next day and picked up two Russian wildlife biologists from St. Petersburg. He flew them to

Churchill for whale watching and to observe polar bears in the wild on one of the famous 'tundra buggies.' Boudreau flew the appreciative Russians back to Winnipeg the same day. Switching planes, he then picked up three American anglers on a pontoon plane, flying them to George Lake for a fishing weekend.

Boudreau made several trips that week transporting equipment to various fishing lodges and he did not have the opportunity to get the rest that he needed. He wondered if he should email Rachel. After thinking about it for a while, he remembered that she would probably be pre-occupied with documenting her findings from the York Factory archaeological project. The following weekend he was just as busy and so he decided he would call her on Monday from his home in Gillam.

On Monday morning he developed flu-like symptoms including a high fever, chills and a headache. He stayed home, called in sick and went to bed. The next day, he was worse with severe back pains and abdominal pain. He began vomiting and could barely keep liquids down. He considered going to the hospital but felt he just had a bad case of influenza, so he stayed in bed taking Gravol, Advil and sipping diluted apple juice.

On Wednesday morning he felt so sick he decided to go to the hospital in Gillam.

Two young medical residents were doing a two-month study on Lyme disease for the Department of Infectious Diseases. This research was in conjunction with the National Microbiology Laboratory in Winnipeg. They were working for Dr. Frank Emberley, head of Infectious Diseases, University of Manitoba, and were collecting blood samples on locals in the Gillam area. Because of climate change, many scientists believed that the incidence of Lyme disease would increase in the province and eventually work its way north.

Indeed, several more cases had been appearing each year, mainly in the southern part of the province. Dr. Emberley was concerned that a few patients from the north were presenting with symptoms of Lyme disease and he wanted to determine the prevalence of the virus north of the fifty-fifth parallel. Several North American studies predicted that climate change might increase the habitat for ticks by 213 per cent by the year 2080. Northward expansions of the Lyme vector in Canada seemed inevitable.

Emberley sent two of his Infectious Disease residents, Dr. Frederick Allan and Dr. Lisa Richardson to several northern communities to collect blood samples during the month of August for his study of Lyme disease in the north. They were also advised to examine and report any suspicious cases of Lyme disease. They had already spent two weeks in Thompson, Manitoba, and would be heading to Churchill in a few days to complete their summer project. As luck would have it, they were both in Gillam this week. They had taken over a hundred blood tests from the local residents and First Nations for Lyme disease and were finished their project in Gillam earlier than expected. At the time of Boudreau's arrival to the hospital on Monday, both medical residents were bored. They were reading medical journals and drinking coffee in the hospital staff lounge when the nurse from the outpatient department interrupted their studies.

"We have a very nice man down the hall with a fever and a rash. The doctor is doing a delivery right now and asked if you would like to examine the patient. His name is Roland Boudreau and he is one of our pilots here in Gillam. His temperature is 39.2 and he doesn't look well."

The two medical residents jumped up and answered by bolting down the hall, with the nurse following behind.

"I guess that means yes!" said the nurse.

The early presentation of an infectious disease can be difficult to identify since many of the symptoms for different infections can be identical at the onset. As Emberley once taught his residents, "Making a diagnosis on clinical grounds alone in the early stages of an infection is like trying to identify the species of a flower erupting in the spring. Only a few green leaves tell you it is a plant of some kind and it may be impossible to tell exactly what kind it is. An astute botanist might identify the flower even before it has revealed its colours a few days later just by the leaves. After a week, anyone's grandmother can tell you what it is. So it is with infectious diseases. Often we need to wait a few days before making a clinical diagnosis. That's why we rely on lab tests in order to make a definitive diagnosis earlier so we can initiate treatment as soon as possible."

After introducing themselves to the pilot, the students took a careful history. As with any infectious disease, they asked Boudreau where he had been. They were astounded at all the places he had flown in the province over the past few weeks. Whatever illness he was suffering from now could have originated anywhere. This case was not going to be easy and, after making a spreadsheet of each town or city with the dates on which he had flown, the two researchers began to see the difficulties they were facing. First, they needed to make a diagnosis. With Lyme disease foremost on their mind, they asked Boudreau about any tick bites he might have had or any rash he may have noticed.

"No ticks, but I noticed I have a rash this morning." He removed his shirt and a generalized maculopapular eruption became obvious.

"It's not Lyme disease, that's for sure," exclaimed Lisa Richardson. "Measles perhaps? Have you been in contact with any children lately? Day care exposure, that sort of thing?" she enquired.

Boudreau shook his head, as his throat was too sore to speak.

"I'll bet this is strep," Allan interjected.

"We need to do a rapid strep test and then get a WBC and cultures," Lisa Richardson added. "But first we need to do a complete physical examination."

The two residents were fastidious in their investigation of Boudreau. Despite limited facilities at such a remote hospital, they were able to do several lab tests. They discovered his streptococcal test was negative after testing it twice. Boudreau's white count had soared to over twenty thousand. His fever remained persistently elevated. After a few hours, they called Dr. Emberley for his advice on the case.

"It sounds like you two have done everything possible considering the limited resources there. But send me copies of what tests you have done and take some pictures of his rash. You might be wise to gown, glove and mask while you're at it," Emberley advised.

"We already put on gowns and masks as soon as he arrived in the emergency department," Lisa advised.

"Good thinking, guys. Just get me those pictures of the rash and lab tests. It's probably some kind of viral exanthem."

The admitting physician in Gillam arrived later in the afternoon, was impressed with the work the younger researchers had done and allowed them to continue. Both Richardson and Allan were reviewing articles on the internet to gain more insight as to Boudreau's diagnosis. They treated him with Tylenol and intravenous fluids. Because he was coughing and complaining of some difficulty breathing, the doctors ordered a pulse oximetry, EKG and a chest X-ray.

The next morning Boudreau's rash developed vesicles or tiny blisters, which Richardson and Allan could not explain.

"Could this be chickenpox?" Richardson asked.

"He's way too old for chickenpox and he probably would have had it as a kid. Besides, with Varicella immunizations available for over fifteen years, chickenpox will soon become obsolete like other poxviruses. Nowadays mainly unimmunized immigrant children get chickenpox. I just read that the incidence of chickenpox has fallen almost eighty-five per cent in the past ten years," Allan responded.

They called Dr. Emberley again and sent more photos of the vesicles and some of the lesions that were now appearing on his face and in his mouth. Some photos showed lesions on the palms of Boudreau's hands, something almost never seen in chickenpox.

"Boy, this is a tough one guys. I wonder if it's a drug-related Stevens-Johnson syndrome. Are you certain he hasn't taken sulpha drugs or any medication at all?" Emberley enquired.

"Negative. We considered that possibility. Syphilis was an option as there are lesions on his palms and soles, but he hasn't been sexually active since his wife died three years ago. And how do we explain his fever, cough and other systemic symptoms, Dr. Emberley?" Lisa Richardson asked.

At this point Frederick Allan interjected, "You know, after doing that research project on smallpox last fall I am beginning to think that this case could fit that picture."

"That's ridiculous, Fred! That is like telling me you have passenger pigeons or dodo birds in Gillam! Where on earth would he have contracted smallpox from?" Emberley erupted over the phone.

"Anyway, ask him where else he has been and re-check his white count and repeat the blood cultures. This is beginning to get spooky. I'm still waiting for our dermatology people to tell us what this looks like. I'll get back to you as soon as possible."

That night, Roland Boudreau coughed up some blood.

Chapter 30

Gillam Containment

Quarantine

The next afternoon, Frank Emberley called Gillam Hospital and spoke to his residents, Lisa Richardson and Frederick Allan,

"This is going to probably scare the heck out of both of you but I asked three dermatology people on staff what this rash looks like. All three said it is classical variola major. It seems you might be right after all, Fred, as unlikely as it seems. I guess I owe you an apology. I'm sending a team up there as soon as possible. We'll need to vaccinate everybody there. Keep asking him where he has been. Something is wrong here. If it is truly smallpox, he had to get it from the CDC lab in Atlanta or from Russia."

"He has never been to Russia although he has flown Russian tourists to Churchill from time to time. But wasn't there an attack on the Russian lab outside Novosibirsk last week by some Chechen nationalists around that time?" Lisa Richardson asked.

"Yes, but I highly doubt that a breach of the lab took place. The Russians are adamant about that. In any event, how would Boudreau contract the virus? I'll contact the CDC and the National Microbiology Lab here in Winnipeg. At this point, we need to think about notifying the public but that will be decided by Public Health of Canada," Emberley asserted.

"What should we do in the meantime?" Frederick Allan asked.

"Just keep Boudreau comfortable. We can't bring a patient with that diagnosis to a city of over 700,000. It's safer to keep him in Gillam and quarantine the town. Meanwhile, I'll be up much of the night arranging supplies, equipment and vaccines for the flight tomorrow. We will also need to coordinate with the people from the National Microbiology Laboratory to obtain Imvamune vaccines for everyone in Gillam."

"Won't that be too late for those of us who have been exposed?" Richardson asked.

"No. The majority of people will benefit from the vaccine even if it is administered within three days following exposure so you should be all right. It's a darn good thing the lab is just down the street from the Health Sciences Centre. Tell everyone there that we will arrive in the morning with vaccinations for everyone in the Gillam area. I'll keep in touch with you," Emberley advised.

The next day, a Dash 8-100 commuter turboprop left Winnipeg with Frank Emberley and several medical personnel from the National Microbiology Laboratory. Numerous aluminum equipment containers, vaccines, hazmat suits and a portable thermal cycler or PCR machine were all loaded carefully onboard. Having a polymerase chain reaction study on Boudreau's blood for smallpox DNA was essential for a definitive diagnosis.

In the meantime, a ring quarantine around Gillam was quickly arranged. No other passengers were permitted on the plane and neither were any other planes allowed to leave Gillam airport. RCMP officers at Gillam guarded the railway station to ensure that no one got on or off the train the following day. A roadblock was set up on Provincial Road 280 that led south to Thompson. Emberley had essentially quarantined the town of Gillam based on a few digital photos and the assessments of a pair of infectious disease residents. He wasn't taking any chances. After flying to Gillam and seeing Boudreau for himself, he was glad he had taken all of these measures.

That day Boudreau's PCR was positive for variola major. Dr. Emberley and the director of the National Microbiology Laboratory in Winnipeg, Dr. Pamela Lindsay, debated over the phone which steps should be taken next. As the scientific director for the NML, Lindsay managed the laboratory public health and emergency preparedness programs under the Public Health Agency of Canada. She listened carefully to Emberley.

"We have quarantined the entire town and vaccinated as many people as we could find. Since no one else in the area is sick, we must assume the pilot acquired his infection elsewhere. My residents have been documenting his itinerary for the past two weeks. It seems he gets around a lot. The big question is where this began and who else has he infected throughout his travels? What do you think, Pam?" Emberley asked.

"My concern is whether he is a victim of bioterrorism. Is he only the first of many cases that will show up in the next few weeks? Frank, it is essential that your residents also document everyone that the pilot has contacted in the past two weeks. His employer will have flight manifests even for short flights. And I want his plane grounded and quarantined, as well as his house in Gillam," Lindsay demanded.

"Currently we don't know if there are any other stocks of smallpox except those sanctioned by the World Health Organization. There has always been speculation that some rogue state might still have stocks. I highly doubt this is the result of a lab accident at either of the two labs. Regardless, I am afraid that an international health crisis will develop because of this case," she added.

"What else do we need in order to identify the source of this outbreak?"

"Frank, you need to obtain a vial of serous fluid from that pilot's vesicles and fly it here in order for us to perform confirmatory DNA analysis. We also need to determine whether this is variola major or minor. If it is the former, he has a one in three chance of dying," Lindsay cautioned. "Hopefully this is a minor strain which has a mortality rate of less than two per cent."

"Yes, but I am hoping the antiviral medication will prove that figure wrong in Boudreau's case. I have already collected the samples for viral culture and DNA analysis. I will get a flight out of here within an hour or so. The patient will be kept here in Gillam and the whole town is currently under quarantine. One of my residents wants to stay here with the patient, the other wants to come with me and follow the investigations at the NML. Since they have both just been vaccinated, I have advised them both to remain here within the quarantine in Gillam."

"Okay, Frank, but be careful with that sample. Remember that smallpox has killed more humans than all other infectious diseases combined. The specter of bioterrorism is frightening and we must seriously consider that possibility with this case," Lindsay cautioned.

Within the next few days, everyone in the Gillam area received vaccinations with the help of Allan and Richardson and two field epidemiologists from the NML. All of the researchers involved in Boudreau's case were given vaccinations with a newer smallpox vaccine. Developed by Bavarian Nordic, it was first approved by the European Union in 2013 as Imvanex before Canada approved it as Imvamune. The FDA in the United States was still researching the vaccine before granting it approval. Fortunately, the NML in Winnipeg had an ample supply. Two days later, the two infectious diseases residents were in the Gillam Hospital lounge having coffee.

"I think I can breathe a sigh of relief, Lisa. After all our research last fall, this bug scares me the most," Allan confided.

"For sure, although Ebola has a much higher mortality rate than smallpox – almost double, I think. For me, that would be scarier. I'm just glad that Dr. Emberley believed us," Richardson added.

"Yes, but those photos you sent were worth a thousand words, Lisa. Look at the staff and equipment they brought to Gillam. A portable PCR machine! How cool is that? This will be a case to remember. I sure hope Boudreau pulls through."

"Yes, he seems like a very nice man. He was delirious earlier today before we treated him with antiviral agents. He was mumbling about someone named Rachel. Do you suppose he has a girlfriend?" Lisa asked.

"I don't know. He's a widower. Maybe that was his wife's name," Allan suggested.

"Anyway, Emberley figures that the combination of vaccination with an antiviral agent might modify the severity of Boudreau's illness. Some studies have suggested that intravenous cidofovir might benefit smallpox victims. But I wonder if the cidofovir might not inactivate the vaccine. I suppose he is already infected so vaccination at this stage probably won't make much difference. There are no scientific studies to refer to in a case like this," Allan added.

"Yeah, and if the cidofovir doesn't destroy his kidneys in the process," Richardson said.

"Yeah, you're damned if you do and damned if you don't. Let's go check on Boudreau. I also want to talk to the NML people. I think after this experience, a job with Canada's Public Health Agency might be interesting, don't you think?" Allan asked.

"Absolutely! As frightening as this has been, I would not have missed it for the world. I just wish I could go with him to Winnipeg to follow the investigations at the NML," Lisa exclaimed.

Just then, Emberley phoned.

"Would you believe there is a press leak about a case of smallpox in Russia? The Russians have tried to hide it but the Moscow State University Hospital has been placed under quarantine and public health officials are vaccinating millions of people in the area. It's almost impossible to withhold that information from the press. Now there is talk again about the Vector Institute attack and whether that might be the source of the infection. Frankly, I have no idea how a bush pilot in Gillam and a Russian in Moscow could get smallpox about the same time. In the meantime, the Russians are saying nothing." Emberley sounded genuinely frustrated.

"Of course, CNN is all over this story and are asking me for another interview. I told them to forget about it, as we have our own case and we are awaiting Dr. Lindsay from the Public Health Agency to make an announcement shortly. This is becoming an international health emergency, folks, and you are in this story from the ground floor. By the way, how is our patient doing?"

"He actually seems to be improving. We think the antiviral might be helping," said Lisa.

"Yes, his fever is down to 38 and he has had no new lesions. He seems to be breathing easier. His oximetry is normal as well," interjected Allan.

"That's good news. However, I still want you two to stay there with Boudreau. He needs your ongoing care and you are under quarantine anyway. You should be writing this up and preparing a paper on your patient while he recovers. There are few doctors in the world who will be able to lay claim to treating a case of smallpox."

Meanwhile, Moscow doctors were learning as much about smallpox as Emberley and his team.

Chapter 31

Rachel

Amor non-reciprocatus

A week later on Friday, August 10, Rachel flew to Winnipeg and booked into the Westin. She had been unwell for several days. The next morning she woke up with a throbbing headache and low back pain. She had been extremely busy since leaving York Factory with her two colleagues and the charming and knowledgeable pilot, Rolly Boudreau. She was delighted that he wanted to see her again but she wondered why, after almost two weeks, she had not yet received an email. Perhaps he was too busy or had just lost interest in her.

She had planned to meet with an RCMP official that day regarding the exhumation at the fort in order to describe their findings and complete the necessary paperwork. Any grave digging required a report to the RCMP since dead people were involved. The fact that the body in question was buried in 1836 was irrelevant.

Besides the severe headaches, Rachel developed a sore throat and began coughing. This was soon accompanied by chills and a high fever. She called her meeting off and stayed in her hotel room, ordering soup for lunch. On Saturday morning, she attended the Health Sciences Centre emergency department thinking she might have pneumonia or the flu. After an initial assessment by the emergency physician, with lab tests and X- rays, an Infectious Disease resident was consulted and examined her.

"Hello, I'm Sara Goldman with the Department of Infectious Diseases. I have been asked to see you by the ER doc as you are sick and they're worried this might be some type of flu. Your white count is quite elevated and your chest X-ray shows some evidence of pneumonia. I would like to take a history and do a physical examination. We are also going to be taking blood cultures and, if you can cough up some sputum, we will culture that too."

"My cough has been dry. Sorry no yucky sputum, thankfully," Rachel joked.

"That's okay. Are you allergic to anything?" Goldman enquired.

"Not that I am aware of," Rachel answered.

"Good, because we want to start you on intravenous antibiotics for your pneumonia. We will keep you in the holding area for a day and hopefully send you home tomorrow," Goldman said. "I'll be back later to see how you are doing."

Later that afternoon, Rachel felt worse despite antibiotics. Her fever persisted. A rash had developed and Goldman was concerned that she might be allergic to the antibiotics.

"Rachel, you seem to have a rash now, possibly from the medication. We will be giving you antihistamines and switching to another antibiotic."

"Okay. Can you give me something for my sore throat? And I feel like throwing up all the time," Rachel whispered hoarsely.

"Certainly. Let me have a look at your throat."

Goldman was shocked to see several sores in her mouth and on her soft palate. The rash soon became redder in spite of the antihistamines. That evening, she decided to phone Dr. Emberley for his opinion. He had just flown back to Gillam to check in on Rolly Boudreau and his two medical residents. Goldman immediately filled him in on Rachel Thompson's symptoms and lab results. She told him her patient was a PhD archaeologist working for the Arctic Institute.

"Sarah, your case sounds very disturbing. Ask Dr. Thompson if she knows a pilot named Roland Boudreau. There may be a connection. In the meantime, put her in isolation. I'll fly back to see her as soon as I re-examine our patient in Gillam." Emberley sounded anxious over the phone.

"What do you think it might be?" Goldman asked.

"Sarah, you're not going to believe this, but we have a pilot here with smallpox quarantined in Gillam. Your colleagues Frederick Allan and Lisa Richardson are with him as well as an intensive care specialist and two field epidemiologists from the National Microbiology Laboratory in Winnipeg. Keep this to yourself – we have inoculated the entire population, including the First Nations living within a hundred miles of Gillam. We used the newer smallpox vaccine, Imvamune. We have also quarantined the town of Gillam and the surrounding area. We have even started our patient on untested antiviral agents," Emberley advised.

"Smallpox! Omigosh, just what are the chances of that happening? And how can you be so sure it's smallpox?" she exclaimed.

"Well, the rash is entirely consistent with variola and we have done a PCR to confirm the diagnosis. I know it sounds unbelievable but Infectious Disease specialists have been afraid of the re-emergence of this pathogen for a long time. As you well know from your presentation last fall, Sarah, bioterrorism with this virus has always been just around the corner. It sounds like your patient may also have smallpox."

"Oh my word, that's terrible," Goldman gasped. It suddenly dawned on her that both she and her patient were in mortal danger.

"Oh, and we have just received word from the NML that a case of smallpox in Moscow has been identified there as well. There are rumours of bioterrorism behind this case. Just turn on CNN if you want some 'breaking news' on that subject. But it may be something as simple as a lab leak.

"No one has seen a case in forty years and now we have three of them. Don't feel bad about not picking this up sooner, Sarah," Emberley added. "It's likely that most doctors wouldn't recognize what smallpox looks like in the early stages. It always presents as an influenza-like illness at the start. I must admit I missed this case here in Gillam even when I had photos of the rash. Historically however, delay in the recognition of this disease is a major factor in its spread."

"That's unbelievable. From what I've read about smallpox, my patient may be contagious. Will I get it too?"

"Not likely at this stage, Sarah. I plan to have you vaccinated this afternoon by physicians from the NML lab on Arlington Street. You will also receive the new Imvamune smallpox vaccine. This vaccine has been shown to be immunogenic in animal models against lethal orthopox viruses. It doesn't cause the post-vaccination side effects and complications with first- and second-generation vaccines. You will be fine, Sarah. But we need to identify all the nurses and staff who were working in the ER when Dr. Thompson came in this morning. Everyone down to the cleaning staff, including other patients. They all need to be vaccinated unless they are pregnant. I will be calling Dr. Lindsay to see if we need to quarantine the entire hospital until we can vaccinate everyone," Emberley added.

"But where would she have contracted this, Dr. Emberley?"

"That's what I want you to figure out, Sarah. Ask her as many questions as possible. There may be a Russian connection to this story with the recent attack on the Vector Institute, although I personally find that hard to believe. As a precaution, everyone must wear hazmat suits. She needs to be in a special isolation ward in the hospital. As I said, you will be vaccinated today as a precaution. It is too late for Rachel, however. In the meantime, there are no reporters in Gillam and we are not making any public announcements until all confirmatory tests on your patient are in."

The next day, the news regarding the story of a smallpox case in Moscow went viral. The buzz surrounding the Vector attack was intense and CNN's *Breaking News* revolved around the scanty details released by the Russians. Non-stop speculation and theories postulated by panels of experts kept the story alive around the clock. Everyone was trying to connect the dots. Everyone except for Dr. Pamela Lindsay, the Public Health Director at the NML in Winnipeg, who had received a phone call from a Russian physician at the Moscow State University Hospital named Alexei Kulagin. She was now aware that the Russian patient was not Russian, but rather a Canadian who was an Arctic researcher based in Calgary. For the sake of preventing panic on a national scale, she decided to keep this to herself for the time being until as many vaccines as possible could be ordered from suppliers in Europe and the United States.

"Is this a coincidence that two patients in Manitoba separated by 740 kilometres were simultaneously afflicted with the dreaded smallpox virus? And a third Canadian dies of it in Moscow?" she asked herself. Once assured that adequate vaccines would be available within a few days, she then issued a statement to the press.

"The Public Health Agency of Canada and the National Microbiology Laboratory in Winnipeg is currently dealing with two cases of smallpox in the province of Manitoba. Quarantines have been established and an aggressive vaccination program has been issued for all health care workers in the province. Additional supplies of vaccine are being flown in from European sources. The patients seem to be recovering. We have also become aware of a third case in Moscow involving a Canadian patient and we understand Russian authorities are dealing with this case in a similar way. The NML is trying to determine the source and we have yet to prove that this outbreak is the result of bioterrorism. Until we learn more about these cases, we encourage Canadians to avoid foreign travel unless absolutely necessary. We also do not feel travel to Russia is advised at this time."

Pamela Lindsay tried to be reassuring but kept her answers to reports as brief as possible, refusing to speculate further on the source of the smallpox, or even whether bioterrorism was responsible.

In the meantime, Sarah Goldman couldn't believe that she had given a lecture just last fall on the subject of smallpox and bioterrorism and now she had an actual case right before her. Smallpox was the last thing on her mind when she first met Rachel earlier but she knew that Dr. Emberley was right. Her initial inclination was that this must have started as a case of bioterrorism and she recalled her presentation on this subject just last year. *How else could smallpox, a disease from the past, re-emerge in two separate countries at the same time?*

Within an hour, Goldman drew more blood from Rachel for a polymerase chain reaction test for smallpox. Sarah wasn't sure if she should tell Rachel right away. She did not want to frighten her. However, it was imperative that she find out where this disease originated.

"So Rachel, we are concerned that you might be suffering from an unusual viral illness and we want to know where you might have picked this up. Has anyone in your circle of friends or co-workers been sick lately?" Sarah asked, mindful of Emberley's instructions to determine if she knew Boudreau.

"Not that I'm aware of. Mind you I haven't seen many people in the past week or two as I have been writing a report on a research project that we did at the end of July."

"And where was that project?" Goldman asked.

"We were at the old Hudson's Bay trading post at York Factory, Manitoba, for five days at the end of July."

"Who else was with you on that project?" Sarah enquired further.

"Just two other scientists from the Arctic Institute in Calgary where I work."

"And how are they doing?"

"Well, I just spoke to Wojeich Jaworski a few days ago. He's okay. But my other associate isn't responding to his emails but that's not unusual for him. He's away at a conference right now." Rachel thought of Gordon Dowling attending the Arctic conference in Moscow.

"Rachel, was there anyone else with you at that project that might have become ill like you?" Sarah asked.

"Only James Klassen and his wife who worked for Parks Canada at the fort and our pilot, Rolly Boudreau," Rachel responded with a harsh cough.

Bingo! Sarah Goldman's mind raced. She knew immediately that she had discovered the connection that Dr. Emberley had requested. There was little doubt in her mind that Rachel also had smallpox and she may have contracted it from Boudreau.

"In fact, I was supposed to go on a date with Rolly sometime this week but he never got back to me. Now I'm so sick I don't think he would want to see me!" Rachel broke into tears at this point.

My Goodness. A couple in a new relationship both afflicted with an extinct disease! Sarah could scarcely contain herself. She would call Emberley as soon as she was finished her interview with her interesting patient. She knew that someone had to tell Rachel about her diagnosis as soon as possible.

"He even saved my life!" Rachel exclaimed.

Goldman was intrigued. "He did? How did that happen, Rachel?"

"I was waiting on the dock for the boat when a polar bear and her cub approached me. I was petrified but Rolly scared it with a flare gun in the boat. I still have dreams about it," Rachel added.

"Wow. That must have been very frightening for you. Rachel, have you or any of your associates been to Russia in the past month?" Sarah asked.

"No none of us have been to Russia. Why do you ask?" Rachel enquired.

"Well, there apparently has been a similar illness recently described in Moscow."

"What do you think I have, Dr. Goldman?"

"Rachel, I'm not sure. Probably some kind of virus. We're doing tests and we should have an answer for you later today. I'm going to call my supervisor, Dr. Frank Emberley, and get back to you soon. Thank you for answering all my questions," Sarah added.

Sarah began to leave the room. Just as her hand was on the doorknob, Rachel added, "But Dr. Goldman, although none of has been to Russia, one of my associates, Dr. Gordon Dowling, is in Moscow right now. He's the one that won't answer his emails. I hope he's okay."

Chapter 32

Jaworski

Revelatio tragica

Dr. Sarah Goldman was shocked to hear that her patient, Rachel Thompson, had a colleague in Russia. That evening she relayed this news to Dr. Emberley before he left Gillam. After learning about Rachel Thompson, Emberley questioned the common source of these patients.

"This doesn't make a lot of sense, Sarah, but since she knows Boudreau, it will hopefully make the source of this disease easier to trace. We need to contact other members of her team as well as the Parks Canada people at York Factory. The prospect of bioterrorism has always been a real concern since smallpox was eradicated in the seventies. What I don't get is how it shows up in northern Manitoba."

"Dr. Emberley, I have already contacted James Klassen, the Parks Canada guide who has a satellite phone at York Factory. He and his wife and family are fine. None of them have had any visitors who have been sick this summer, which makes this more confusing," advised Goldman.

"I also contacted Dr. Wojeich Jaworski, a forensic pathologist who was with Rachel at York Factory. He is also not showing any symptoms of smallpox. He sounded quite anxious about Rachel, though. He was also concerned that he hadn't heard from his associate, Gordon Dowling, either. Apparently, Dowling had flown to Moscow to deliver a lecture at an Arctic conference. When I asked Jaworski if he had been vaccinated before, he replied that, as a forensic pathologist, he has vaccine updates every five years. But he had no idea whether Dowling had been previously vaccinated," Goldman added.

"Good work, Sarah. By the way, did you get your vaccination yesterday?"

"Yes I did, and I'm praying it works in case I contracted smallpox from Rachel. On Dr. Lindsay's orders, the entire hospital staff has been vaccinated. The ER has been closed because of the quarantine so you can imagine how upset the public is. All the ambulances have been diverted to other hospitals and the place is crawling with staff from the virology lab," Goldman said.

"Yes. I can imagine. The town of Gillam is all abuzz and so is Moscow with their case, I'm sure. There have been no new cases yet, which is good news. Listen, Sarah, I'm just hopping onto a plane and returning to Winnipeg in about an hour and I will see your patient when I get there. I think you are doing everything possible. Good work on making the connection between the two cases. In the meantime, I have asked Dr. Lindsay to find out about this fellow, Dowling, in Russia. "

"Thank you, Dr. Emberley."

"By the way, it appears that our patient, Mr. Boudreau, is improving. I am sure he will pull through although he will have a few pockmarks as a reminder of his ordeal," Emberley said.

"When should we tell Rachel about her diagnosis, Dr. Emberley? The PCR for smallpox was positive as we expected and we should let her know the diagnosis soon. She will be upset, of course. She is already emotionally upset for another reason. It appears she had just started a relationship recently with your pilot in Gillam but she hasn't heard from him for several days. She will be glad to know that Boudreau has not stood her up and that he is sick too. So, from an epidemiological standpoint, I wonder if they contracted the virus at the same time through their relationship with each other."

"Good point. Sarah, you seem to have developed a good rapport with Rachel. Give her the diagnosis now and I will see her in a few hours when I get back to Winnipeg. Tell her that Boudreau is improving. She may be devastated in the loneliness of her isolation room with this horrible diagnosis so stay with her," Emberley advised.

That evening Rachel gasped when Sarah Goldman told her that she had smallpox. By this time, her rash had become full blown with a high fever. Intravenous antivirals infused her bloodstream and she took oral Tylenol with codeine for the fever and pain from the sores. She was also shocked to find out that Roland Boudreau was being treated for smallpox at the same time in the Gillam Hospital. *That explained why he never called me*, Rachel thought.

"What about the others?" Rachel asked hoarsely.

"I have already spoken with Dr. Jaworski and he is fine. Being a forensic pathologist, he was vaccinated a few years ago. Nevertheless, he will also receive an Imvamune booster. He will be coming here tomorrow to see you. Dr. Dowling is still not answering his calls or emails. We are currently trying to find out which hotel he booked into."

"Thank you, Dr. Goldman. I have never felt so sick in my entire life. What are my chances of dying from this?" At this point Rachel coughed a clot of blood into a Kleenex and started to cry.

"Well, your friend, Rolly Boudreau, seems to be pulling through and we think it's the cidofovir that's helping. We have started you on a similar drug called Brincidofovir, which is another intravenous anti-viral agent that is quite effective in animal models. We are very optimistic for you, Rachel. I will be following you closely but there will be epidemiologists from the Public Health Agency who will be asking you questions if you are up to it." Goldman tried her best to encourage her patient.

"Okay, but how do you know this drug will work on me?"

"We don't," Goldman replied, "but it has been used success-fully in treating cases of widespread vaccinia infections. These are people, usually friends or family of American military personnel, who contracted the infection from soldiers who had been vaccinated within a week or two before going to Afghanistan. Most of them had eczema, which allowed the vaccinia virus to spread. It seems that this drug helped them get well. We believe it should work in other orthopox infections."

"Why would they vaccinate soldiers?" Rachel sputtered.

"Because the U.S. military feels that smallpox could still be out there as an agent of bio warfare. They have been vaccinating soldiers sent to Iraq and Afghanistan after 2002 and boosting them every five years. But Rachel, enough questions. It is important that you get your rest now. I will be looking in on you frequently and you have the top specialists in infectious diseases in the country involved with your case. You will also be receiving vaccinia immune globulin, which should help you to recover," Goldman reassured her.

Rachel thanked Sarah Goldman again and cried herself to sleep that evening. In fact, she slept for most of the next three days, rousing only when her doctor visited her or when the lab people, dressed like spacemen, came to draw blood. She felt like a leper and became more depressed with each passing day. Finally, on Wednesday, Jaworski paid her a visit. By this time, Rachel seemed to have turned a corner. Her fever and headache had resolved and the sores in her mouth and throat were less severe. She was, however, mortified when she looked in a mirror to see numerous scabs covering her face and her bloodshot eyes. Jaworski stood at the foot of her bed wearing mask, gown and gloves.

"Rachel, I am very sorry I did not come to see you sooner but they wouldn't let me travel once they knew I was associated with you and the pilot. Even though I had been vaccinated, they weren't taking any chances. They wouldn't let me fly either as a public safety precaution so I drove from Calgary." Jaworski sounded genuinely remorseful.

"That's okay, Wojeich. I seemed to have slept the past three days. I have totally lost track of time and what's happening in the outside world while I have been in this isolation room. What is going on, anyway? How on earth did I get this virus and how is Rolly?"

"Who is Rolly?" he asked.

"Our pilot. You remember him from York Factory, don't you? He saved my life."

"Ah, yes, the pilot. You two became friends, didn't you Rachel?" Jaworski broke into a smile.

"Yes, sort of. We had planned to get together this week but I heard he got sick too. Do you know how he is doing?" Rachel asked.

"Well, the pilot has pulled through and is much better, I'm told by your doctor. He may still be contagious until all the scabs have fallen off and then he will be discharged from the Gillam Hospital in the next week or so. It appears you will be fine too," Jaworski replied.

"Has anyone heard about Gordon yet? Has he returned from his conference in Moscow?"

Jaworski swallowed hard. "Actually, Rachel, we just learned that Gordon also contracted smallpox and died in the Moscow State University Hospital. In fact, he was the very first Russian smallpox patient, according to the Russian news media. They have not revealed his nationality yet because of security reasons as they think he was a victim of bioterrorism that may have originated here in Canada. I found this out from an old classmate who is a pathologist at the MSU Hospital. They're all going crazy over there."

"That's awful, Wojeich. You and he were such good friends and worked on so many projects together over the years. I am so sorry. How did we all manage to get this?" Rachel exclaimed.

"I have no idea, Rachel. Something we dug up from the project perhaps."

"There must have been something in the plane. Omigosh, the blanket! There must have been smallpox on that Bay blanket. It's all my fault, Wojeich!" Rachel swore at the idea of causing Dowling's death.

"No, Rachel, it's not all that simple. Maybe we were exposed to something in the blanket, but two more Russians from St. Petersburg came down with smallpox on the tenth, about the same time that you flew to Winnipeg. They must have been exposed to smallpox in Russia before you were. How do you explain that?"

"You have a good point, Wojeich. I don't know how to explain that. I don't know what's happening out there," she responded.

"Well, the entire country is in a panic. The Russians are no longer worried about bioterrorism. Now they are blaming the Vektor people for a cover-up regarding the amount of damage sustained in the attack by the Chechens. The President's popularity just went down the drain this week with these new cases. There are several more cases suspected as well, so you must not blame yourself. Besides, we all wanted that blanket, which, by the way, is still in our freezer in Calgary. We took all the necessary precautions and sealed it in the bags but it must have leaked somehow during our trip home. It is being sent to the National Microbiology Laboratory tomorrow for analysis," Jaworski explained.

"Well, that would explain the duct tape on the bag. I told you that the bag was punctured. We should never have taken that blanket from the next gravesite. I suppose they will probably burn the blanket if it has smallpox," Rachel sighed.

"Probably, but look Rachel, you need to get your rest and not worry about this," Jaworski commiserated. "If the blanket was a fomite for smallpox, we will find out soon enough, but there may have been another source from the sounds of it." He then left a bouquet of flowers for Rachel with a get-well card on the bedside table and turned on the television for her. As soon as he turned on her TV, the CBC news made a disturbing announcement.

Chapter 33

Russian Epidemic

Sic parvis magna

The evening news on CBC did indeed make a dramatic announcement regarding the smallpox outbreak in Russia.

"Dr. Leonid Yakov, director of Russia's Vector Institute issued a public statement today regarding the recent outbreak of smallpox in Russia. It appears two Russian biologists from St. Petersburg who had been working in Siberia have contracted the variola virus, otherwise known as smallpox."

An older, distinguished looking male wearing a bright white lab coat appeared on the screen. Leonid Yakov spoke in sombre tones for his announcement.

"Smallpox is very dangerous and, in the hands of terrorists, it is a lethal weapon. It is elegant in its simplicity and can be delivered without any sophistication. The recent outbreak of smallpox in Russia, however, was not the result of a breach at the Vector Institute. The terrorists caused limited damage and the negative pressure was unaffected during the attack of July 29. In fact, not one of the labs was even close to being damaged."

After brief footage of the Vector Institute and the front entrance, which appeared intact, Yakov continued. "The Moscow case involved a patient from Canada where we believe that bioterrorism originated. We have in fact learned from Canada's Public Health Agency and their National Microbiology Laboratory that two other cases of smallpox originated in the province of Manitoba in the past few weeks."

Yakov went on to disown any responsibility for the Moscow smallpox case and blamed the Canadians entirely. He made no comment regarding the outbreak in St. Petersburg.

Following this announcement by the Russian Ministry, many Canadians who had believed that the smallpox outbreak had originated in Russia following the Chechen attack on the Vector Institute became alarmed. As Canada's leading public health infectious disease laboratory, the National Microbiology Laboratory was responsible for the identification and prevention of infectious diseases. Managing the recent cases of smallpox and notifying the public was no easy task. The announcement by the Russian Ministry of Health did not make things any easier.

A state of panic ensued, with massive vaccination programs beginning in Canada that week. Russia and the CDC in America followed suit, vaccinating all medical personnel who might be exposed to any new cases. The Israeli government, however, long ago had issued vaccinations for all its military and medical personnel and for most of its citizens who worked in government agencies. Sufficient quantities of vaccine had been stockpiled in that country for the entire population in the unlikely event that smallpox was ever used as an agent of bioterrorism against Israel.

A week later Yakov reversed his earlier accusations towards Canada. He stated that there were no new cases in Moscow associated with Gordon Dowling's case thanks to the rapid response of Dr. Kulagin and the Vector scientists. Nevertheless, many other people who had been exposed to the Russian biologists became sick. By the end of the summer, dozens of new cases of smallpox appeared and Russia was witnessing the beginning of an epidemic.

DNA analysis of the virus using gene sequencing revealed that the Russian smallpox was an ancient strain likely from the previous century. It appeared to be unrelated to the modern strains of smallpox stored at the Vector Institute lab. This presented an enigma to the Russian researchers, who felt that this strain must have been resurrected from some source where smallpox had struck in the past. They began to look at Siberian sites where the permafrost yielded to climate change. How Dowling acquired his infection was still a mystery but he, too, had a connection to permafrost research.

Leonid Yakov had spoken too soon in pointing his finger at Canada. The revelation of the story of the two biologists from St. Petersburg with smallpox forced him to reverse his stance.

Following his state of delirium, Roland Boudreau recalled his trip to Churchill with the two Russian biologists in his Cessna. He wondered whether the interior of the plane had become the source for the virus once it was released from the storage bag. Shortly after their visit to Churchill, the two Russian biologists had flown to Siberia to do permafrost research. Not long afterwards, it was announced that two biologists became ill with smallpox. When he learned of this, Boudreau seriously questioned whether their smallpox had come from a source in Russia where the permafrost was thawing just as it had affected the Canadian researchers, or whether his plane was the source of their infection. He feared that the connection between the Russian biologists and their trip to Churchill remained unreported, mainly because he had been incapacitated with smallpox in the Gillam Hospital. This fear and uncertainty would come to haunt him for several months.

A week later, Leonid Yakov appeared again on national television, this time explaining what Russian scientists believed to be the source of the smallpox outbreak in his country.

Frowning, Yakov tersely announced, "Last year on the Yamal Peninsula of Siberia, dozens of people were hospitalized from an outbreak of anthrax and thousands of reindeer in the area were infected. Our scientists are blaming a heat wave for thawing permafrost and causing infected reindeer from the last century to be unearthed. It would appear that the source of the current smallpox outbreak did not originate in Canada or from the Vector Institute. We believe that smallpox may have resurfaced from the permafrost with infected bodies from an epidemic in the last century. "

As expected, there were no apologies from the Russian Ministry of Health nor any other government officials. Without using the expressions 'climate change' or 'global warming,' the Russian Ministry's announcement implied that the temperatures in the Arctic were rising very quickly.

"The soil in the Yamal Peninsula is like a giant freezer," Yakov announced. "Those are ideal conditions for bacteria and viruses to remain alive for a very long time."

By September, in spite of a massive vaccination program, thousands of new cases of smallpox flared up in Russia as well as eight other border nations. The mortality rate, not surprisingly was around thirty-five per cent. Patients with access to acute care facilities and intravenous therapy fared better than those in remote or rural areas. The Russian Ministry of Health was expending all of its resources on containment with ring quarantines and its vaccination program. Health care workers could barely keep up. Russia's economy was showing the effects of the epidemic. Tourists and business people were prohibited from flying to any part of the country. The President as usual remained silent on the issue.

"We are hearing some interesting statistics on this Russian small-pox epidemic," Frank Emberley announced to his residents at the Health Sciences Centre in Winnipeg during a seminar in September.

"First of all, it is growing exponentially as one might expect from the study of epidemics from the nineteenth century. Furthermore, those patients who were immunocompromised showed much higher mortality rates, as did those patients on biologic medication for rheumatoid arthritis, Crohn's disease and psoriasis. In addition, diabetics and those with autoimmune disorders likewise suffered more deaths in the Russian epidemic. It's interesting to note that no cases showed immunity from previous vaccinations, since antibody levels diminished years ago. This proves that the ancient art of variolation is superior to vaccination in that it confers lifelong immunity, whereas vaccination can only give seven to ten years of immunity at best," Emberley expounded.

"Yes, but at what cost?" Lisa Richardson asked. "Variolation caused one to two per cent mortality. Vaccination is much safer, especially with the newer vaccines, isn't it?"

"Indeed, but it is debatable as to whether there will be enough doses for Russia's population of 144 million people. Furthermore, there is no herd immunity as with many other infectious diseases, and smallpox is spreading like wildfire in spite of the current ring quarantine measures," added Emberley.

"In that case, the Russians could be in for a major disaster," Lisa Richardson declared.

"Well, the current situation in Russia is already catastrophic," Emberley responded. "I think with global travel and with the number of people who fly daily, there could be trouble for us all, Lisa, in spite of the international quarantine. Still, if we had to, we could probably vaccinate the entire country of Canada within a week or so. We could train anyone to use a vaccine stylet in ten minutes. In a true emergency," he added, "schoolteachers, police officers, firefighters and others could all be vaccinators."

"But are there enough vaccines to go around, Dr. Emberley?" Lisa asked.

"That's a good question. It is estimated that there are only 700 million doses of smallpox vaccine for a world of seven billion people. Only the United States, Japan and Israel have enough doses for their entire populations. However, we don't know about the Russian vaccine supply. Russia, in spite of all the research they have done on smallpox, may have fallen behind, in which case you may be right about them."

Chapter 34

Emberley's Interview

Aequanimitas

The same day in which Emberley discussed the Russian smallpox epidemic with his residents, a reporter from CNN interviewed him. Emberley never felt comfortable with these interviews, but his own colleagues encouraged him to speak to the reporter.

One of his heroes in the field of medicine was the great Sir William Osler, who had written a book for graduating physicians called *Aequanimitas*. Frank Emberley received a bound copy of that book when he graduated from medical school almost thirty years ago. In this classic tome, Osler exhorted his students to acquire the personal quality of equanimity or 'imperturbability.' In other words, he advised his students to "not to let anyone ruffle your feathers" and to remain calm even under the most trying of circumstances. Emberley strived for this noble quality in spite of his own choleric temperament. He leaned towards pragmatism and a certain insensitivity, traits that were undesirable in a medical doctor and perhaps more appropriate for a researcher. His logical reasoning and aloofness often left colleagues wondering what they had done to upset him. His natural inclination was to strive to be neither polite nor respectful, nor friendly. Often his residents and colleagues walked on eggshells around him. He was painfully aware of this facet of his personality. Sir William Osler admonished him otherwise. In preparation for the interview today, he read the first chapter of *Aequanimitas* for the umpteenth time.

"So Dr. Emberley, it appears that this outbreak originated in Canada and then spread to Russia. Do you feel that someone in your country is involved with bioterrorism?" asked the CNN reporter.

"Not at all. The Canadian outbreak may have originated with an archaeological dig at one of our northern outposts. The virus may have been preserved in permafrost for over two centuries before the thaw reactivated it. This was totally an accident and there was no intention to spread this disease by bioterrorism I can assure you.

"Three of the researchers at the site contracted the disease, so clearly the exposure to smallpox was entirely accidental. The Russian outbreak, I believe, is a separate matter. It is common knowledge that Russian scientists have been exhuming bodies from the Siberian permafrost, looking for anthrax and smallpox for several years," Emberley explained. "It is certainly possible that the current epidemic in that country coincidentally emerged under similar circumstances."

"We understand that the patient who died in Moscow in August may have been an American. Can you explain that?" the reporter asked.

"No, he trained and lived in the United States and obtained his PhD from Stanford University. But he was a Canadian and was born in Portage la Prairie," Emberley advised.

"Oh, so he was from Quebec then?" the reporter asked.

Emberley sighed. "No, he was from Manitoba. I really don't think it is relevant where he was from. The fact is he was a brilliant researcher who was greatly respected by his colleagues. He will be greatly missed."

"Of course. Dr. Emberley, can you tell us how extensive this smallpox epidemic in Russia will become? Do you see any end in sight?" the reporter asked.

"Frankly, no. The smallpox virus has an infectivity rate that is three times that of influenza or polio. We know from the history of outbreaks in an unimmunized population that smallpox has an R Naught number of around seven, which is quite worrisome."

"Can you explain what an R Naught number is, Dr. Emberley?"

"The R naught number or $R0$ for short, or the basic reproductive rate of an infection, gives us an idea as to how contagious the infection is in a susceptible population. For example, an $R0$ value of less than one means the infection will not spread at all and it will die out. On the other hand, an $R0$ value of greater than one means the infection will spread. The larger the $R0$ number, the more contagious it is and the more difficult it will be to control the epidemic." Emberley didn't want to get too technical with this reporter but he couldn't ignore this important question.

"Why does smallpox have such a higher $R0$ number when compared to polio, doctor?"

"Because it is spread by airborne droplets, which means all you have to do is breathe or cough near someone to infect them. Polio is spread by contaminated water or food," Emberley replied.

"Does smallpox spread as readily as Ebola?"

"Actually the $R0$ value of Ebola is only around two, based on the 2014 epidemic. Smallpox, however, spreads three times as readily as Ebola. This is because Ebola is spread only by direct contact with bodily fluids," Emberley answered.

"Do you see any obstacles in keeping this epidemic from spreading further, Dr. Emberley?"

"Keeping this epidemic in check will depend entirely on the effectiveness of the World Health Organization in obtaining vaccines and on how quickly we vaccinate the seven billion people in the world who are at risk for this lethal virus. Unlike the Ebola epidemic in 2014, the WHO has been involved at an early stage with smallpox and it is taking this epidemic very seriously."

"Do you feel that enough is being done to keep this epidemic from spreading, doctor?"

"Let me assure you, that public health agencies in all the affected countries are working around the clock. In the United States, I understand that the CDC has also initiated mass vaccination programs in spite of no cases of smallpox being reported so far," Emberley responded.

"But just how safe are these vaccines, doctor? Haven't people died or become sick from getting vaccinated?"

"It all depends on which vaccine is being used and that varies from country to country. Here in Canada, as in Europe, we are using the Imvamune vaccine. It has proven quite safe and there have been no deaths associated with it. As of today, all Canadian military and health care personnel have been vaccinated initially because of their inherent risks and the limited supply of available vaccines."

"Just how many doses of vaccines does Canada have, Dr. Emberley?"

"The Public Health Agency of Canada currently has around 400,000 doses, but we feel that these can be diluted and still be effective. This could double or triple the current supply. More vaccines are being manufactured as we speak," Emberley said.

"And just how many people live in Canada, Dr. Emberley?"

"About thirty-six million." Emberley looked uneasy, anticipating the next question.

"Well it seems that Canada has been unprepared for this disease, wouldn't you agree, doctor?"

The reporter could certainly be an annoyance, thought Emberley. He decided, perhaps unwisely, to retaliate at this point. However, he reminded himself of Osler's *Aequanimitas* and managed to remain professional.

"Canada is in no better position than most countries for this unexpected virus," Emberley announced. "Keep in mind that smallpox was virtually eradicated in Canada by 1946. Furthermore, over the forty years since global immunizations stopped, smallpox immunity has all but disappeared among the majority of Canadians. So there has been no need for the level of vigilance that you suggest."

"Will all Canadians eventually be vaccinated?"

"No," Emberley advised the obnoxious reporter, "we are careful not to give it to pregnant women or people who have a compromised immune system."

"What does that mean, doctor? Can you explain what a compromised immune system is?"

"It means anyone who has HIV/AIDS or is taking steroids or methotrexate, which is used in treating rheumatoid arthritis. Many newer drugs called 'biologics' are taken by patients for psoriasis, inflammatory bowel disease and various types of arthritis. These agents all suppress the immune system. A smallpox vaccine could be devastating to these patients."

"So what happens to these people if they get smallpox, doctor? Do you just let them die?"

Emberley was beginning to find this reporter to be extremely annoying. He felt the interview was becoming sensationalistic rather than informative fact-finding. Nevertheless, he soldiered on with the questions, keeping Osler's injunctions in mind.

"Well, of course not, we try not to let anyone die. We believe that, with the judicious use of ring quarantines, as was proven effective in Gillam and in Winnipeg in August, we can avoid further cases. We also believe that 'herd immunity' will eventually prevent the spread of the virus. In other words, mass vaccination will protect even those who are not vaccinated. The disease cannot spread as easily if a sufficient number of people in a population are immunized. Herd immunity is a type of indirect protection against infectious diseases including smallpox." Emberley wondered what was next.

"I see," said the reporter. "But what if someone whose immune system is, uh, compromised, as you say, contracts the smallpox virus because they weren't vaccinated? What then, Dr. Emberley?"

"In that case, we would use variola immune globulin."

"And how exactly does that work, doctor?"

"The vaccinia immune globulin is a blood product made from the blood of people who have been recently vaccinated. It contains antibodies against vaccinia, which is the virus used in the smallpox vaccine. Now that we have patients who have actually survived small-pox, we are saving their antibodies to manufacture variola immune globulin. Hopefully, we can use this serum in the event that we have a case of smallpox in an immunocompromised host."

"Well it certainly sounds as if you are on top of this epidemic, Dr. Emberley."

"I wish to correct you on that last statement. Two cases in our province of well over a million people does not constitute an epidemic. For information on epidemics, I am afraid you will have to interview someone from Russia." Emberley was clearly incensed by the ignorance of the reporter. Before he could accuse the reporter of creating fake news, the reporter cut him off suddenly.

"Thank you for this interview, Dr. Emberley, and for taking time from your busy schedule to share the situation in Canada with us."

As a Canadian, Emberley could hardly appear to be impolite on American television. 'Imperturbability,' Osler had said.

"You are most welcome," he said. "Good evening."

Chapter 35

The Fourth Horseman
Nil desperandum

The minister adjusted his microphone at the lectern and read from the Apocalypse of St. John in the King James Version to the rapt attention of his congregation and some special visitors that day in his church.

"'I looked, and behold, an ashen horse; and he who sat on it had the name Death; and Hades was following with him. Authority was given to them over a fourth of the earth, to kill with sword and with famine and with pestilence and by the wild beasts of the earth.' Revelation 6:8."

By October, over 100,000 people were afflicted with smallpox and over 30,000 had died, mostly in Russia. Numerous other countries were desperately fighting the spread of this disease. There was no end in sight and it appeared that a global pandemic was inevitable. Today, the church minister incorporated the epidemic in his sermon topic, 'Pestilence in Scripture,' and for his text, he alluded to the passage from Revelation Chapter 6.

"The Bible states there will be a great plague during the end times that will consume a quarter of the world's population. It would appear that the current smallpox epidemic with a mortality rate of over thirty per cent could very well be the pestilence described in this passage of Scripture," the evangelical minister solemnly pronounced to his spellbound congregation.

"In Ezekiel 5:12, we read 'One third of you will die by plague or be consumed by famine among you, one third will fall by the sword around you, and one third I will scatter to every wind, and I will unsheathe a sword behind them.'"

Middle Eastern countries like Syria and Turkey were also grappling with outbreaks of their own. Many Chechens had likewise suffered and died. Some Chechens still blamed the Caucasian Mujahideen attack on the Vector Institute for this disaster. Public health officials in these countries undertook drastic measures such as compulsory vaccinations and ring quarantines. International air travel had fallen by fifty per cent; isolation wards in hospitals were expanding each day and church attendance was up, especially in North America. Not a day went by without 'smallpox' on the front page of every national newspaper.

"The Bible states elsewhere that a great pestilence shall engulf one-third of mankind. The only infection that could achieve these numbers is smallpox. If this epidemic is a fulfilment of scriptural prophecy, then we can expect many more deaths. We must prepare ourselves spiritually for this possibility," the minister solemnly emphasized.

Roland Boudreau squeezed Rachel's hand at this pronouncement by the eloquent and charismatic pastor. They had been dating since their recovery over a month ago. Both of them had been cradled in the arms of death, which drew them closer to each other. Boudreau had been encouraged by one of his friends to attend this church and meet with the pastor. He asked his sister to drive them to church this morning; he was prepared to ask this minister to marry them.

After hearing his sobering sermon, they were not so sure they had done the right thing in attending this church. Neither Boudreau nor Rachel felt comfortable with this sermon. They were not expecting a 'doom and gloom' message today and, after what they had been through, it was unnerving for them both.

Having suffered through and survived one of the worst scourges known to humanity, they were intrigued by the apocalyptic prophesy from the Book of Revelation. The sermon did not seem too far off, considering the rapid spread of smallpox in recent weeks. *But a third of humanity?* Surely modern medical science would prevail against this epidemic, they reasoned.

Both Rachel and Rolly realized they were in love with each other. They had spent much time together since their illness over the ensuing months. In spite of a ten-year age difference, they shared a love of history and a love of the north. They also shared a bond known only to survivors of near-death experiences. Moreover, they both bore the pockmarks that reminded them of the variola virus that had laid them so low less than three months ago. It was a physical reminder of what they had in common, which set them apart from the rest of the population. The scars on her face still bothered Rachel tremendously.

"You know, Rolly, I have been reading up on the history of smallpox. Did you know that Queen Elizabeth the first almost died from it when she was twenty-nine? Just like me, she had a high fever for two days and then the rash appeared all over her body, but her face was spared for some reason. She was in critical condition and deteriorated to the point that a successor to the throne was sought. Apparently, her life hung in the balance and then she suddenly improved and made a rapid recovery," Rachel explained.

"Just like you," Boudreau added.

"Yes, she took time to recover completely and her body was pock-marked but not her face, which is not like me at all. It's not fair!" Rachel exclaimed.

"Rachel, you are just as beautiful to me as you were on the first day I met you at York Factory!" he exclaimed. Boudreau was telling her the truth; he had never met a more vivacious, intelligent and beautiful woman.

Rachel had always been an independent woman, confident in her own strength. Her illness, however, had left her vulnerable. Rolly Boudreau was the only other person who knew what she had gone through. His knowledge of the north and the history of its people gave him a mystique that she found appealing. He possessed a quiet strength of his own and a gentleness that she admitted to herself she could not live without. *And he's not bad looking either.*

"Do you feel comfortable with having this minister marry us?" Boudreau asked.

"I don't really care, Rolly, I just want to get married and get on with our lives. To be honest, I really didn't come to church to hear about smallpox. Couldn't we just get a justice of the peace to perform our ceremony?"

"Absolutely, but I thought it would be kind of nice to have a traditional church ceremony, that's all. Why don't we meet the minister after the church service and talk to him?"

In the end, they agreed to have a Christmas wedding with this minister after meeting with him. This would give the couple two months to prepare. They watched the national news that evening together and the announcement by the CBC news anchor shocked them.

"The World Health Organization, with its headquarters in Geneva, Switzerland, has found that diluted smallpox vaccines are still effective. This has allowed more people to receive vaccines. However, it has become painfully obvious that stockpiles in both Canada and the United States are becoming rapidly depleted. In Europe, the three million doses stockpiled at the WHO headquarters has likewise quickly evaporated. Pharmaceutical companies cannot seem to meet the demand in spite of lucrative contracts with federal governments. Rumors are circulating that wealthy individuals in Europe are paying huge sums for the vaccines from corrupt officials," the announcer said.

"I still feel this is entirely my fault, Rolly. I should have left that damned blanket in its gravesite. It's like a curse! Look at what's happening now!"

"But Rachel, you are an archaeologist. Come on, sweetheart, this was part of your job to reclaim ancient artifacts. Besides, your colleagues went along with it and you took all the necessary precautions," Boudreau commiserated. He was aware of Rachel's guilt and did his best to assuage her emotional pain.

"How were you to know that there was a 235-year-old trading knife tucked inside the blanket? It was my fault for pushing the bag to make more room in the plane. That's probably when it ruptured. According to the scientists from the NML, the blanket was loaded with smallpox. They said the blanket was a fomite, whatever that is."

"It means the blanket was a carrier for smallpox. I just don't know how the other Russians in St. Petersburg got smallpox."

Boudreau remained silent. He felt he knew exactly where the Russian scientists may have contracted smallpox. He had tried to find the flight records from that trip with them, but they had been taken by the Public Health Agency of Canada after he contracted smallpox. He didn't want Rachel to know that the scientists' infection had indirectly originated from the blanket as well. She would never forgive herself if she discovered that the blanket that she had unearthed at York Factory last summer was the source of the current Russian smallpox epidemic. Besides, if the Russians hadn't figured it out by now, there was no point for him to inform them. *Let them think they contracted smallpox from their own permafrost, if that's what they believe.*

Yet he wrestled daily, bearing the burden of this secret, wanting to help authorities in their search for the source of the epidemic and yet at the same time wanting to protect Rachel. The emotional stress from this contradiction was huge and he slept poorly at the best of times. Boudreau was suffering from what psychologists refer to as 'cognitive dissonance.'

Boudreau felt guilty about lying to the woman he loved even if it was to protect her. He faced the dilemma of disclosing the truth now, which would not change things for those in Russia. But by keeping this secret to himself, he had to cope with all of its psychological consequences. He reasoned that at some time in the future he would speak to Dr. Emberley regarding the Russian scientists, if only to ease his own conscience. For the time being he could not hurt the woman he loved, even if he had to withhold the truth from her. Yet the weight of carrying this secret was at times overwhelming and Boudreau had considered visiting their pastor for counselling.

"Rolly, the Russian scientists think they acquired smallpox from the Siberian permafrost, the same way we got our infection. It's frightening to think that the permafrost is like one giant freezer that can hold all kinds of infectious diseases for centuries and then release them with global warming. I suppose smallpox vaccinations will be the norm from now on," Rachel commented.

"Yes, I'm sure you're right," Boudreau tersely agreed and kissed her on the cheek.

"Hopefully, this epidemic will burn itself out by the time we get married at Christmas, Rolly. I am just happy we have each other through this difficult time." Rachel smiled.

"Exactly. Look what we have gone through. I love you, Rachel," he said and kissed her again.

By Christmas smallpox had infected a million people in Russia and there was no sign that the epidemic was abating.

Chapter 36

Emberley's Lecture: Smallpox, WHO and Vaccinations

Eczema vaccinatum

On October 18, 2018, Dr. Frank Emberley stepped up to the lectern holding a memory stick. After inserting it into his laptop, he adjusted the microphone. A year had passed since he had met with his three residents to discuss the principles of the transmission of infectious diseases. They were now capable second-year residents who had experienced the care and management of patients with smallpox. Emberley smiled when he recalled their enthusiasm for this subject and how they had thrown themselves into researching an extinct disease. At the time, he had considered it a pointless endeavour. Today, however, the irony struck him and he was thankful for the three bright young doctors.

Today he was giving a lecture to a packed house in the Gaspard Theatre, Health Sciences Centre in Winnipeg. Emberley was the guest lecturer for Grand Rounds with the Department of Internal Medicine. His audience was a mixed bag of doctors, interns, residents and numerous medical students. Because of the controversial nature of his subject, several journalists from the *Globe and Mail* and the *National Post* also attended. A writer was also recording his talk for the *Canadian Medical*

Association Journal and a CBC camera crew stood nearby. The small-pox epidemic attracted huge media attention and put the National Microbiology Laboratory and Winnipeg on the map. Numerous questions regarding vaccinations had arisen. The purpose of this medical symposium was to answer these questions. The title for Emberley's talk was 'Smallpox, WHO and Vaccinations.'

"As you all know we have seen two cases of smallpox in our province this past year. The victims were an archaeologist and a pilot who survived after suffering from severe illnesses. And now a global pandemic claims new victims every day.

"With the virus having been extinct for forty years, it was not easy to determine just how prepared the world should have been in the event of a smallpox outbreak. Few doctors have ever seen a case until recently. Concerns about an accidental leak from existing labs or the intentional release of the virus through acts of bioterrorism or through natural re-emergence have always existed. Now the World Health Organization faces what it has always feared, namely an epidemic of an infectious disease that killed more people in history than all other infectious diseases combined. Whereas diseases such as rabies or Ebola have much higher mortality rates, they are not nearly as contagious as smallpox. And whereas an infection such as the common cold may be more contagious than smallpox, it does not carry the mortality rate of smallpox," Emberley announced.

Emberley showed signs of stress from the past few months. He had developed a slight resting tremor recently and he intentionally kept his hands at his sides, away from the lectern.

"The World Health Organization came under fire for its slowness to respond to the 2014 Ebola outbreak in Africa in which 11,000 people died. In fact, you may recall that Paris-based Doctors Without Borders, or MSF, severely criticized the WHO for contributing to the deaths of thousands of lives by dragging its feet before it raised an international alarm. Even its own officials admitted to being behind the curve, and MSF described the WHO response in 2014 as a 'global coalition for inaction.'

"With the smallpox pandemic of 2018, however, the WHO has reacted swiftly and effectively. It has incorporated principles used in the famous smallpox eradication program of the 1960s, which successfully made smallpox an extinct infection for the past forty years. The man responsible for that historic and sentinel public health program was Dr. Donald Ainslie Henderson, Director of the World Health Organization's Smallpox Eradication Unit from 1966 to 1977.

"Currently the World Health Organization now follows the methods of Dr. Henderson. It has employed thousands of workers in the infected countries, vaccinating everyone within a specified radius of those infected. Back in the sixties, Dr. Henderson was challenged with the colossal task of eliminating this virus from the planet using ring quarantine and vaccination. Smallpox had killed at least 300 million people in the twentieth century alone. Therefore, it's easy to see that this was probably the greatest public health success story of all time.

"Before Henderson began this heroic endeavour in 1967, smallpox was endemic in more than forty countries with ten million cases annually. Yet after only ten years, the virus had been completely eradicated. It is amazing that Donald Henderson did not receive the Nobel Prize for his amazing accomplishment. The eradication of smallpox is considered as one of the greatest moments in history."

Emberley paused and showed a few slides relating to the great Smallpox Eradication Programme from the 1970s. A photo of Dr. Henderson appeared on the screen.

"When Dr. Henderson ran the great Smallpox Eradication Unit of WHO in the 1960s and 1970s, most of the world's population was already immune to smallpox thanks to vaccinations. Not so today. Only a handful of North Americans have been vaccinated within the past five years, mainly military and medical workers. For this reason, the current epidemic is taking off like a prairie wildfire and has already killed over 300,000 people within a matter of three months since it was released from the permafrost in Russia last July. At least that is where we think it originated, although there have been doubts cast on this source. Mathematical projections by the CDC for this epidemic are ominous. By this time next summer, it is conservatively estimated that over three million people could be infected with smallpox. If it spreads to China or India, we could be facing an epidemic affecting hundreds of millions."

Emberley paused for a sip of water. He shifted his slide from a photo of American soldiers in the Afghan war receiving inoculations at a military hospital to a graph, which extrapolated the death rate for the next year.

"The United States has vaccinated thousands of soldiers going to Iraq and Afghanistan since 2002. Whereas the real possibility of bioterrorism existed in those countries back then, most American casualties were victims of roadside bombs or IEDs rather than small-pox. Unfortunately, thousands in those countries have now fallen victim to smallpox."

Emberley's next slide showed a gruesome picture of a child with a generalized rash that looked like either chickenpox or smallpox, but the caption stated 'eczema vaccinatum.'

"This photo shows a child with severe eczema vaccinatum. Vaccinations can have serious side effects. There are anecdotes of wives, girlfriends and children of American soldiers who developed eczema vaccinatum, a rare but potentially lethal condition. This serious adverse reaction affected those with eczema and caused a generalized eruption that looked for all the world like smallpox.

"Patients with eczema vaccinatum were treated with vaccinia immune globulin and many ended up in intensive care. For that reason, patients with a simple skin condition like eczema have been excluded from having vaccinations. Hopefully, in due course, they will benefit from herd immunity. But the point is that vaccination saves lives and we must renew what Dr. Henderson began in the sixties regardless of the risks to a few."

Emberley paused and took a deep breath.

"In view of this global disaster and the accelerating nature of this smallpox epidemic, I believe that an immediate and global vaccination programme must take place. Canada has set the stage for this endeavour even though we have only had two cases of smallpox. It is inevitable that the virus will return and we must be better prepared for this eventuality using the most modern and effective vaccines."

Suddenly a voice at the back of the theatre screamed out, "No vaccinations for smallpox! Vaccinations kill!" An anti-vaxxer wearing a lab coat carrying a stethoscope around his neck had made his way into the lecture theatre. He tried to commandeer the presentation with his own contrary message that he had written on a placard for the cameras in the room.

"So we have an anti-vaxxer here today," Emberley quickly responded. "I won't argue with you because we have history and science on the side of the argument. But I would really like to know from our anti-vaccination protester whether he believes the world is flat or whether gravity really exists."

Emberley's taunts resulted in a further outburst. Security people then stepped into the lecture theatre and quickly removed the protester to the echo of jeers and boos.

Returning to his interrupted lecture Emberley quipped, "He's probably more afraid of gluten than he is of smallpox."

A few guffaws erupted from the audience. Emberley returned to his presentation.

"When Dr. Henderson began his eradication program, some two million people a year were dying of smallpox in 1966. Ladies and gentlemen, we cannot let that happen again. There are just too many sources whereby this deadly virus can be resurrected. We know of two level four labs in the world where smallpox is stored. There may be labs in other countries including rogue states that we don't know about that may also have stocks of variola. There is always the possibility of laboratory leaks or bioterrorism from these labs.

"Furthermore, malevolent forces that have the technology to create a smallpox virus by biomolecular engineering might effect a resurgence. Since the DNA sequence for several strains is known and the genetic code is readily available on the internet, this possibility is no longer science fiction."

Emberley's next slide showed the headline 'Scientists Warn World Is Now More Vulnerable to Smallpox After Controversial Virus Synthesis.'

"At the University of Alberta, scientists have been researching the horsepox virus and have actually recreated the viral genome from scratch. By purchasing DNA fragments of the virus over the internet for 100,000 dollars, they have embarked on a dangerous journey in which the next step is the recreation of the variola virus or one quite similar. In so doing, we have yet another source of smallpox with which to contend. This is an example of bioengineering of the worst kind. What is of greater concern is the fact that it is being researched right here in Canada and this study has now been published. The point is if they can synthesize a horsepox virus, then why not a smallpox virus? Hence the need for a universal vaccination program." Emberley paused briefly to change slides and then continued,

"Allow me to quote from Dr. Tom Frieden, former head of the Centers for Disease Control and Prevention regarding this research: 'It is a brave new world out there with the ability to recreate organisms that existed in the past or create organisms that have never existed.' This comment is taken directly from *The Washington Post*." Emberley left this slide on the screen for the duration of his presentation.

"Lastly, as we have already witnessed in our own province this past year, there may even be other sources of the smallpox virus. Artifacts from a person killed by smallpox centuries ago and preserved in the Arctic permafrost have re-emerged. We are fortunate that three of our medical residents were able to make an early diagnosis on two cases that originated from the permafrost. A third patient, who flew to Russia, unfortunately died from smallpox that he contracted from the same Arctic permafrost."

Emberley then looked up and pointed to Drs. Richardson, Goldman and Allan sitting in the front row.

"Considering these events, it is obvious that every additional experiment involving live smallpox viruses increases the risk of an accidental release. While the 1978 accident in the UK was contained, this was attributed largely to the high degree of smallpox vaccination with immunity in the British population at that time. A similar lab accident today could wreak havoc in a large population because virtually no one has any immunity to smallpox. Even if all experiments with live smallpox virus were conducted under maximum containment conditions, the risk of an accidental release always exists. Therefore, my second recommendation is for the destruction of all laboratory stocks of smallpox in spite of the current outbreak and the potential to synthesize the virus."

Emberley concluded his lecture with one of his favourite quotations from Dr. Henderson, another one of his unsung heroes.

"If you can think like a virus, then you can begin to understand why a virus does what it does. A smallpox particle gets into a person's body and, in a way, it's thinking 'I'm this one particle sitting here surrounded by an angry immune system. I have to multiply fast. Then I have to get out of this host fast. It escapes into the air before the pustules develop.' By the time the host feels sick, the virus has already moved on to its next host. The previous host has become a cast-off husk (and is now becoming saturated with virus), but whether the person lives or dies no longer matters to the virus. However, the dried scabs, when they fall off, contain live virus. The scabs are the virus's seeds. They preserve it for a long time, just in case it hasn't managed to reach a host in the air. The scabs give the virus a second chance."

Emberley then added, "Fortunately the immediate quarantine and ring vaccination prevented the spread of this virus in the two cases this past year in Manitoba. We were very lucky to have the resources of Canada's National Microbiology Laboratory just down the street."

Emberley awaited questions from the audience. He expected a flurry of questions regarding the safety of vaccines, however, the encounter with the anti-vaccination ideologue had somehow quieted the spirit of scientific inquiry and people left the auditorium. A few reporters stood by, but Emberley was tired and slipped out the side door, glad for the escape from the usual barrage of questions. However, just as he left the lecture theatre, a reporter stepped in front of him.

"Dr. Emberley, can you tell us how the archaeologist and the pilot are doing? Have they recovered completely, sir?"

"Yes, they have recovered and they are both doing well. In fact, they are getting married at Christmas here in Winnipeg. They have invited many of their caregivers, including myself to the wedding. I am looking forward to attending along with my senior residents."

Chapter 37

Dark Winter

Amor vincit omnia

At fifty degrees north latitude, November and December in Winnipeg, Manitoba, can be the darkest and coldest months of the year. With the smallpox epidemic raging on the other side of the world and threatening to advance to North America, specialists in the Department of Infectious Diseases at the Health Sciences Centre were busy reviewing a subject long forgotten. Several medical consultants were even unaware that smallpox vaccinations required boosting every five years and were surprised to learn that vaccinations did not confer lifelong immunity.

Newer textbooks of pathology made no mention of Guarnieri bodies, as they were considered a medical oddity. The average internist had no idea whether smallpox was an RNA or DNA virus. Not that it mattered much, as no new cases of smallpox in Manitoba or the rest of the country had reappeared since the summer. The aggressive vaccination and quarantine program conducted by the Public Health Agency of Canada, together with the staff of the National Microbiology Laboratory, miraculously prevented any further cases. After a few months, however, even gas jockeys and hair stylists knew all about smallpox, thanks to all the media attention given to the current epidemic in Russia. The anti-vaccination voices had finally fallen silent once the numbers of smallpox-related deaths mounted in that country.

As the smallpox epidemic spread from Russia to Europe and the Middle East, North Americans lived in fear that it might 'jump across the pond' in spite of a continental quarantine involving the cancellation of all airline flights and shipping across the Atlantic. Public health authorities worked against time to complete the vaccination of the three North American countries before the dreaded disease could reappear on the continent.

Experts felt that, once the virus had spread to China and the Far East, all Pacific flights and shipping would be likewise postponed indefinitely. By this time, the economies of all the countries in the world were taking a hit. Tourism revenues fell dramatically and the cruise ship industry ground to a halt. Stock markets had fallen almost fifty per cent and students studying overseas were not permitted to return home for the holidays. Christmas would very different for many families this year. Even domestic travel was down and people were driving instead of flying to get to places. Radio stations played the popular Christmas song *I'll be home for Christmas* more often than any other song that year. Even letters and parcels from the European continent were forbidden from entering the country for fear of smallpox contamination via fomites. Indeed, it was a bleak Christmas for many that year. Some economists feared a complete economic collapse.

Nevertheless, in the middle of this dark and depressing time, a joyous celebration took place on Saturday, December 22, 2018, one day after the winter solstice. Dr. Rachel Thompson, archaeologist, married Roland Boudreau, northern bush pilot, in Winnipeg's Elim Chapel on Portage Avenue. Both smallpox survivors, they felt comfortable getting married in this delightful 110-year-old stone church.

Among those invited were the nurses and doctors who had cared for them during their hospitalizations in July and August.

In attendance with families from both sides were Drs. Frank Emberley, Lisa Richardson, Frederick Allan and Sarah Goldman. Rolly Boudreau had his sister stand up for him as Best Woman and Rachel had Dr. Wojeich Jaworski by her side as Man of Honour. It was not a wedding in the traditional sense, but the bride looked radiant and the groom beamed when she came down the aisle. It was an emotional affair and there were few dry eyes after the minister pronounced them 'man and wife.' The audience cheered when Boudreau kissed Rachel. They walked down the aisle together with the *Star Wars* movie theme blaring from the massive forty-year-old Casavant pipe organ. Everyone had a good chuckle at the unconventional music that Boudreau had chosen to present his bride to the world. The grand symphonic overture from the organ imbued a sense of victory as the radiant couple walked down the aisle, lifting the spirits of all in attendance.

The medical people clustered in the back pews had seen both of them close to death. They cheered the loudest, throwing confetti as the happy couple left the church and climbed into a white limousine in the cold December air. Boudreau and Thompson had survived the worst that life could throw at them.

They were now able to face life's challenges together. Everyone felt that nothing further could touch them. Some of their friends felt that they may have married too quickly, while others understood that they were made for each other and there was no rationale for waiting any longer. Unlike most people on the planet, they were immune for life from smallpox. With their antibody-enriched sera, they could now save others.

A cocktail reception a few blocks away in the La Verendrye Room of Winnipeg's Hotel Fort Garry took place an hour later. As waiters served hors d'oeuvres, the newlyweds greeted guests and passed out pieces of wedding cake, which they had carefully wrapped with colourful ribbons. After everyone was served champagne, a cluster of the doctors surrounded Rachel and Rolly Boudreau to congratulate them. Sarah Goldman warmly embraced Rachel. She was astounded at the resilience of this remarkable woman who had painstakingly applied facial cover up and dermal soft tissue filler to hide her pox marks for her wedding day. *Boy that took guts.* Goldman poured herself a glass of wine and raised it to Rachel with an admiring smile.

Many guests brought gifts to the wedding, some of which included Hudson's Bay point blankets, towels, mitts and toques, all emblazoned with the distinctive stripes of the Bay logo. The labels on these items showed the old York Factory grand depot, an irony that was not missed by the bridal party. Rachel had prepared herself for this possibility and just laughed it off. Some of her nerdy scientific friends could be insensitive.

Near the front, a table covered with a white tablecloth held a wedding cake in the shape of a scaled down replica of the York Factory depot building. A tiny Hudson's Bay flag adorned the cupola. Beside it, a model Cessna airplane and a toy polar bear and cub garnished the unique wedding cake. One of Rachel's girlfriends used her lipstick to paint a small red circle on the bear's backside. Rachel and only a few of her friends including Wojeich Jaworski appreciated the prank. He smirked at the small polar bear and whispered to Sarah Goldman, "Now there's a couple in love with each other. I never would have expected a Christmas wedding for them. But I am happy for their sakes, considering all they have gone through."

"I believe people should fall in love only if there is a great story about how they met each other. I guess I am too much of a romantic," Goldman responded.

"Well, if meeting each other under the circumstances of smallpox isn't a great story, I don't know what is," Jaworski added. "You know, Sarah, I think they should write a book about their experiences. It could be a bestseller," he stated with a smirk.

"And what would they call it?" Goldman asked.

"How about *Love in the time of Smallpox*?" he quipped.

"Ha-ha! I think that title has already been used, Wojeich! Very funny, though," Sarah laughed. "And they all lived happily ever after!" she added and laughed again.

There were high fives between Frederick Allan, Frank Emberley, and Rolly Boudreau. Several of Boudreau's pilot friends likewise congratulated him with warm embraces. Holding a champagne glass with one hand and Rachel's hand with the other, he approached Frank Emberley and said, "If it wasn't for you and your residents, we wouldn't be here today. I don't think I have properly thanked you for the several trips you made to Gillam on my behalf during my illness, and for saving Rachel while I was recuperating. We are both eternally grateful."

"Yes," Rachel chimed in. "Thank you, Dr. Emberley. You also prevented an epidemic by putting both Gillam and the hospital under quarantine and for vaccinating all those people. If it wasn't for those aggressive measures, we might be fighting an epidemic like they have in Russia and the Middle East right now."

Frank Emberley, for the first time in recent memory, was at a complete loss for words. He could not deny that what they were saying was partly true, but he had to give credit where credit was due.

"Listen, I am just thankful I had these three medical residents who played a major role in diagnosing and treating both of you. I could not have done it without them. And of course, the Public

Health Agency of Canada was invaluable," Emberley added as an afterthought.

"But Dr. Emberley, do we know when this epidemic will come to an end?" Boudreau asked. "Will it ever stop?"

"It's funny you ask that, Rolly. We were just making a few projections earlier today at the Public Health Agency and we resorted to an exercise that the Americans used after 9/11 when they feared an act of bioterrorism was likely. They called it 'Dark Winter.' It was a simulation of what might occur if smallpox were to be introduced in three states during the winter of 2002. The current situation overseas in Russia and the Middle East isn't much different from what was projected from the Dark Winter exercise," Emberley replied.

Lisa Richardson winked at Frederick Allan and Sarah Goldman. They all knew Emberley was now on a roll and they were prepared for his usual off-the-cuff dissertations.

"What was the outcome of that exercise?" Rachel asked.

"In short, Dark Winter predicted three million cases and one million dead after seven months. We are on track for a similar scenario in Russia, although we are not receiving all the information we need in order to extrapolate the extent of their epidemic.

"There are several variables in the current situation, the most important one being the speed with which their vaccination program can take place. We have been in secret communication with a Dr. Kulagin at the Moscow State University Hospital and he tells us things are worse than the government is willing to divulge. Apparently, a few Russian dairy farmers own cows with cowpox on their udders. They have been making a fortune using them as a source of vaccination to those willing to pay for it. Entire herds are being infected on purpose just so that people can receive the same vaccination that Sir Edward Jenner used in 1796. It's not a bad idea when you think about it," Emberley said.

"Fascinating. It amazes me how people can improvise when they have to. I guess if it worked in 1796 it will work today," Jaworski added.

"Exactly. But getting back to the Dark Winter exercise of 2002, the Americans learned that in addition to a high death rate, there would be a huge breakdown in essential institutions such as the police and fire department, as well as the military. This hypothetical epidemic was then followed by civil disorder and widespread panic. Eventually martial law was necessary to control the ensuing chaos. Shortages of vaccines as we are now seeing were a major problem in keeping the epidemic in check. The Dark Winter exercise revealed that an attack on the United States with biological weapons would threaten its national security. Our current leaders are unfortunately not prepared for an attack with bioterrorism and I think the public knows that," Emberley stated.

"Yikes, that's scary," exclaimed Rachel, almost spilling her champagne. "I can't imagine the current president managing an epidemic on American soil. Thank goodness it hasn't infected people in the United States."

"No, Rachel. At least not yet. Since the smallpox outbreak, the CDC has implemented a mass voluntary vaccination program using diluted vaccines from stocks that were stored after 9/11. People have been lining up by the tens of thousands for vaccinations. The news media have been airing stories recently about Dark Winter and they are frankly scaring the heck out of people," Emberley said.

"Many Americans still believe that both of you were victims of an act of bioterrorism rather than an archaeological exploration. Even several of the CDC specialists are finding it hard to believe that your smallpox was acquired from a 235-year-old variola major strain from

York Factory. The Americans have the DNA analysis, but they are still skeptical and think the Russians started this whole epidemic by either a lab accident or bioterrorism. They just cannot figure out the Canadian connection in spite of what we have told them. For years, the U.S. Centers for Disease Control and Prevention has been warning doctors to watch for any unusual outbreaks of a disease that could be consistent with bioweapons. Hence, their skepticism."

A waiter briefly interrupted the conversation to refill their champagne glasses. Everyone was fascinated with Emberley's knowledge of biological weapons and the Dark Winter exercise.

"The Russians, on the other hand, are saying that their epidemic started with archaeological explorations of their own in Siberian permafrost. And of course, CNN and other networks create more questions than answers with all their sensational news reporting. So it all becomes very confusing," Emberley emphatically stated.

"Yes, but we know the truth. We acquired our smallpox from a blanket buried at York Factory. I wonder how many other bodies have been preserved in the permafrost with their viruses," Wojeich Jaworski enquired.

"That's a good question, doctor. We may never know the answer to that but you can be sure that any scientists involved in further projects that require permafrost excavations will be better prepared, thanks to what we learned from the York Factory cases," Emberley advised.

A string quartet began playing a mix of classical favourites and popular Broadway tunes while the crowd mingled with each other. For Rachel and Roland Boudreau, this wedding was psychologically therapeutic. To see so many friends and family supporting them at their wedding without fear of smallpox was reassuring.

Of course, all of their contacts as well as the entire population of the country had been vaccinated months ago once it was revealed that the two had contracted smallpox. The stigma of their illness dissolved that evening and they knew that their illness was now a part of history. They still had to deal with media interviews and a few reporters had snuck into the reception because of the huge human-interest story unfolding before them. The next day, a half-page story in the *Winnipeg Free Press* described not only the nuptials, but also a few of Emberley's comments regarding the Dark Winter exercise that the reporter overheard. The headlines stated, 'Smallpox Victims Happily Married; CDC Has its Head in the Sand.'

Chapter 38

To Russia with Love

Euphoria

On the evening of the wedding reception Dr. Frank Emberley answered his cell phone and spent ten minutes focused on his call in a corner of the room. After hanging up, he approached the newlyweds, who were still celebrating with their friends in the Fort Garry reception room.

"When did you two say you were flying to Mexico for your honeymoon?" Emberley asked innocently.

"On Monday, the day after tomorrow," Rachel replied. "Why, do you want to come with us, Dr. Emberley?" Rachel joked. The champagne was definitely going to her head.

"Yes, actually I want to go with the two of you, but not to Mexico. Why don't we all fly to Russia tomorrow, courtesy of the Russian Ministry of Health?" Emberley asked.

"You've got to be kidding, Dr. Emberley!" Rachel gasped. "Why would we go there for our honeymoon? It's as cold there as Winnipeg is in the winter."

"Well, I just received a call from the Director of the National Microbiology Laboratory of Canada, Dr. Pamela Lindsay, who has been in contact with the Vector Institute in Novosibirsk. They have asked if we can 'lend' the two of you to help save some high-level researchers whom they suspect of having smallpox in the early stages."

"We were told that our antibody levels are still elevated against smallpox and that we are protected for life. But why us? There must be thousands of Russians who have survived smallpox and have elevated antibodies that could help them," Rachel said.

"True, but they specifically want the two of you as they are planning to use your sera with that of others to make a more comprehensive smallpox immune globulin. They think that the strain that you suffered from is slightly different from what they are seeing over there," Emberley explained.

"I'm not sure I completely understand all this. What exactly do they want us to do?" Rolly Boudreau asked.

"Yes, I'm sorry, Rolly. Our Russian counterparts want the two of you to go to the Moscow State University Hospital where a Dr. Kulagin and his team will meet you. They will take blood from you just as if you were giving a unit of blood for a transfusion. They will then separate your red cells from the plasma and then give you back your red cells. The procedure is known as 'plasmapheresis.' Following that, they will then use your plasma to infuse a patient whom they believe is in the incubation period of smallpox. The immunoglobulins that your immune system manufactured during your illness are still quite elevated. They can be taken from your plasma and used to prevent or reduce the severity of the illness if given shortly after exposure."

"Well, this is all very interesting but I will do whatever my bride says we will do," Boudreau replied.

"Why don't we go, Rolly? I'm familiar with this procedure from my university biology class. It's no big deal and I've always wanted to visit Moscow. Maybe we can fly to St. Petersburg and see the Hermitage!" Rachel exclaimed. However, her real reason for volunteering so readily was to help others afflicted with smallpox. She thought of her colleague, Gordon Dowling, who died in Russia of smallpox. She hoped to mitigate the guilt she still bore for his death by serving in this way.

"There's your answer, Dr. Emberley. My question is, how do we get there with an international quarantine separating the continents and who is this guy we are saving, anyway?" Boudreau asked. Inwardly he felt torn about going to Russia. Knowing that the smallpox epidemic originated from his plane would make it difficult to meet people who had survived the infection. Worse still, what if he were to meet any Russians who had lost loved ones from smallpox? He hoped this would not happen and it frightened him to think about the possibility. Nevertheless, he put on a brave face for Rachel's sake.

"We have special arrangements between the two countries. The Russians are sending a private jet to Gander, Labrador, that we will board for a direct flight to Moscow. They will cover our expenses starting now – even your hotel expenses here at the Fort Garry will be paid for, courtesy of the Russian government. They have also offered a generous honorarium for your cooperation, but they require complete secrecy. Since most of your friends and family know you are leaving for your honeymoon anyway, this should not be too difficult for you. As far as this individual is concerned, you must appreciate we are sworn to secrecy, so it is just as well you don't know," Emberley advised.

"What a surprise, Dr. Emberley. This is so exciting!" Rachel gushed with enthusiasm.

The next day, the three flew to Gander where two Russian Ministry of Health officials met them at the airport with a warm welcome. A flight attendant escorted them onto a Russian Sukhoi Superjet 100. It was the VIP version of a regional airliner similar to the Canadian Bombardier or the Brazilian Embraer with a range of 3800 kilometers. Once aboard, they were served a light dinner with vodka and caviar shortly after take off. With the exception of Frank Emberley, the Russian health officials and a flight attendant, they had the whole plane to themselves. The flight attendant opened a bottle of Krug's Vintage Brut 2000 champagne, which delivered a stunning bouquet of complex fruitiness and depth. They raised their glasses to each other and laughed, enjoying this opulence at 35,000 feet. The attendant then served them Sachertorte with unsweetened whipped cream. Rachel was beside herself.

"Rolly, I can't believe how good this tastes. I feel like we have died and gone to heaven. How do they know I just love dark chocolate?" she exclaimed.

"Beats me, but my last recollection of dying wasn't anything like this!" Boudreau deadpanned.

Rachel laughed and scolded Boudreau disapprovingly, wagging her finger with a petulant look while savouring the rich chocolate dessert. She laughed again and the attendant poured more champagne for them.

"I wish we could offer these amenities to our clients flying into Gillam," Boudreau said. "I think business would definitely improve!"

"Yes, but your airline would go broke offering this kind of service, sweetheart," Rachel replied.

Later the officials invited Rolly Boudreau to visit the pilots in the cockpit where he sat intrigued for the next hour. One of the Russian pilots spoke English and explained the various instruments and the specs of the fifty million dollar Superjet to the fascinated bush pilot. It had been years since Boudreau sat in the jump seat of a commercial jet and he was thrilled with this experience. Once the fly-by-wire jet was over Greenland, Boudreau returned to the cabin to join his new bride.

Rachel was fast asleep, stretched out comfortably in business class, covered by two blankets. The flight attendant sat close by and smiled at Boudreau, offering him a glass of Canadian ice wine. He passed on the wine, grabbed a blanket and lay down on three empty seats near his wife. At the rear of the empty plane, Frank Emberley quietly worked on his computer and spoke on a cell phone at the same time. The Russian officials sat near him reading from their own laptops, the glare from their screens casting an unnatural glow on their sombre faces. No one left the plane during a brief refueling stop in Iceland.'

At 530 miles per hour, the Sukhoi 100 was quiet and the flight was smooth. Boudreau could not believe that they had this entire plane to themselves and he had many questions. He wondered how much it had cost the Russian government to send a jet of this size for so few people. He wondered how the Russians managed to get Canadian ice wine in view of the current international quarantine. He again questioned whether they would really be able to help if their antibodies were against the same strain of smallpox that currently afflicted millions of Russians. Moreover, he wondered who it could be who needed them so badly as to fly them with such urgency and luxury. *Why are they really doing this?*

"Must be somebody very important," he mumbled as he pulled a blanket over himself.

The strains of soft Russian chamber music drifted throughout the cabin and soon Rolly Boudreau was sound asleep, snoring softly. Boudreau's week had been hectic preparing for the wedding.

Five hours later, he awoke to the softness of his wife's kiss and the overwhelming feeling of contentment and well-being. Still groggy from the champagne, he tried to remember the name of Rachel's perfume. *Was it Obsession or Euphoria? Or was it Mystique?* He knew it was one of those exotic names that evoked romance and sensuousness that had put a spell on him when he first met her six months ago at York Factory. He put his arms around her in a warm embrace and then remembered that her perfume was called *Euphoria*, which rather described how he now felt. *Just who comes up with these names?*

"Where have you been all my life?" Rachel whispered in his ear.

"I've been around. Where are we? Where is Emberley? Gad, I must have slept!" he said.

"Yes, Rolly, you have slept and I didn't want to wake you but we are landing in half an hour. Dr. Emberley and the Russian people want to brief us on our meeting with the doctors at the Moscow hospital before we land. This is all so hush-hush and he doesn't want us asking any questions when we meet them," Rachel replied.

"Right. Too much champagne for someone who only drinks the occasional beer," Boudreau said as he looked outside.

"Good morning, Rolly! How was your sleep last night?" Emberley asked. "You seemed to be quite comfortable after that great dinner and dessert."

"I slept well, thanks. Perhaps too much champagne, though," Boudreau replied.

"That was a wonderful evening, Dr. Emberley," Rachel exclaimed. "We must be sure to thank our hosts when we meet them."

"You will have the opportunity to meet only a few of the medical people, I'm afraid, Rachel. At any rate, this is the Russian Ministry's way of thanking the two of you for coming here on your honeymoon.

We will be picked up at the airport shortly after landing, which is soon, so you might want to buckle up," Emberley advised.

An hour later, a limousine drove the three Canadians from Sheremetyevo airport to the Moscow State University Hospital. Dr. Alexei Kulagin and his chief resident, Dr. Viktor Markov, greeted them warmly in a large office lined with medical textbooks and a picture of Kulagin posing with a large fish hanging on the wall. Several medical degrees in Cyrillic script adorned the oak paneled walls.

"Welcome to Moscow State University Hospital, Dr. Emberley. It is so good to see you after the many discussions we have had over the phone over the past few months. This is indeed a pleasure. Let me introduce you to my chief resident, Dr. Viktor Markov. And you must be the newlyweds. Thank you very much for coming here on your honeymoon. As you know, I cannot disclose the details of why you have been asked to help us but we do need to borrow your blood for a while," Kulagin said with a smile.

"As you may know, giving a vaccine for a disease stimulates the body to produce antibodies against that disease. This is known as 'active immunization.' But once the disease process has started, it is too late to administer a vaccine, so we use immune globulins, which contain antibodies that have been obtained from someone who has had the infection and survived. We call this 'passive immunization.' You might recall several Ebola survivors gave their sera for this purpose and saved lives during the Ebola crisis in 2014. But of course, Dr. Emberley has probably explained all this to you," Kulagin said.

Viktor Markov also shook their hands and then stared at Boudreau, analyzing the pockmarks on his face. Before Kulagin could remonstrate against the rudeness of his chief resident, Boudreau interrupted him.

"That's okay, Dr. Kulagin. We find most doctors tend to stare at us analytically ever since we recovered from smallpox," Boudreau said.

"Yes, we have many patients in Russia with these types of scars and, although they are now immune to smallpox, we still keep them under quarantine ever since we looked after your colleague, Dr. Gordon Dowling, last summer," Kulagin replied.

"Oh dear! You took care of Gordon? He was my colleague and mentor. He was a brilliant physical anthropologist and a dear friend. Would you please tell us about him? I hope he didn't suffer much? I know he had a few health problems, but to die of smallpox is just unheard of, Dr. Kulagin," Rachel lamented.

Alexei Kulagin cleared his throat and fidgeted with his watch.

"Yes, we will go over all of this with you but, keep in mind, our epidemic here in Russia has spread very rapidly beyond our borders and has caused the deaths of two million people. We expect many more in the next few months until we can catch up with our vaccination program. So, contrary to what you say, dying of smallpox is not a rarity any more. In fact, on this side of the planet it has become all too common," Kulagin solemnly advised.

"I do have a favour to ask you, however. We have a package of Dr. Dowling's papers and personal belongings that has been decontaminated and I wonder if you might take it to his family?"

"Certainly, Dr. Kulagin. It would be an honour for me to do so," Rachel wiped a tear from the corner of her eye.

"But why don't we take your bags and get your blood tests done to prepare for the plasmapheresis. You will have several forms to fill out and I am sure Dr. Emberley can help explain the procedure to you. There is an urgency with this procedure as you can appreciate. Smallpox waits for no one. Afterwards we have a special dinner prepared for you with several officials from the Ministry of Health and from the Vector Institute."

Roland Boudreau remembered the two Russian biologists that he had flown to Churchill and suddenly felt very uneasy about this whole experience.

"Dr. Kulagin, do you think I could speak to you privately for a few minutes about the smallpox epidemic?" he asked.

"Certainly, Mr. Boudreau. Anything you want," Kulagin answered.

Both Rachel and Frank Emberley gave the bush pilot a questioning look. Rachel shrugged.

"I just have a few questions for our Russian hosts. It's okay," Boudreau replied awkwardly.

Chapter 39

Plasmapheresis

A riddle, wrapped in a mystery, inside an enigma

Dr. Alexei Kulagin led Roland Boudreau at his request into a medical examining room next to his office. "What's on your mind, Mr. Boudreau?" Kulagin smiled warmly wondering what secret scientific questions a bush pilot might have to ask.

"Please, Dr. Kulagin, just call me Rolly. Now as I understand this, you want our blood serum because of the antibodies to smallpox that we still have, correct?" Boudreau questioned.

"That is correct, Rolly. We spin the blood in a centrifuge separating the serum and then give you back your red blood cells so you should feel no ill effects. It is a procedure known as plasmapheresis. I assumed that Dr. Emberley would have explained all this to you," Kulagin said.

"Well wouldn't that only help if our smallpox strain was different than the smallpox from the epidemic here in Russia?" Boudreau asked.

"Yes, but your strain is in fact, slightly different and we want to mix your sera with that of Russian smallpox survivors to make a more comprehensive smallpox immune globulin. It might be unnecessary, but we want to try this to ensure success with our patient. Of course, a medical study will likely follow this experiment as well if it is successful. In addition, sequencing the DNA of Dr. Dowling's smallpox enables us to establish the timeline of the evolution of this virus. His strain is 250 years old, as are yours. But why are you so concerned, Rolly?" Kulagin was interested in where the pilot was going with his line of questions.

"I am confused because I have always felt that this epidemic came from North America. You know that Rachel and I got smallpox from digging at a gravesite in the permafrost up north. The day after flying the scientists back to Gillam, I flew two Russian biologists up to Churchill to see some of our polar bears. They also seemed interested in the permafrost in northern Canada, as they had been doing their own research on it. They flew back to Russia a few days later. I can't help but feel that there were still smallpox viruses in my plane and that this was the source of their infection. I didn't know whether to say anything as my wife feels bad enough about Dr. Dowling getting smallpox and then dying over here. If she knew that the smallpox epidemic in Russia came from the same gravesite, she would be devastated. I want to tell her but I can't." Boudreau's lip trembled slightly as he spoke.

"Ah Rolly, we know all about those two biologists. Yes, they have also done work in our own melting permafrost and discovered animal and human remains from a century ago that have surfaced with the climate change in Siberia. But those researchers had been vaccinated against smallpox because of the type of work they are doing here. So in fact, they would have been protected, even if there were smallpox viruses in your plane. The Russian media however, has identified two other biologists who apparently contracted smallpox from archaeological projects in the Siberian permafrost. The fact that you are here should tell you that your strain is different from the epidemic strain we are currently fighting," Kulagin assured.

"You're kidding me? How is that possible?" Boudreau exclaimed with great relief.

"No, I tell the truth, Rolly. Dr. Emberley and I have had some secret conversations about the source of our smallpox epidemic. The people from the Vector Institute have also exchanged information about the DNA of the Russian strain and it appears that they are different. There is no way the epidemic came from North America. We knew this from DNA sequencing on Dr. Dowling's smallpox last fall and his strain is a much older type than the current Russian strain. Let me assure you this has nothing to do with you or your plane." Kulagin could see that a giant weight was slowly lifting from the Canadian pilot as he reassured him.

"So there is no York Factory connection to the Russian epidemic?"

"No, there is no York Factory connection, Rolly," Kulagin softly replied.

"Well isn't smallpox all the same? How can you tell the difference between strains, Dr. Kulagin?" Boudreau further enquired.

"Two distinct varieties of smallpox have always existed, variola major and variola minor. Variola major is what killed Gordon Dowling and what you and your wife suffered from. Variola minor has disappeared – in the past, it was a much milder variety with a lower mortality rate. Long ago, people tried to become infected with variola minor in order to prevent them from getting variola major, which is much deadlier," Kulagin explained.

"So the Russian epidemic is from variola major?" Boudreau asked.

"Yes, variola major has a mortality rate of up to forty per cent. Yet even within variola major there are different strains based on the DNA sequencing, which allow us to identify the differences. I can see why you assumed that the Russian epidemic arose from the visiting biologists who flew with you that day. But, my friend, that is not the case."

"Well, where did the Russian epidemic come from then?" Boudreau was clearly relieved but baffled nevertheless.

"The Russian government has wanted to avoid that question. They have issued a statement that other biologists contracted it just as you did, only from diseased bodies resurfacing from the Siberian permafrost."

"But that would be an incredible coincidence, Dr. Kulagin. What are the chances that smallpox returns from two separate sources from the permafrost at the same time after forty years?"

"Ah, Rolly Boudreau, for a bush pilot you are quite astute. Many people are asking that same question. Some authorities are explaining the coincidence by using climate change as a common factor in releasing this deadly scourge from different permafrost sources at the same time," Kulagin explained.

"And? You make it sound as if there is more to this than coincidence, Dr. Kulagin," Boudreau asked.

"It is not a coincidence, Rolly. I think I can trust you to keep this to yourself. Only a few people including Dr. Emberley and some of his Canadian colleagues know about this. You see, Vector was dealing with the Russian smallpox epidemic before you and your wife contracted smallpox and before Dr. Dowling's death. Several scientists thought the Chechen terrorists may have caused a breach at Vector but the terrorists did little damage except to its security reputation," Kulagin explained.

"So where the hell did it come from?" Boudreau persisted.

"The fact is, Rolly, this smallpox epidemic arose from a lab accident that went unrecognized until it was too late. You see, the Vector Institute operated under a massive biological weapons program in the 1990s called Biopreparat. There were tons of anthrax, smallpox and other weapons-grade infectious disease agents manufactured there during that time. It was sheer madness, but with the break-up of the Soviet Union, this bioweapons program fortunately ended. However, not all of these agents were destroyed and another lab in Russia under Biopreparat had some remaining clandestine stocks of variola for their own research.

We always knew that these unaccounted-for stocks of smallpox could present a problem as a possible bio weapon. I cannot tell you which lab that was as there were eighteen labs employing well over 30,000 people at the peak of the Biopreparat program. Suffice it to say, a few scientists secretly kept some of the viruses for research at this particular lab. Last May, a lab worker was accidentally exposed to smallpox, probably from an unrecognized tear in her positive pressure personnel suit. She spread it to her family who then spread it to friends who travelled to various places in Russia. Once the virus began to spread, it provided rogue elements the opportunity to wreak havoc," Kulagin explained.

"What rogue elements?" Boudreau asked.

"We think a terrorist, possibly a Chechen, eventually learned about this and allowed himself to become infected from someone he knew. He then spread it to shopping malls and airports over the course of a week or so until he finally collapsed in a department store, covered in pox blisters. It was simple and elegant: no bombs, no IEDs, no suicide vests. He just walked close to as many people as he could while he was infected in as short a period of time as possible."

Boudreau swore. "That's just evil, Dr. Kulagin. Why do these people do these things?"

"They follow a perverse ideology and adhere to a religious fanaticism that we do not completely understand. Sadly, word has spread and now there are dozens of these 'suicide viral bombers' spreading smallpox to thousands of people in other countries. Keeping North America on quarantine may have impeded the spread to that part of the world but, unless the vaccination programs can be completed in time, smallpox will arrive on the shores of America likely within the next few weeks. The only way to stop it from spreading is to vaccinate the entire planet as quickly as possible. Simple ring vaccination will not work as it did in the 1970s with the Smallpox Eradication Programme. With terrorists intentionally spreading the virus while they themselves are sick, it makes ring vaccination obsolete. As soon as everyone within the ring of exposure is vaccinated, a bioterrorist infects others outside the ring," Kulagin explained.

"The strongest argument for mass vaccination is that it would eliminate the threat of smallpox as an agent of bioterrorism. We need to immunologically quarantine the virus you see," he added.

"I think I am beginning to see the picture now. Thanks for explaining this to me. You have taken a huge load off my shoulders, doctor. Rachel will be happy to know this if I can share it with her."

"Yes of course, but I beg you to keep this to yourselves. Imagine if the press discovered that the epidemic originated from a laboratory within the famous State Research Center of Virology and Biotechnology. It would be very embarrassing to the Russian government, you see. Many heads would roll, including mine, if this information should ever be leaked. Better, the public believes that the smallpox epidemic originated from the Siberian permafrost. However, it was a catastrophe on par with Chernobyl and the initial cover-up was becoming more and more difficult to manage. Therefore, they invented the story of Siberian permafrost as the source of the epidemic. They were looking for smallpox there for years, anyway. And then when the Canadian smallpox story emerged, well it played right into their hand, you see?"

Rolly Boudreau nodded and suddenly it became clear to him.

"The problem has been rectified too late since we are now on the verge of a global epidemic. As far as I am concerned, Vector and all the other labs under the Biopreparat program should have destroyed all their stocks of smallpox years ago. However, if the scientists at the CDC in Atlanta were keeping their smallpox stocks alive, there is no way that the Russian government would destroy theirs. The situation is similar to the standoff in the nuclear weapons programs. 'Détente in the laboratory,' as Dr. Emberley has described it," Kulagin added.

"So Rolly, your confusion about the source of the epidemic is certainly justified. As you can see, there is even more confusion with the cover-up story that the Russian government released. The smallpox cases in Manitoba occurred at just the right time for them. If it could happen there, then why not in Siberia? It offered an alternative explanation. Once it became known that smallpox was in the permafrost in Canada, it became the perfect cover-up story to explain the lab leak in Russia, even if it was not the truth," Kulagin explained to Boudreau.

"This is amazing. Does Dr. Emberley know all about this, Dr. Kulagin?"

"Yes, he does know. He is one of the few people outside of Russia who knows the truth about the source of the epidemic. He and I have been in conversation as soon as he recognized that you and Rachel contracted smallpox last July. Dr. Pamela Lindsay, the director of the NML in Winnipeg also knows about this situation. She has agreed to maintain confidentiality about the lab error at the behest of the Vector Institute and the Russian government. I felt it necessary to inform them lest the Russian epidemic was blamed on Dr. Dowling's case, which would suggest that it originated in Canada. We were very fortunate to recognize and isolate him at the very start. The entire city of Moscow was quarantined and an immediate ring vaccination program prevented an epidemic from originating there.

"But you see, Rolly, as I have explained, Russia had its own smallpox epidemic brewing earlier from a laboratory leak that was kept secret. At this point, however, the origins of the epidemic are all academic. We need to focus our attention on how to keep it from spreading. It seems, however, that the terrorists have the upper hand and are making it spread faster than it might otherwise. Hopefully, once a critical mass of the population has been vaccinated, the terrorists can do no further harm."

"I can't believe how complicated this epidemic has become. Just when you think you have it figured out, the plot thickens."

"Yes indeed, Rolly. The explanation of the Russian smallpox epidemic unfolds like one of our Russian Matryoshka dolls. The story is always contained within yet another story. As Winston Churchill once said, 'Russia is a riddle, wrapped in a mystery, inside an enigma.' So is the explanation for the Russian smallpox epidemic, Rolly. Welcome to Russia." Kulagin smiled and gave Boudreau a slap on the back.

"We should get back to the others. They will be asking questions about your absence. And you need to give us your blood for the plasmapheresis. After all, that's why you are here."

"Right. Thank you for explaining this to me, doctor."

Kulagin sensed Boudreau's relief but he silently questioned whether he had given too much information to this affable bush pilot. He trusted Boudreau, however, since he had nothing to gain from this information. It also relieved Boudreau of a great emotional burden. *Besides who would believe him, anyway?* Kulagin reasoned.

What Kulagin did not reveal to Boudreau was the ongoing argument he had had with his own government about the cover-up story regarding the source of the smallpox epidemic. The Russian government, influenced by the Vector Institute, was initially quite willing to put the entire blame on Canada for the outbreak. After all, Dowling brought the disease from Canada to Russia last July. After this, it would have been a simple matter to impugn the Canadian research project at York Factory for the Russian epidemic. It was Kulagin, however, who had opposed this plan from the start. He liked the Canadians and refused to participate in such a lie that would make Canada a pariah among the nations for causing a worldwide epidemic that really began on Russian soil.

Instead, he sent an encrypted email to Drs. Emberley and Lindsay in Winnipeg, explaining the lab accident that had released smallpox into the Russian population last May. After doing so, he threatened the government officials that they needed to come up with a better explanation for the cause of the epidemic or the Canadians would reveal the truth about the lab accident. It took great courage on Kulagin's part to confront his own officials and essentially blackmail them into changing their story. A compromise was finally reached in which the scientists working in the Russian permafrost of Siberia would be blamed for inadvertently releasing smallpox, just as the Manitobans had done at York Factory in July.

Of course, this story would play into the hands of the environmentalists and climate change ideologues. In the end, global warming was blamed as the real cause of the outbreak. Kulagin was prepared to live with that story instead of falsely incriminating the Canadians. Both Emberley and Lindsay agreed in return to keep the Vector lab accident a secret to protect Russia's reputation. It was more expedient to blame global warming and the permafrost than the carelessness of one of Vector's labs. In the end, the Russian government agreed to this lie to protect itself from the truth. Canada agreed to the same lie to protect itself from another lie.

"Ah, such is politics!" Kulagin reasoned.

Chapter 40

The Hermitage

O s p a

The actual procedure of the plasmapheresis took less than an hour. As the newlyweds reclined in lounges drinking Russian tea and eating glazed Christmas spice cookies known as *pryaniki*, they discussed the rapid and unexpected series of events that had transpired since their wedding day. Plastic bags with their own red cells emptied into intravenous lines that ran down to their forearms as curled ribbons. A nurse monitored the rate of flow from the bags and then covered the donors with a blanket.

"It's hard to believe that we are spending our honeymoon in Russia hooked up to IV tubing," Rachel quietly said.

"Yeah, no kidding. I was really hoping we could spend our honeymoon in a more romantic place, Rachel, especially for Christmas," Boudreau lamented.

"Like the Mexican Riviera?"

"Nah, I was thinking York Factory actually," Boudreau joked.

"Ha-ha! Funny man. Can you just imagine how cold and dark it would be there in the winter? Actually, I try not to think about that place too much as it gives me anxiety. I have even had bad dreams about York Factory," Rachel answered solemnly.

"At least we would be on our own, Rachel. However, Dr. Kulagin has arranged for us to have a private tour of the Hermitage in St. Petersburg before flying us back to Canada. He said it would be a gesture of appreciation from the Russian Ministry of Health. He was also aware that you wanted to visit St. Petersburg. Would that be more romantic for you?" Boudreau asked.

"Oh, yes. Now we're talking. How did you arrange that, Rolly? And what were you and Dr. Kulagin discussing for so long in that examining room, anyway?" Rachel drank some more tea and dipped another cookie into her teacup.

"I was asking him if the smallpox epidemic that started here in Russia could be related to the same infection that we had from York Factory, that's all," Boudreau said.

"And?" Rachel had also pondered this question over the past few months. She was always afraid to ask Dr. Emberley in case the epidemic could be traced back to her archaeological project at York Factory. It was her greatest fear that she had somehow been responsible for the Russian epidemic by unearthing the Bay blanket during the York Factory project. This possibility had kept her awake at nights as she questioned the coincidence of the Russians unearthing smallpox from the Siberian tundra at the same time.

"No way. Kulagin explained that they have a method to distinguish the different strains of smallpox called 'DNA sequencing.' They are different strains so you can put aside any fears that our smallpox from York Factory spread to Russia. Dr. Dowling's case made it appear that the disease originated back in Canada but, apparently, the epidemic occurred from bodies in Siberia resurfacing at the same time. At least that's what they have been telling people," Boudreau explained to his wife. He did not want to tell her what Dr.

Kulagin had shared with him about the Biopreparat lab incident. As Kulagin had said, it was all academic, anyway. *Or was it?*

"Thank goodness for that. But Geez, Rolly, that is an amazing coincidence, don't you think? Like, what are the chances of that happening? Most scientists have always believed that, if smallpox were to re- emerge anywhere in the world, it would be from a lab accident or bioterrorism. At least it didn't come from our York Factory project. I don't think I could live with myself if that were the case."

"Well, Rachel, you can put that fear to rest. Kulagin was adamant about that. It seems that climate change may have been the culprit in this case," he said, knowing he was not telling his wife the whole truth. Nevertheless, Boudreau could live with this falsehood to maintain the trust Dr. Kulagin had placed in him. He would tell her everything later when they were all back home in Manitoba.

"But can we really visit St. Petersburg and see the Hermitage? Is it even open with all that's been going on in Russia the past six months? It's not like there are any tourists here anymore. The Russian economy has been devastated from this epidemic. Rolly, are you sure about this?"

"Absolutely. But you are right about the Hermitage being closed with the smallpox epidemic. Kulagin has made special arrangements for us to visit, since we are immune. Who knows? We might have the whole place to ourselves, Rachel."

"Rolly, have you wondered just why are they showering us with all this kindness? Just who is benefitting from our blood serum in this country?" Rachel asked.

"Beats me, but it must be someone important."

The nurse checked their intravenous lines as the red blood cells emptied from the hanging bags. She poured them some more tea and turned on a television set, giving Rachel the remote control.

CNN Europe was suddenly featuring a *Breaking News* story about the Russian smallpox epidemic and several pundits were discussing why the public had not heard from the Russian president for several weeks.

"He's been incommunicado and even the Russian News Agency, TASS, has been enquiring after the President's health," one of the commentators said.

"It's possible that he has been overwhelmed with the work involved in dealing with one of the worst epidemics in Russian history and the unprecedented economic consequences," pointed out a professor of medicine from London in a clipped British accent.

Another expert on Russian affairs stated, "The President has always been in excellent health. Why would he not refute rumours to the contrary if he wasn't sick?"

Rachel reached over, grabbed Boudreau's hand, and whispered, "Rolly, do you think that's why we are here? Could the President have smallpox?"

"I doubt it, Rachel. I mean, wouldn't they vaccinate all the top brass after the epidemic began last year?" Boudreau protested.

"Yes, but what if the vaccination didn't take? I mean that does happen, doesn't it?" Rachel whispered.

"Honey, I'm just the bush pilot, remember? And we have been warned not to ask questions about why we are here."

"Exactly. That even makes it more suspicious that the President could be the mysterious person who will get the immune serum globulin from our antibodies," Rachel pondered.

"Wouldn't that be something to tell our grandchildren someday?" Boudreau smiled.

Just then, Dr. Kulagin entered the room. He picked up a *pryaniki* cookie, turned up the volume on the television and leaned over towards the reclining couple.

"Be careful, everything you say in this room is recorded. Please keep all speculations to yourself. I have arranged for a private jet to take you to St. Petersburg tomorrow morning for the day and then you will fly home in the evening on the same plane that brought you here. Before I leave, I just want to thank you both on behalf of the Russian government. As you know, we have now lost at least two million Russian citizens from this disease. We feel that the epidemic should die out shortly, thanks to a very aggressive vaccination program that has been ongoing since the outbreak began. I should mention that when you arrive back in Gander, you will be given a new set of clothes when you leave the plane as a safety precaution. Nothing fancy. Just jumpsuits after your landing in Newfoundland," Kulagin advised.

"Why do we need to do that, doctor? I just bought my honeymoon outfit last week," Rachel moaned.

"Because your government and the Canadian Public Health Agency doesn't want to take any chances. Smallpox can survive for months on clothing, as you know. I suspect that, even though you are both immune to smallpox, you could spread it from your clothing if you were to be in contact with the Russian strain while you were here.

"You will also go through a special decontamination procedure that Dr. Emberley has set up in Gander. You will not be wearing the jumpsuits for more than a few minutes and then they will be burned as well. Dr. Emberley will arrange for you to have other clothing that you will wear until you get home. Sorry about all of this, but you do not want a smallpox epidemic in your own country," Kulagin added.

"Certainly not," Rachel stated firmly. She considered that she had almost been responsible for starting an epidemic in Manitoba six months ago. Only the quick thinking of Frank Emberley and his team had prevented that from occurring.

The next day the newlyweds arrived in St. Petersburg, which appeared as a ghost town with very little traffic and few planes taking off from the airport. A limo drove them to the famous art museum where they were met by a pock-faced docent who spoke broken English.

"Welcome to Hermitage Museum," the tour guide greeted them warmly. "Museum not opened to public with people sick. Just people who already have sickness allowed to visit," he advised.

"Boy, this museum looks like a place where a hermit might live. No wonder it's called the Hermitage. You could shoot a cannon in here and not hit anyone," Boudreau dryly remarked to his wife. "I am impressed they opened it just for us."

"No kidding. We would certainly need days or weeks to see everything." Turning to the Russian docent she asked, "Could we see the Dutch masters and the French impressionists today?"

"Of course. But must not walk slow. Very big place. Lots to see."

After five exhausting hours of viewing hundreds of classical works of art, the two were given a light lunch before leaving for the airport. After noticing his facial pockmarks, Boudreau decided to ask the tour guide about how he acquired smallpox and what it was like to have suffered with it. Rachel visited the ladies room as the two men chatted.

"I get sick from my wife. Chechen gave her big hug at shopping mall. She not thinking such a bad thing but then she get sick. Then kids get sick and I get sick. Then my wife die. Terrible sickness. Kids not die. Many people in my town get sick and many die of this sickness. Russian word for sickness is *ospa*. American call it 'smallpox.' This sickness is not so small I think," the docent smiled sheepishly at his own dark humour.

Boudreau recalled from researching his own illness that an infected person could spread the virus for up to fourteen days before his or her own symptoms developed. The thought of a bioterrorist spreading smallpox throughout the realms of an unwary public was terrifying. He didn't know what to say to the docent except that both he and his wife had also suffered from *ospa* as well.

"I see you have marks on face like me from *ospa*. You are American?" the docent asked.

"No, we are from Canada," Rolly replied.

"Ah. Canada. Play good hockey. Beat Russian hockey team. Me, I like Alexander Ovechkin. Good hockey player I think."

At this point Rachel walked up and smiled at the tour guide.

"We thank you very much for showing us this magnificent museum today. It has been wonderful but we have to leave now. Our ride has arrived and we must go."

The couple shook the docent's hand warmly and Rolly slipped him a few bills in Canadian money. Two older five-dollar bills with their distinctive blue colour featuring children playing hockey fascinated the Russian docent. He smiled and turned the bills over holding them up to the light. One of the newer polymer bills featured a spaceman with the Canadarm acknowledging the Canadian Space Agency.

"Nice pictures. Canada money very pretty. Hockey picture on money is nice I think. *Spasibo*, thank you." The docent expressed his gratitude and escorted them to the exit. He had not seen foreign tourists in months and had enjoyed his time with the Canadian couple as much as they had touring the museum.

"*Dos vedanya!* Come again." The docent waved as the couple exited down the massive stairs from the museum.

After this warm farewell, a limo sped them to the airport in St. Petersburg where they boarded the same Sukhoi jet. Dr. Frank Emberley was on board and greeted them with a small gift of Russian Matryoshka dolls wrapped in shrink wrap.

"What a lovely gift, Dr. Emberley. How thoughtful of you," Rachel exclaimed.

"Don't thank me. It's from Dr. Kulagin and his team. They really seemed to like the two of you. It's a wedding gift and a gesture of their appreciation for your sacrifice in helping them. But you won't be allowed to open it until it is decontaminated at the National Microbiology Laboratory even though it has been sterilized here. I assume everything went well today. Did you enjoy your own private tour of the great Hermitage Museum?"

"Oh, yes. It was fabulous, Dr. Emberley. But I'm still curious as to the identity of our benefactor." Rachel fastened her seat belt as the Sukhoi jet started its taxi down the tarmac.

"Ah, you promised not to ask, Rachel," Emberley gently scolded. "I also heard from Dr. Kulagin that you were discussing this question during the plasmapheresis procedure. You probably weren't aware that private conversations are often monitored in Russia because of the bioterrorism that has taken place here since the beginning of the epidemic. Weaponizing smallpox for ideological purposes has made the epidemic much worse than expected and they trust no one. They are all paranoid, and rightly so."

"We were just speculating whether the Russian president might be the one who had smallpox. The television news even questioned that possibility. I didn't think a private conversation between husband and wife would cause such controversy," Boudreau answered.

"Don't worry about it. Dr. Kulagin won't tell me anything either but your speculations are probably not far off. At any rate, it appears that with the massive vaccination program going on, the epidemic in Russia has plateaued. When we get home, you will be able to continue with your honeymoon. It's possible, that we will likely never know the true nature of our mission here," Emberley added.

Chapter 41

Return to the Fort, July 2019

Catharsis

Winter and spring came and went. Millions more around the world suffered and died of smallpox. Quarantines along national and continental borders continued. Economies fell. Eventually, the effect of mass vaccinations slowed the infectivity rates and the Russian epidemic finally ground to a halt. By June, borders reopened and international travel resumed from North America to Europe. Newspapers referred to the epidemic as the 'Dark Winter of Smallpox' and the 'Great Plague of Modern Times.' People grew weary of the ongoing interviews and endless speculations by medical experts on whether the smallpox virus would once again be eradicated as it had been in the seventies by the World Health Organization under Dr. Henderson.

In Russia, Dr. Alexei Kulagin received the highest award given to civilians, the Hero of the Russian Federation. The purpose of this award was to recognize persons who had been of service to the Russian state and nation, usually associated with 'heroic feats of valour.' The President of the Russian Federation presented the title. In receiving this prestigious award, Kulagin would wear a 'Gold Star medal' for the rest of his life. He was also nominated along with the Vector Institute for the Nobel Prize in Medicine for his work in containing the smallpox virus in the Moscow case and in fighting the epidemic.

Dr. Frank Emberley and his three residents were becoming well published in the medical literature as the 'Canadian smallpox experts.' The *New England Journal of Medicine* was asking them for articles to publish, a reversal from the days when it was next to impossible to be published in this prestigious medical journal. Emberley obliged willingly and recruited his capable residents to do much of the work.

After their return from Russia, Boudreau and Rachel bought a condominium in Winnipeg. They were able to continue with their work for awhile from this city even though they both commuted weekly to Calgary or to northern Manitoba. Both slept poorly after the events of the past year. Rachel began to suffer from anxiety attacks and nightmares about York Factory and especially the grisly scene at the graveyard with Joseph Charles' frozen stare. A psychologist diagnosed her as having a form of post-traumatic stress disorder and she attended weekly counselling sessions. She was no longer her chatty self and had lost her appetite. She was losing weight and, had she been permitted to wear her honeymoon outfit back from Russia, it would hang loosely as many of her clothes now did. Her husband became increasingly concerned about Rachel and did his best to help her.

"Rachel, I think you might be getting depressed with this problem. What does your psychologist think you should do?" Boudreau gently asked his wife.

"She thinks I need to desensitize myself to whatever is bothering me. She thinks I'm suffering from PTSD. She thinks I need to face my fears head on."

"And how does she propose we do that?"

"I don't know. It all started with our York Factory project last year and my subsequent infection with smallpox. I keep dreaming about it and most of my dreams are ghoulish. I don't want to start taking sleeping pills but I am afraid I might not have a choice," she lamented.

"Hmmm. I have an idea if you are up to it, Rachel. But it means returning to where your fears all began."

"What do you mean, Rolly?"

"I mean we need to go back to the fort and revisit the cemetery to get you through this funk," Boudreau suggested.

"Oh my goodness, I don't know if I could handle that. How would we get there? Would you fly us in?" Rachel inhaled deeply.

"No, Rachel, I have a better idea. Why don't we fly to Gillam, stay at my place for the night, and in the morning we'll take a jet boat down the Nelson River to Hudson Bay. Then we'll head south up the Hayes River to the fort, just for the day. You will get a totally different perspective on the river than from flying in," Boudreau advised.

"Do you really think so, Rolly?"

"Absolutely. Perhaps you might want to discuss this idea with your therapist first though. But you did say that she wants you to face your fears, right?"

"Okay, I guess. I'll discuss it with her tomorrow."

Rachel was uncertain about this venture. Yet she knew that to get over the fears and the nightmares generated from the previous summer's experience something drastic had to be done, as difficult as it might be. She swallowed hard. "When would we go, Rolly?"

"I can set it up for next week. I know the guy that operates the jet boat out of Gillam and he has two cancellations. I'll give him a call now if you like."

After obtaining her therapist's approval, Rachel packed a small bag for the trip, and a week later the couple flew into Gillam and stayed at Rolly's old house. The next morning they were up at 4:30. A van picked them up in the twilight and drove them downstream along the Nelson River past the three huge dams, about an hour's drive.

Driving past the massive Limestone Dam, they saw an eight-ton jet boat waiting for them; the operator was cleaning the windows and loading equipment for the day's journey. His name was Cliff and he whistled a country western tune as he prepared for the trip. An assistant with the nickname 'Bear' helped transfer equipment onto the boat and then loaded his twelve-gauge shotgun with five slugs in the chamber. Bear sported an armful of tattoos and wore a Harley Davidson muscle shirt. He was a man of few words but seemed to know what he was doing.

"That's the kind of guy who probably butts his cigarettes out in the palm of his hand and hunts with a bow and arrow," Boudreau whispered to Rachel with a smirk while they waited to get onto the boat.

Rachel smiled at her husband's humour, something she had not done for weeks.

Dawn sunlight suffused the rising mist along the sand-coloured cliffs of the Nelson's shores. Colourful wildflowers grew profusely along the shore where the jet boat was anchored to the rocks. The roar of water rushing through the colossal spillway of the Limestone Dam nearby reminded them of the ongoing efforts to harness the mighty Nelson River. A few other passengers showed up, bleary-eyed, huddled together, wearing heavy jackets that would soon be shed once the sun had risen.

"Good morning, everyone! Welcome to the Nelson River. It will take about three hours to get to York Factory. The first part is a bit rough but we can handle the rapids. We have a very sturdy boat with only eight inches of draught so it is no problem for us to get through them. Please put your lifejackets on and leave them on until we arrive at York Factory," Cliff announced.

The thirty-foot jet boat came to life with the roar of the two massive 400 horsepower engines and soon it was speeding downstream past islands and rocks with an ever-increasing turbulence of the river. The boat slowed as it entered the roughest part of the river and, for four miles, bounced and banged over the rapids, sending huge waves and spray over the bow. This violent stretch of river actually qualified as level-five rapids on the international grading scale of white-water rapids. Wide-eyed and white-knuckled, Rachel hung onto her seat and scowled at her husband during this stretch of the river. Boudreau was enjoying every minute of it and even stood up in the boat for a few minutes, laughing at the wild ride the rapids provided. As a pilot who often flew in rough weather, he was in his element.

"I haven't had a ride like this since the Red River Exhibition when I was a kid!"

"Rolly, for goodness sake, sit down! You're going to fall over or hit your head," Rachel scolded.

After ten minutes of the turbulent white-water rapids, the Nelson suddenly became calm and the river widened. The boat accelerated to eighty kilometres an hour for the rest of the trip, cruising past rugged shorelines and vast forests of spruce and fir with surprising smoothness. The gravelly cliffs held scraggly coniferous trees that clung tenaciously to the steep slopes. Numerous bald eagles fed on an animal carcass near the western shore and ravens soared nearby, looking for an opportunity to claim their share of the kill, their echoing croaks heard above the motor's roar. Moments later several Sandhill cranes foraged near some sandy shallows, their long black legs and white bodies clearly visible as they scrambled to fly away at the sound of the approaching jet boat.

Rachel looked back at the enormous wake the boat created, its waves dashing against the rocky shores in the distance. The Nelson River presented a kind of perverse grandeur that had not changed much in a millennium.

"I don't think I have ever gone this fast in a boat or seen such beautiful scenery," she shouted in her husband's ear.

"It certainly gives you a different perspective that you don't see from the air." Boudreau shook his head as the boat roared past an island in the middle of the river. The operator was acutely aware of shoals and rocks and constantly relied on a GPS program during the trip. He invited Boudreau to sit at the front in a captain's chair beside him. Rachel felt her spirits lifting, seeing her husband so happy with the gorgeous scenery whipping by. Beams from the early morning sun began to break through the thinning spruce trees along the sandbank cliffs. Several low-lying pink clouds quickly evaporated as the sun rose.

As they entered the estuary of the Nelson River, a multitude of white beluga whales and their calves began to leap and dive in the shallow water. The riverbanks widened until they were barely visible in the horizon. Soon a series of block-like structures appeared on the port side, as if a train with boxcars ran right into the river.

As the boat drew closer, Cliff announced, "That is the old railway bridge built in 1918 that was supposed to transport grain to waiting ships. But the channel was too shallow for ships so they built the largest dredge in the world at that time. This plan was doomed from the beginning, with huge storms that made it impossible to navigate these waters. After a year, the dredge beached itself on an island during a storm where it rests to this day. The port was then moved to Churchill. I'll try to get closer for a better look."

The rusted remains of this fractured monstrosity lay draped over the small island like the carcass of some colossal animal, a mute monument to an engineering folly one hundred years earlier. Rachel thought the dredge was foreboding and gave a shudder as she fought her fears of returning to the fort.

The jet boat sped on into Hudson Bay. The waters were calm and the whales appeared as white flakes upon the murky water. Two beluga whales dove right in front of the boat and the tourists took out their cameras hoping to get a picture of the elusive mammals. Several curious seals frolicked on the starboard side. The Hayes Estuary was smaller with very few trees. They arrived at the fort twenty minutes later.

Cliff soon announced, "Welcome to York Factory!"

Bear secured the jet boat to the dock where a year earlier Rachel had encountered the polar bear. A Parks Canada guide who also sported a twelve-gauge shotgun greeted the group. He described the history of the old fort and then took them along the boardwalk to the cemetery. Rachel was familiar with this narrative but she wasn't paying attention to any of it. Feeling her anxiety return, she reached out for Boudreau's hand and grasped it firmly. She felt dizzy with strong feelings of apprehension. She did not want to follow the group to the cemetery. Suddenly she stopped on the boardwalk. Boudreau put his arm around her, aware of the painful memories of the preceding summer. He knew she had to go back there and he gently led her along.

Rachel never heard the words of the Parks Canada guide. Keeping her head down, she did not want to look around at the all-too-familiar cemetery. Before she knew it, she was standing beside the tombstone of Joseph Charles. She gasped.

"Rolly, this is the grave of the man that we exhumed last year. I can't believe I am back here after all that we have been through," she sobbed.

She read the epitaph once again. "'Sacred to the memory of Joseph Charles, a native of Hudson's Bay, who departed this life at York Factory, the 29th day of May 1836, the 29th year of his age. Deeply regretted by his friends and ...'" Rachel could not make out the last part of the writing because of an overgrowth of moss and lichens. She stooped over and was surprised that she had not seen this part of the epitaph a year earlier.

The Parks Canada guide watched her trying to read the weathered face of the tombstone.

"Some of these graves are so old that the inscriptions are difficult to read. Like the one there of Joseph Charles. That tombstone is almost 200 years old," he announced.

Rachel was enrapt by this tombstone. She slowly reached out and touched it gently as if she had personally known Joseph Charles. The group became silent during this time, watching Rachel who suddenly broke down and wept, releasing a year of grief and guilt all at once. Boudreau knelt with her at the graveside. Anticipating this reaction, he reached into his pocket and pulled out a package of Kleenex and a few brightly coloured ribbons, which he gave to her. They were the same ribbons from their wedding cake that he had saved. She took the ribbons and placed them on the tombstone just as the Cree people might have done for their ancestors buried there. This was liberating for her and she recognized that she was one of two remaining people on the planet who had actually seen Joseph Charles face to face. *How could I possibly explain this to the rest of the group?*

Fortunately, the guide moved on with the rest of the group, explaining the remains of the old Powder Magazine, the crumbling wall of stones that once housed gunpowder and munitions at the fort. Rachel remained at the tomb of Joseph Charles for a few more moments and whispered something that the others could not hear. Boudreau nodded knowingly. It dawned on both of them that Joseph Charles was not just a historical oddity who suffered from a mysterious ailment over 180 years ago and whose remains lay buried in the Sloop Creek Cemetery at York Factory. He had become a real person. Rachel quietly talked to Charles, apologizing for desecrating his grave.

Boudreau also wiped a few tears away, knowing many of his own ancestors lay buried only a few yards away. He knew his great aunt and uncle were buried in this cemetery and others as well. He recalled visiting their graves as a boy. What he could not know was that Crooked Legs remained interred only a yard or so beneath his feet. Crooked Legs was the unfortunate Chipewyan from the summer of 1782 whose Bay blanket began a series of events that continued to unfold dramatically in the lives of this couple. What he did know from Rachel was that Joseph Charles lay buried within the permafrost beneath the ancient tombstone dated 1836.

Rachel recalled the image of his icy grimace at the very moment the coffin had been opened a year ago. She recalled her shock at seeing a frozen face preserved in the permafrost from the remote past, yet as if he had been buried only yesterday. She had so many questions as an archaeologist, but her enquiries always led to the philosophical and then to the theological. She questioned the possibility of resurrection from the dead. In a way, she had witnessed it personally in the exhumation of Joseph Charles. Memories of the resurrection of smallpox made her even more philosophical. *How could something from the past return with such a forceful and harsh reality?*

Turning away from the tombstone, she looked at other graves. A large white marble slab stood over the graves of two children dated 1907. Engraved at the bottom of the headstone was a scripture that jumped out at her: 'I am the resurrection, and the life: he that believeth in me, though he were dead, yet shall he live.'

Rachel immediately remembered this verse from the musings of the character Sydney Carton in Charles Dickens' classic novel, *A Tale of Two Cities*. It gave her comfort. A weight seemed to lift from her shoulders. The rest of the group by this time had left the cemetery. Bowing her head at the tomb of Joseph Charles, she silently prayed for several minutes, Boudreau at her side.

Then standing up, she quickly left the cemetery arm in arm with her husband. They followed the group towards the old depot building. The sun was shining brightly now and she could see the grand old fort with its white cupola that she had once visited. A carpet of green grass extended to the riverfront. Rachel remembered stumbling on it last year when she first arrived at the fort. Warm memories of the fur trade and the Bay men and the factors that supervised the great monopoly of the Company over hundreds of years rushed in to erase the dark images from the graveyard.

Near the stairs to the dock, Bear was cooking hamburgers on a portable barbecue. He sliced tomatoes and onions and glanced around from time to time, his shotgun slung around his tattooed shoulder. Rachel suddenly smiled and wondered if Bear really did butt out his cigarettes in the palm of his hand.

Striding briskly along the wooden boardwalk, Rachel sniffed the air. The aroma of hamburgers cooking was too much for her. Turning back to her husband, she smiled and exclaimed, "I'm starved, Rolly. When can we eat?"